## REMO FLEW AT THE CAR

It was racing into the street.

A sudden voice behind him. Frantic in the crystalline night air.

"Remo!"

Chiun was framed in an upper-story window, small and frail against the burning backdrop.

"Help me!" he pleaded. He flapped his kimono sleeves at the smoke that was curling up from the lower story.

Remo hesitated. He could still catch them. Even driving full out he could outpace the rapidly accelerating car.

But he couldn't abandon Chiun. Ever.

Remo let the men who'd set fire to his home go.

Sliding to a stop beneath the open window, he threw out his arms.

"Jump, Little Father!" Remo yelled up through the roar of flames. "I got you!"

A scowl formed on the old man's soot-streaked face. "Don't be stupid!" Chiun snapped down through the choking smoke.

Created by Murphy & Sapir

# THE
## Destroyer™

# SYNDICATION RITES

## A GOLD EAGLE BOOK FROM
# W RLDWIDE.

TORONTO • NEW YORK • LONDON
AMSTERDAM • PARIS • SYDNEY • HAMBURG
STOCKHOLM • ATHENS • TOKYO • MILAN
MADRID • WARSAW • BUDAPEST • AUCKLAND

First edition January 2001

ISBN 0-373-63237-1

Special thanks and acknowledgment to James Mullaney
for his contribution to this work.

SYNDICATION RITES

To the Biancos:
Hector, Caroline, Vincent, Douglas and Thomas.

And to the Glorious House of Sinanju,
e-mail: housinan@aol.com

Offering quality service in the field of professional
assassination for over 5000 years.

(see our coupon in this month's Regicide Quarterly)

*Discretion and decapitations guaranteed!*™

**1**

Drugs were Cal Dreeder's stock-in-trade. He had realized this sad truth in an alcohol-inspired epiphany just a few short days before his untimely death. That cold winter night—the last of his dreary life—he mentioned his revelation to Randy Smeed.

"Stock-in-trade means you deal it, Cal," Smeed explained to the older man. He tried to force a bored tone, but there was a tightness to his voice.

The two men were crammed along with twelve others in the back of a windowless van. They jounced uncomfortably on their hard seats as the nondescript vehicle turned off the New Jersey turnpike. The road soon became rough.

"It's what you do business with," Cal said knowingly. "I looked it up. And without drugs, we're out of business." He sounded almost disappointed.

"We'd find something else to do," Randy insisted dryly.

"You, maybe. Not me. I've been in this business nearly thirty years. It'd be hard for me to find something else. At my age, it's hard to change."

"You're old enough. Why don't you put in for a desk job?"

Cal laughed. "That'd be even harder. No, my only hope is that the drugs hold out until I retire."

A few hard faces glanced his way.

"Joking," Cal said, raising his hands defensively. "Jeez, you guys've gotta learn to lighten up."

One of the young men held Cal's gaze for a long time. He was still scowling when he finally turned away.

Cal shook his head. So serious.

The young men in the truck all wore matching windbreakers. The letters DEA were printed in block letters across the back. Cal wore one, as well.

He'd worn some form of official ID for most of his life. From his stint in the Navy, he'd gone straight to the Drug Enforcement Administration. Most of the men who surrounded him now were still watching Saturday-morning cartoons when Cal was going on his first hippie drug raids.

Thirty years of undercover, crappy pay and putting his life on the line on an almost daily basis. And the drug problem had only gotten worse.

These days, people would drink a gallon of cough syrup if they thought they could get a buzz off it. Cal had heard of kids sealing their nostrils shut while sniffing glue, housewives who had been hospitalized after guzzling rubbing alcohol and one case where a teenager had died after sucking on the nozzle of a can of spray paint.

Society was crumbling. Cal Dreeder was charged

with the impossible job of holding it together. As a result, Cal had been depressed for more years than he cared to remember.

The young punks around him didn't get his bitter joke. It had been a stupid thought. Drugs weren't going anywhere. Not as long as there were people willing to pump the junk into their veins and snort it up their noses. Not as long as there were creeps eager to push it in schoolyards and playgrounds. And especially not as long as it was profitable for the bigwig scum-suckers abroad and at home who supplied it.

No, Cal Dreeder's job was secure. And on this mid-January night on a back road in Jersey, the cold stink of the factories in the distant frozen swamps curling on winter's wind into the van's fetid air, the thought that he would never be out of work filled Cal with an infinite sadness.

They drove for another half hour.

The road became almost impassable. The men who were sitting were practically thrown from their seats. Those standing banged their heads on the steel roof more than once.

"They could've picked a better location," one of the young men complained.

"Better for who?" another grunted.

Eventually, the van slowed to a stop. What little conversation that had been going on within the confines of the truck died along with the engine.

Guns were pulled out of holsters. Safeties were

thumbed off. The men formed a silent sweating row as the side door of the van rolled open.

"Out."

The voice of the DEA field agent in charge was a soft growl. The men dutifully piled from the van.

Cal felt a small knot deep in the pit of his stomach when he saw the dull amber squares through the naked trees. The light shone through the windows, casting weird shadows around the nearby frozen woods.

On the surveillance photographs he'd seen, the building looked as if it had been an airport hangar at one time. If so, there was no sign of the airstrip it had served. It might have been used by a crop duster during some bygone age in the Garden State. Now, it was just another rotting hovel commandeered by society's dregs.

The rusting tin building had the benefit both of being in the middle of nowhere while remaining convenient to Jersey City, Newark and New York. The drugs that had found their way to America would be shipped from here.

At least that was the drug merchants' plan. But they were about to find out that the DEA had learned of their warehouse.

Cal gently fingered the trigger of his Colt as he fell in with the other, much younger agents.

The kids were nervous. Although he'd never admit it, Cal was, as well. He didn't feel the same depth of shivering apprehension as the rest, but it was there. His was the anxiousness of experience.

The men began to break away, circling through the woods in the prearranged deployment pattern.

Cal pulled in a few deep, steadying breaths before pushing away from the side of the van. He hadn't taken a single step before a firm hand pressed against his shoulder.

It was his superior. He was younger than Cal by a good twenty-five years. His expression was grave.

"Cal, you and Smeed are backup," Agent Wilkes said.

Cal Dreeder was stunned. "Excuse me?"

"Stay here," Wilkes insisted. The words came out in an angry hiss. His breath on this cold night was white.

Cal wanted to press the issue but knew he couldn't. The field agent in charge turned away, marching purposefully after his group of silent commandos.

There was no reason to ask why he was being left behind. He already knew the answer. He was old.

Harry Wilkes had made it clear time and time again that this was a young man's game. He didn't want to entrust a rickety old fossil like Dreeder with his life.

Cal glanced at Randy Smeed. In the pale light cast from the drug warehouse windows, Cal saw an expression of anger mixed with confusion on the much younger man's face.

Smeed was his partner. Because of Cal, he was losing out, too.

This wasn't the first time Cal's age had been an

issue. The doubts had been expressed for the past few years. Never like this, however. This was maddening, humiliating. Under the circumstances, even inappropriate.

Maybe the higher-ups were right. Maybe it was finally time for him to pack it in.

Right now, there was still work to be done.

Cal holstered his gun.

"Inside," he ordered in a growling whisper.

Cal preceded his partner into the rear of the van.

Two more men still sat in the back. They didn't even look up from their monitoring equipment as the pair of discarded agents climbed into the van's interior.

The other two men each wore a slender radio headset. They were monitoring the DEA agents who were even now making their way to the old tin hangar.

Cal slipped on a headset, as well.

All he heard at first was heavy breathing. The agents were maintaining silence as they approached the building.

"How many are in there?" Cal whispered.

A bowllike unit that resembled a small satellite dish was secured to the roof of the van. Aimed at the hangar, it was used to amplify sound.

"Two," one of the men said, sounding annoyed that the question was even asked. He didn't look at Cal.

Suppressing his anger, Cal fell silent.

"Raffair," one young man barked to the other. It

was a word he'd just heard on his headphones. "Any idea?"

"Guy's name?" the other suggested.

Cal wasn't even listening.

Two. If their source was right, this would be a big bust. With only two men in the makeshift warehouse and more than a dozen DEA agents converging on the place, there wasn't much doubt who was going to come out on top. And Cal was stuck sitting in a van with three wet-behind-the-ears kids.

Grumbling, he pulled the headset down around his neck.

Probably just as well. Maybe everybody was right. Maybe at his age, it was time to get out.

Rubbing his hands for warmth, he glanced over at Smeed.

The kid was sitting anxiously by the half-open rear door. He hadn't bothered to reholster his gun. It was sitting on his thigh. Every once in a while, he'd switch hands, wiping the sweat from his palms across his knee.

Smeed was cleaning off the latest cold perspiration when Cal Dreeder heard a distant pop. It was echoed on the headset around his neck.

Cal's eyes widened. A gunshot.

It was followed by another. All at once, a chorus of soft pops filled the freezing woods like winter crickets.

Smeed shot to his feet. "What's happening?" the young agent asked, gun raised. A gloved hand reached for the door.

"Stay put," Cal snapped, whipping his headset back to his ears.

Cal was instantly assaulted by the closeness of the gunfire. Between shots, men shouted.

It was an overlapping gibberish, back and forth. Although he couldn't make out what was being said, he'd heard enough. The number of voices shocked him.

"There's more than two," he said, his heart thudding.

The agents manning the equipment shook their heads in helpless confusion. "There were only *two*," one said, his eyes registering the first hint of panic.

"It's an ambush," Cal muttered hotly to himself.

That was all Randy Smeed needed to hear. Gun in hand, the young agent hopped from the back of the van.

"Hold it!" Cal shouted, ripping away his earphones.

Too late.

A sudden grunt from outside. The door slammed shut.

Cal was diving for the door when he heard the muffled shots. Too close.

"Damn," Cal swore. He wheeled to the two stunned agents. They were like ice statues, frozen in their seats. "Draw your weapons," he ordered.

The men behind him dutifully dragged guns from holsters. Depositing their headsets on their eavesdropping equipment, they stepped woodenly up behind Cal.

"Cover me," he snapped.

But as he reached for the handle, Cal froze. He cocked an ear. Listening intently, he wiped a sheen of cold sweat from his upper lip with the cuff of his windbreaker.

"What is it?" one of the young agents whispered.

Cal's voice was flat. "Gunfire's stopped."

So scared were they, the men hadn't realized it. Straining, they tried to make out the familiar pop of weapons' fire. There was none. The woods had fallen silent.

Cal Dreeder knew that could mean only two things. The DEA had either won or lost. Judging from the number of nongovernment voices on the squawk box, he had a sick feeling it was the latter.

In an instant, the air within the van seemed to grow noticeably hotter. More difficult to breathe.

"We've got to get out of here," one of the men said, his voice tight. It was the young agent who had scowled at Cal's drug comments not an hour before.

Cal shot the man a withering look.

There was only one real option, and Cal Dreeder wasn't happy with it.

There was no access to the cab from the rear. Someone would have to physically step outside the van and walk around to the front.

Smeed was dead. The bullets that had doubtless ended his young life had been fired right outside the door.

Yet there was silence now.

Maybe they'd retreated. Maybe if they gave Cal enough time, he could—

There came a wrenching from the rear of the truck.

"Ready!" Cal growled, falling back.

He aimed his gun at the door. The other agents followed suit, their faces sick.

When the door sprang open, Cal caught a glimpse of a hulking figure with a crowbar. Squeezing his trigger, the DEA man buried a slug in a spot below the edge of his stocking cap.

As the man collapsed, another sprang into view. This time, Cal's shot was wide. His opponent's was not.

The bullet caught Agent Cal Dreeder dead center above the bridge of his nose. With a meaty slap, it formed a deep black third eye between the fifty-four-year-old agent's shocked baby blues.

Cal toppled onto his back. Even as he fell, more scruffy faces appeared at the rear of the van.

The other two agents fired wildly. One shot clipped an assailant in the shoulder. The rest missed completely.

The shots fired into the van were far more accurate. In a matter of seconds, the last two agents joined Cal Dreeder in a bloody heap on the van floor.

Silence flooded the woods once more. The bodies were left where they fell. The gunmen hurried away from the van, back to the big building with the sickly yellow light.

THE VAN WOULD BE discovered at dawn the next morning. By that time, the five hundred million dollars of cocaine that had been stored in the old hangar would have already been shipped to a safer location.

That dreary post-New Year's day, four things would happen in the wake of the botched DEA raid.

ON THE NEW YORK Stock Exchange, a company called Raffair, which had recently gone public, would be the center of a buying frenzy. As the day progressed, the value of Raffair's stock would skyrocket in brisk trading.

AT A WROUGHT-IRON TABLE on a polished-granite Old World veranda overlooking a cold, dormant vineyard, an old man would open a newspaper. His weathered face would grow quietly pleased while reading of the unsuccessful raid across the Atlantic. It was all part of the master plan....

THE FAMILIES of the fifteen dead DEA agents, including Cal Dreeder's, would begin making funeral arrangements. In their grief, they would neither know nor care to know that the deaths of their loved ones were not in vain.

The audio recordings made within the bloodsoaked DEA van would be duplicated and analyzed by every concerned agency in the U.S. government.

Through circuitous means, the information would be brought to the attention of a dull gray man in a small sanitarium in Rye, New York.

FINALLY, the most awesome force in the arsenal of the United States would be released against the agents' killers. So terrible would be his wrath that the very earth would tremble beneath his feet, and when vengeance finally came, it would be swift and brutal.

But before America's last, best hope could set out on this most violent path, he needed to do one tiny little thing first. He had to stop the future from happening.

**2**

His name was Remo and there was a time in his life when he didn't believe in ghosts.

Back when he was a simple beat cop in Newark, New Jersey, Remo didn't have time to worry about ghosts or goblins or any of the other supernatural beings that sprang to frighten children from the minds of the Brothers Grimm. In those days, he was too busy just trying to stay alive.

Another lifetime and a million years ago, Remo Williams thought as he stared out the small airplane window.

The setting sun was an orange island of fire. On the ground far below, it was already growing dark.

The commercial plane on which he was flying was bound for Puerto Rico. Unbeknownst to the other passengers, it had begun its descent a few seconds ago. Like a mild itch, the barely perceptible shift in altitude was registered by Remo's sensitive eardrums.

Only one other set of eardrums on the face of the planet would have detected the first subtle slide the U.Sky Airlines plane had made over the Caribbean island. At the moment, that pair of ears and their owner were back in Massachusetts. Chiun, Reigning Master of the House of Sinanju, the greatest house of master assassins ever to ply the art, was contemplating the future. Both Remo's future and his own.

Remo wasn't in the mood to think about the future. In fact, when Upstairs called with this assignment, Remo was more than eager to accept it. He had hoped that activity—any activity at all—would keep him from thinking about anything other than the here and now.

The seat-belt light abruptly began flashing. Over the PA system, the pilot muttered something both in Spanish and in English. Alone with his thoughts, Remo listened to the words without hearing. His mind was somewhere else.

The eerie sensation was finally starting to go.

It all started a few months ago at the wake of an infant child in Illinois. Remo had gone there to find the baby's killer. Instead, he found himself troubled by repeated ghostly visitations from a young Korean boy. In time, Remo discovered that the child was in fact the son of his very own adoptive father. In a sense, this sad young boy was the spiritual brother the orphaned Remo Williams had never known.

Chiun's first pupil had died many years ago, and in so doing had helped to fulfill Remo's destiny. Under the strict tutelage of the Master of Sinanju, Remo had himself ascended to full Masterhood. In full command of his entire being, Remo was able to do things that could only be considered superhuman for the average man. Apparently, the ability to host visitations from the occasional Korean ghost was one of those things.

The boy had prophesied of Remo's coming years. Of the time that Remo would take a pupil of his own and when Chiun would retire to his native village of Sinanju in North Korea. He had also told of the unseen hardships Remo would yet face. As phantom apparitions went, this one had cribbed a lot from Dickens. His cryptic words of Remo's life-to-be made the youngest Master of Sinanju feel a lot like Ebenezer Scrooge. But, unlike Scrooge, by the sound of it there wasn't a damn thing Remo could do to change his life one way or another.

After that time a few short months before, it had taken Remo a while to stop looking over his shoulder every two seconds. Even now he caught himself glancing around every now and then, looking for...

Well, he didn't like to think about what it was he was looking for. He certainly wasn't looking for his future. That was a long way off. He hoped.

Anyway, this day wasn't about the future. This day, thank God, he had work to do. Something to distract him from the bleak words of his ghostly visitor.

When the plane touched down at Luis Munoz Marin International Airport, Remo was the first passenger down the air stairs. He found a cab in front of the main terminal.

His destination was in a seedier part of the capital, San Juan. He gave the driver the address from the scrap of paper he'd brought from the United States and settled back on the taxi's worn seat.

Twenty minutes later, the driver deposited Remo on a sidewalk in front of an old brick building that slouched along the edge of the road like a two-story vagrant. A faded rectangle above the door indicated where a sign had once hung. The sign, along with the business it had advertised, had long since fled the neighborhood.

The street was dark, but like most streets in San Juan it was crowded. A few weak lights pinched the heavy shadows.

"Thanks," Remo said to the anxious taxi driver. Without bothering to count, he peeled a number of twenties off a thick roll of bills.

"It is not safe here," the cabbie warned as he accepted the money. His accent was soft, his voice tense. "MIR owns this neighborhood. This is their stronghold."

At this, Remo offered a flat smile. It was a smile devoid of even a hint of warmth. "According to my guidebook, it's Menudo world headquarters. Tell you what." He peeled off another eight twenties. "I won't be long. Circle the block and meet me back here in ten minutes. If I don't come out with Ricky Martin's signature, this is yours." He held out the bills for an enticingly long moment before depositing them back in the pocket of his tan chinos.

The driver frowned as he eyed Remo's hard face. The fare looked to be in his early thirties. His white T-shirt was spotless, and his hand-sewn leather loafers held not a single scuff or scratch. Apart from the man's startlingly thick wrists, there wasn't anything outwardly extraordinary about him. Except for his eyes.

The driver found himself studying Remo's eyes. Set deep in his skull-like face, the passenger's brown eyes glinted with a quiet menace that stilled the cabbie's heart between beats. There was somehow the promise of otherworldly menace buried in the depths of those penetrating eyes.

The cabdriver nodded with slow fear. "Very well," he agreed. "I will return in ten minutes."

When Remo turned to go, the cabbie called after him. "I am not for independence," the older man blurted.

On the darkened sidewalk, Remo turned silently.

"I love America," the cabbie insisted. Realizing the building in front of which he was proclaiming his fealty for the United States, he pitched his voice lower. "I have never missed an opportunity to express my patriotism. In fact, in November I voted for the man who is to be the new President."

Remo considered the man's words for a long moment. At last, he gave a knowing nod.

"Too late to take it back now," commiserated Remo Williams, a man who yet possessed some vestiges of childlike patriotism, but who rarely found use for those who governed.

And turning on his heel, Remo headed for the building.

Behind the wheel of his cab, the driver didn't see

the front door of the old building open. One moment, Remo was there; the next he was gone, swallowed by shadows.

The driver gulped. Although he did not agree with MIR or its tactics, the older man found himself saying a silent prayer for those inside that crumbling building.

Doors locked on the dangerous San Juan slum, he pulled out into the street.

EDUARDO SANCHEZ HAD SPENT nearly twenty years of his life as a political prisoner in a foreign land.

That his incarceration had taken place not in Russia, China or even Cuba, but in the United States of America did not matter. Freedom was freedom and prison was prison. And he had spent a large part of his adulthood in a cold stone cell in a hellish New York maximum-security federal prison.

That he had been imprisoned for his politics, there was no doubt. Oh, there were those who would have said that he was a murderer. Sanchez wasn't one of them. The bombs he'd set had been the first salvos in the war for liberation.

That his victims had been largely innocent civilians mattered not. America was guilty of oppression. America was its people. Therefore, all Americans were guilty.

Back in the U.S. in the 1970s, Eduardo Sanchez's Movimiento de Izquierda Revolucionaria, or MIR for short, had set off dozens of bombs intended to liberate Puerto Rico from beneath the grinding heel of its American oppressors. The only things the bombs succeeded in liberating were a few American arms and legs from a handful of worthless American torsos.

Prison had kept MIR silent for years. Not anymore.

The time had come. Finally.

In a grimy old garage in the back of an old factory in the most squalid San Juan slum, Eduardo Sanchez and most of the upper echelon of the *movimiento* were in the process of planning the first in a series of events that would oust the rulers of their island nation once and for all and install a new leader of the People's Puerto Rico.

"My friends, the time is upon us," Eduardo Sanchez announced solemnly to those gathered around. There were sixteen of them in total, all dressed in the drab paramilitary chic of the 1970s. The same clothes most of them had worn during their trial years ago. "We exchanged inactivity for our freedom. The silence of the past year has been difficult for all of us to endure. Yet for our benefactor, we embraced the silence. For *her*, we have kept this temporary truce."

A small shrine had been constructed on an upended wooden crate. On it, surrounded by flickering votive candles and rose petals, was a lovingly framed picture of a woman. The photo was meant to show its subject as pensive and caring. Instead, it looked as if she'd had a bowl of glass for breakfast and was ready to spray fragments from her eyes at whoever had the misfortune of gazing at the picture too long.

Careful to keep his own eyes from meeting those in the photograph, Sanchez raised his hands in supplication. His dark, pockmarked face was somber.

"To you, Señorita Primera, we dedicate this new, fresh wave of bloodshed."

With the reverent tone taken by Sanchez, silence had descended upon the wide two-stall garage in which they were assembled. And in that moment of respectful, solemn silence, the gathered leadership of MIR was shocked when the woman in the picture seemed to speak.

"Oh, great, not *her* again."

It was disorienting. The picture was in front of them, but the voice came from behind. The *man's* voice.

The men and women of MIR wheeled around.

A thin young man stood behind them, arms crossed in disgust over his chest. He was looking beyond the group of scruffy terrorists. The photograph of America's First Lady glared back at him.

"You know," Remo griped, walking closer, "I have this feeling that you can trek into the middle of the Sahara, you could jump from a plane in the dead center of the Arctic Circle, you could hide out on the dark side of the moon, for God's sake, and I don't think you'd ever find a place in the universe where you're gonna be safe from those two."

Only a few MIR members carried guns. Confusion quickly surrendered to professionalism. The weapons flew up and were leveled on Remo. The unarmed terrorists, including Eduardo Sanchez, took safety behind the rest.

"Who are you?" Sanchez demanded. "What do you want?"

"Besides mandatory muzzles for every politician and his wife in the forty-eight contiguous states?" Remo said, his voice thin. "What I want is for dirtbags like you to slither back under the rocks you climbed out from. And before this turns into twenty questions, I know what you're up to. I know part of the secret deal you cut for your pardons was to keep your noses clean until the President was out of office. I know he's gone by the end of the week, and I know you planned to celebrate this great peaceful exchange of democratic power by blowing up a couple of planes heading for the mainland from the San Juan airport. I knew everything but *that.*" He pointed to the First Lady's picture.

For the first time, Remo noticed something lying on the floor beneath it. The thing had feathers.

"Dammit, don't tell me you're sacrificing chickens to her?" he demanded.

Sanchez's spine stiffened. "We owe her our freedom," he sniffed. "If she had not wished to curry favor with the Hispanic community during her Senate campaign in New York, her husband would never have released us."

"Yada-yada-yada," Remo droned. "Let's just get this over with. I have a cab waiting."

When he took a step toward Sanchez, the raised

guns rattled more alert. Remo was a hair away from the nearest gunman.

"I do not know how you learned of our plans, but you are not from the pig United States government," Sanchez insisted. "The President who released us still serves. He fears the wrath of his wife, so would not send anyone against us."

"You only heard from one part of the government," Remo assured the terrorist. "The part that studies polls and does focus groups and reads frigging tea leaves and Ouija boards to see what's the right or wrong thing to do on any given day. I'm not from that part of the government. I'm from the other part. The good part."

"There is no other part." Sanchez grinned malevolently. "We were given pardons by the President himself, thanks to the intercession of his lovely wife. We are free men. Free to do whatever we want. And you are a dead man."

The smile Remo returned was cold. "Been there, done that," he said. "At least five times. I've lost count." Not a facial muscle twitched as he studied the MIR leader.

Sanchez couldn't believe the stranger's nerve. He was as cool as they came, not even giving a hint of concern at the weapons that were trained on him.

"Presidents come and Presidents go," Remo continued. "The part of the government I work for isn't even really part of the government. We've lasted through eight presidents, about to go on nine, and we're still standing. We say the hell with what

Jeanne Dixon and Dick Morris have to say. We do what's right because it's the right thing to do.''

And nearby, another terrorist spoke.

"We protected," the rotten-toothed man said, sneering. His cunning eyes were rimmed in black. A crooked yellow smile split the dark swath of his five-o'clock shadow.

Remo didn't like the satisfied smirk the man wore. In fact, he didn't like it so much that he decided to wipe the smile off the man's face. He did so with a sideways slap so fast that none in the room could hope to follow his hand.

Remo succeeded in wiping away the smile along with the rest of the man's face. Dislodged flesh and bone struck the grimy black wall of the garage with a hard wet splat.

So fast did this happen that the man didn't have time to relax his smile. As his body fell, his face remained fixed to the wall, a now toothless grin gaping like a happy mask at the other shocked MIR terrorists.

Seeing how quickly the stranger in their midst could move, the men and women of MIR, so used to delivering faceless death from safe distances, reacted like true terrorists confronted by risk to their own precious lives and limbs. They threw down their guns and threw up their hands.

"We surrender!" several cried.

"Prison in America is not so bad," Eduardo Sanchez agreed numbly as he eyed the smear of bloody bone that was once the face of his most trusted lieutenant. "Maybe if we go back to jail, Ed Asner will start returning my calls."

"Nope," Remo said firmly. "No jail. Not this time."

He was looking beyond the forest of raised hands. An old Ford Escort sat rusting in one corner of the garage. The car belonged to Sanchez.

"You are not here to arrest us?" the MIR leader asked. When he tore his gaze from the bleeding skull on the floor, his eyes were deeply worried.

Remo didn't answer. At least not directly. "Hey, you guys like the circus?" he said cheerily.

Hesitation from the crowd. "Uh…"

"Of course you do," Remo insisted. "Everyone likes the circus."

Like an elderly woman herding a flock of park pigeons, Remo guided the fifteen remaining terrorists back toward the car. When one or two tried to escape, he coaxed them back into place with a sound smack to the side of the head.

Going around the far side of the car, Remo quickly sealed the doors. Coming back around, he sprang the two doors on the nearer side.

"Everybody in!" he proclaimed.

A wash of fresh worry passed over the crowd. "We will not all fit," offered a male terrorist.

"That's negative thinking," Remo warned. "We don't allow negative thinkers in the circus."

And lifting up the man bodily, he tossed him onto the far side of the rear seat. The terrorist cracked his forehead on the door. He fell back into the seat, dazed.

Sensing no escape, the others began to climb nervously inside the car. By the time only five of them were in, the sitting room was gone. The three in the back were already squeezed uncomfortably in place.

"The car is full." The next terrorist in line shrugged. She was a woman in her early fifties. She licked her lips nervously.

"That attitude'll get you thrown out of the big top, missy," Remo cautioned with a waggling finger.

And grabbing her by the neck, he tossed her onto the laps of the three men. When she tried to sit up, she found she couldn't. Another terrorist had been thrown in on top of her. His broad bottom pressed down on her face.

Another, then another terrorist flew in through the door. When the back was full, Remo piled more men and women in the front.

"There isn't room!" one voice cried desperately.

"Sure, there is," Remo insisted. "The nuns from the orphanage took us all to a circus when we were kids. There must have been thirty clowns stuffed in a car even littler than this. Just think skinny."

He braced the front door shut with his foot. He'd already slammed and sealed the back.

There was only one terrorist left. Heel holding the door in place, Remo reached for Eduardo Sanchez.

"No, no, no," Sanchez insisted. He shook in fear even as Remo dragged him to the car. "This cannot be. You cannot be from the government. We were promised that we would be protected as long as the current President served.''

''His term's up January 20,'' Remo said. ''Yours is just running out a couple of days early.''

Springing the door, Remo stuffed Sanchez inside. It was a tight fit. The fourteen other terrorists inside moaned and yelped as Remo jiggled the door closed on the press of warm human flesh. He sealed the door with a metal-fusing slap.

Someone opened the sunroof. Hands clawed the air.

''Please keep your hands and feet inside the clown car at all times,'' Remo said. As a warning, he slid the sunroof sharply into the cluster of up-raised arms. A few bones cracked audibly. The arms quickly retreated inside the car.

As the MIR leadership groaned, Remo did a quick search of the surrounding area. In one of the many crates stacked in the garage, he found something that looked like a cartoon bomb Snidely Whiplash might use. Several sticks of dynamite had been fastened together with black electrical tape. A digital clock was fastened to the side of the bomb, ominous wires strung to the explosives. The LED display of the clock was dark.

Remo brought the bomb back to the car. By this time, the windows were filled with nervous fog. Remo rapped his knuckles on the rooftop.

''Quick question before the finale,'' Remo called

at the nearest steaming window. "How do you set this thing?"

There was a squeak of damp flesh on wet glass. A scrunched-up eye looked out from a mass of limbs.

The eye widened in abject fear.

"Let me out and I will show you," came the muffled voice of Eduardo Sanchez.

The terrorist's fat lips were plastered across the small triangular vent window on the passenger-side door.

Remo frowned at the pursing flattened lips. "Didn't they teach you anything in clown college? No one exits the clown car until the final act," he warned. "How 'bout if I press one of the little buttons?"

The car began to rock on its springs. A chorus of nos filtered out through the ball of crammed flesh.

"Okay, maybe not."

Remo's frown deepened as he studied the bomb more carefully. The look of confusion on the face of his captor was not lost on Eduardo Sanchez.

"If you let me go, I will show you how to set it," the MIR leader promised, his strained voice growing crafty.

Remo looked down at the man's one visible eye. "I don't believe you," he said.

"I *promise*," Sanchez insisted. "I give you my solemn, most holy and sacred word."

Remo gave the terrorist a deeply skeptical look. "You've made other promises in the past," he suggested. "Like not to blow up any more innocent people, for instance."

"That was politics," Sanchez dismissed. "This is a personal pledge. From me, Eduardo Sanchez, to you..." His voice trailed off. He suddenly realized that he didn't know the name of the scary, bomb-holding man who had stuffed him and the entire future ruling congress of the People's Puerto Rico into his hatchback.

"Tell you what," Remo offered. "I give you a counter promise. Show me how to set this, *then* I'll let you go."

Sanchez was reluctant to take the man at his word. On the other hand, he didn't appear to have much of a choice.

"Very well," the terrorist relented.

Nodding, Remo used the suction of his fingertips to pop open the small triangle of glass at the corner of the passenger-side window. A gush of nervous body odors flooded from the car's interior.

Wiggling like a snake shedding its skin, Sanchez managed to work one arm out the window.

"How long do you wish me to set it for?"

Remo considered. "Three minutes," he decided.

"That will not give us much time," Sanchez warned.

"Plenty of time," Remo assured him.

As Remo held up the bomb to the terrorist's eye, Sanchez carefully entered the time. When he took his finger away, the clock had begun to tick a three-minute countdown.

"Now let me out," Eduardo Sanchez insisted, wriggling his arm back inside the car.

Remo leaned in close to the terrorist's one visible eye. "Sorry." He smiled. "That was just a terrorist's promise. Besides, the Local Brotherhood of Clowns, Mimes and Tumblers would put my ass in a sling if I violated the sanctity of the clown car."

With a gentle push, he slipped the bomb through the small triangular window. It bumped against several thrashing legs on its way down to the foot well.

The small car began to shake like a can of paint in a hardware store mixer. Screams and muffled curses rose from out of the car's sweat-drenched interior.

"I know one group of clowns who don't know the clown code," Remo warned. "I'm gonna have to report you to Bozo. And if you thought America was tyrannical, wait'll you see what he does with a seltzer bottle."

And with that, he left the garage and its carload of terrified terrorists.

The last image the horrified eye of Eduardo Sanchez saw before the window in front of him steamed up for the last time was the First Lady's grinning face. As the fog enveloped her image, votive candles surrounding her carefully coiffed hair in an ethereal nimbus, the soon-to-be-late Eduardo Sanchez had a sickening realization.

"She is angry with us," the terrorist whined as her face faded forever from his sight. "I told you we should have sacrificed more chickens."

WHEN REMO SLIPPED out the front door of MIR headquarters, his cab was already slowing to a stop. He hopped into the back seat.

In the rearview mirror, the driver noted the cruelly satisfied smile on his fare's face.

"You ever wonder how they fit all those clowns into that little car in the circus?" Remo asked in satisfaction.

The driver frowned confusion even as he began to drive down the winding street. "There is a trap-door on the bottom of the car. The clowns climb up from beneath the floor."

Remo snapped his fingers. "I *knew* there had to be some kind of trick," he said, his brow creasing.

And as his fingers snapped, there came a muffled thud from somewhere far behind them. Remo alone felt the gentle rumble of earth beneath the cab.

He felt good. For the moment, he had forgotten about the future. It was a feeling he could get used to.

He settled back comfortably in the seat of the cab for the winding trip back to the airport.

WHEN HE SAW the thin man leaving MIR headquarters, Corporal Rolando Rodriguez stopped dead. He loitered on the street corner near a group of rowdy drunks until the cab drove away. Tucking the small box he was carrying tightly under his arm, he hurried across the street to the rotted old building.

The first thing Rodriguez did upon entering the garage was vomit. The walls were smeared with globs of flesh—like hurled meat. Eduardo Sanchez's car was curled apart at the top like a stubbed-out cigar. Twisted black metal sent threads of smoke into the fetid room.

Rodriguez backed into the office. As he put his box down, the contents rattled. They were the new identifying pins. The ones designed by their leader. Had he not been sent to retrieve them, Rolando would be dead, too.

With shaking hands, he found Sanchez's little black book and dialed the special number. When the woman answered, he felt his frightened breath catch.

*"¡Hola!"* she said with quiet menace. In the background, a man spoke Spanish in slow, measured tones.

"There has been a catastrophe!" Rodriguez wailed. "Many of the *movimiento* are dead." He quickly described the grisly scene in the garage.

"Who did this?" she demanded once he was through. The white-hot rage roiling below the barely controlled surface threatened to crack the ice in her tone. So softly did she say the words that her Spanish accent seemed to disappear, lost in her swelling anger.

"I don't know," Rodriguez cried. "A man. He was thin, with short hair. He wore a T-shirt. I couldn't really see that well. It was dark." Something suddenly came to him. "But his wrists were thick. Very thick. Like the trunk of a tree."

There was a soft intake of air on the other end of the line. In the ensuing moment of silence, the muffled man's voice continued to drone in the background. When the woman finally spoke, there was fresh menace in her tone.

"I've met him before," she snarled.

Rodriguez was surprised. "What do you want me to do?"

Her voice was perfectly level. "He is a threat to my goals. I will find him, then you will kill him."

The oblivious man continued to drone continuously in the background as she slammed down the phone in Rolando's ear.

**3**

Lippincott, Forsythe, Butler had been the most prestigious brokerage house on Wall Street since before the time horse-drawn surreys filled the muddy lane that would one day become the most famous financial district on Earth.

Legend had it that an agent of LFB brokered the original purchase deal for the island of Manhattan between the Dutch governor general and the indigenous Indian tribe. It was a testament to the reputation of this distinguished old house that the story was not dismissed out of hand as apocryphal.

The firm occupied one of the original Lippincott buildings in lower Manhattan. There were several. Pricey real estate was easy to come by to the family that had practically dived like lemmings over the side of the *Mayflower* in order to shout dibs over much of the new country.

Over the years, the Lippincott family—along with its poorer millionaire relatives, the Butlers and Forsythes—had weathered all the financial storms of a young nation.

It was a comfort of sorts to all who worked for

the Lippincott family of corporations to know that the businesses for which they spent their days slaving would last long after they had passed from this realm into the next.

Lawrence Fine was just the sort of employee to derive such solace. Whenever he passed through the opulent lobby and rode the gilded elevator up to the fourteenth floor, Lawrence marveled at his small role in financial history.

The founding Lippincotts had worked in buildings on this very location. Of course the original structures had been replaced over the years, but beneath the tar and concrete of Manhattan was the same soil trod upon by builders of a commercial empire that had stretched across centuries. Atop that same hard-packed earth, future Lippincott generations would preside over financial markets yet to develop.

There was history here. In a sense, the entire economic history of America. Lawrence Fine usually felt it as a palpable presence around him. Usually. But not this day.

This day he found the lobby a garish distraction and the elevator a confining box pulled too far off the ground by too-slender cables. Why did it remind him of a coffin?

On the fourteenth floor, Lawrence stepped into the recycled air of the main LFB offices. His head swam as he made his way down the hallway and into the rows of cubicles.

In strategic locations around the floor, scrolling electronic boards kept track of the movements of the

New York Stock Exchange. Company abbreviations and numbers ran across the long rectangular boxes from left to right, moving so quickly only a trained eye could see anything more than just an endless yellow blur. Lawrence Fine possessed such an eye.

The scroll on one board was nearing the end of its repetitive cycle. Flashing quickly, it reached the *R*s.

Behind his wireless glasses, watery eyes took in the latest information. Although he had just come from the trading floor, information could change in a heartbeat.

Pausing, Lawrence watched the latest data on the company that most concerned him fly by. When it did, he breathed a relieved sigh. Up a quarter point in the past ten minutes.

Lawrence started through the cubicle aisle. His leather briefcase swung in alternate time to his pumping legs.

Behind him, heads stuck out from cubicles. It was a morning ritual. The taunts trailed behind him.

"Nyuk-nyuk-nyuk."

"Soitenly, Moe."

"You had a hallucination. No, I had a hunk of pipe."

The words were meant to be insulting. However, as usual he had no idea what they meant. This morning, Lawrence Fine didn't care. He had a very important meeting to get to.

They had given him his own office while he was working with this special client. For the past three years, this had been a career goal, but thanks to the client he'd been given, Lawrence found himself missing his old cubicle.

He stepped from the cubicle sea and into the adjacent hallway. The vague sick-building smell was replaced by an odor of rich wood and leather.

Lawrence had only just stepped into the corridor when he caught sight of the man coming toward him.

His heart sank.

He didn't need this. Not today.

It was Arthur Finch. Distantly related to the Butlers, Finch had been with the firm for only three months and had already moved from the cubicles to a small office. The privilege of breeding.

Finch's face broke into a broad smile when he spied Lawrence coming toward him.

"Hey, Moe, where'd you get the sunglasses?" LFB's latest management trainee called down the hall to Lawrence.

Lawrence frowned at the non sequitur. He hardly ever knew what Finch was talking about.

"I'm not wearing sunglasses."

"Of course not, knucklehead," Finch smiled.

They were side by side now. Finch was still wearing the same idiot's grin he had sported since the moment he learned Lawrence's name. He was the one who had inspired the taunts from the other workers during his three months of goofing off in the cubicles. When he'd left, the jokes had stayed.

It was a quarter of a year later, and Lawrence still

didn't want to admit that he hadn't the foggiest idea what everyone was laughing about.

"Hey, I saw the Corleones a few minutes ago," Finch said, stopping Lawrence with a palm to the shoulder. With his forefinger, he pressed his nose to one side.

"They're here already?" Lawrence asked anxiously.

Finch nodded. "They brought a washtub full of cement. One of them wanted to know your shoe size."

Lawrence tensed visibly. "You shouldn't make fun of them," he whispered.

"Why? They can't hear me."

"Please," Lawrence begged. "And they're not thugs." He pulled out a handkerchief, wiping sweat from his forehead.

"Gee whiz, Larry, lighten up."

Larry. All his life he'd been Lawrence. That had stopped the minute Finch showed up at the brokerage house.

"Excuse me," Lawrence said. He stepped around Arthur Finch. Spine rigid, he marched down the hall.

"If they try any funny stuff, start a pie fight and escape in the confusion," Finch called after him.

Doing a quick one-legged shuffle, the Butler progeny backed up. Spinning, Arthur Finch marched merrily down the hall in the direction opposite the terrified Lawrence Fine.

Lawrence arrived at his small office thirty seconds later. When he opened the door, his nostrils were assaulted by the sickeningly familiar mixture of noxious colognes.

There were three men in the room. Two were huge mountains of flesh and muscle. They stood just inside the door. The third was an oily little man in a shiny blue suit. He sat in a chair before the tidy oak desk.

"I'm not late, Mr. Sweet," Lawrence pleaded with the attorney as he pushed the door closed. He whimpered as he eyed the two behemoths.

"Not to worry," Sol Sweet replied. "We're early."

Lawrence breathed a sigh of relief. His briefcase a makeshift leather shield, he stepped past the two bodyguards and sank into his chair.

"The stock's performing well." Sweet smiled as Lawrence settled his briefcase onto the blotter.

In his element now, Lawrence Fine nodded. "I just checked the board. It's gone up another half point since I entered the building."

"What about block trades?"

"Not many now. But remember, it's only 9:00 a.m. And because of the nature of this, um, business, word of mouth is carrying us at the start. I'd say things are going very well. Better, in fact, than I predicted."

"What about clearing and settlement? Has everything been ironed out?"

Lawrence nodded. "Absolutely. We're a clearing corporation, as well. You chose LFB specifically because we were a large enough concern to handle all financial requirements and responsibilities.''

At this, Sweet flashed a row of barracuda teeth. ''LFB was chosen, Larry, because its guiding principle has always been greed,'' the lawyer said. ''Your founders ran guns to the Indians, as well as to the pilgrims. Their descendants backed the Colonies and the Crown during the Revolution. *Their* sons secretly swore allegiance to the North *and* South during the Civil War. LFB was even a clearinghouse for Nazi funds during the end of World War II. Don't think you can coast on prestige with us. This company is big, corrupt and well-connected. *That's* why we picked it.''

As he spoke, Sweet leaned across the desk. Lawrence Fine sat quietly as the man stabbed out a long-distance number on the touch tone. Sweet turned on the speakerphone.

Lawrence realized the moment the voice came on the line that the phone call had been set up in advance. Otherwise, the man who spoke would never have answered.

''Is that you, Sol?''

It was a warm rasp. The overpronunciation of every word was familiar to Lawrence Fine. He had heard it on television a number of times. Always on the news.

Don Anselmo Scubisci. The ''Dandy Don'' of the Manhattan Mafia. Although he was the one behind this operation, Lawrence had never actually spoken to the man before. When he heard the familiar voice, he felt his stomach clench.

"Yes, Mr. Scubisci," the attorney replied. "I'm here with Larry Fine."

"Lawrence!" Don Scubisci's voice enthused. "It's a pleasure to finally meet you. How are you today?"

"I'm—" Lawrence's voice was a barely detectable squeak. He cleared his throat. "I'm fine, Mr. Scubisci."

"I'm so glad to hear that. I understand from Solly that you have been quite successful in your handling of our little business venture. The powers that be at LFB were wise to give you this assignment. I'm very pleased."

Pride mixed with fear. "Thank you, Mr. Scubisci."

"No, I thank you, Lawrence. I've been monitoring the situation from here. We are up two points since trading began this morning. Up overall for the week. Very nice."

Sol leaned in to the speaker. "New Jersey helped, Mr. Scubisci," the attorney said. "Since the story hit the wire services today, we've been performing well. The discreet word we put out on the street has pushed the value up."

"Excellent," Don Scubisci said. "Now, Sol, what about Raffair corporate headquarters?"

"Renovations and remodeling are finally complete. We'll be up and running tomorrow. The day after at the latest."

"And my office?"

"Will be waiting for you, Mr. Scubisci."

"Good, good," Don Scubisci said. "Sorry, but this is going to have to be a quick call, Lawrence. I have an appointment with my physical trainer in five minutes. I just wanted to call with a personal expression of gratitude for the long hours you've put into this for us. It's greatly appreciated. Keep in touch, Solly. Goodbye, gentlemen."

The line went dead.

Their business over, Sol stood. The two flanking bodyguards bundled in beside him.

Lawrence Fine remained at his desk, holding his breath as he stared at the speaker. Until now, the man who was his de facto boss in this matter had stayed firmly in the abstract. But now...

The way he studied the speaker, it was almost as if he expected the most notorious crime figure in modern New York history to come crawling out through the plastic mesh.

"This is the last face-to-face we'll need for a while," Sol Sweet announced, breaking Fine's trance. "Now that Raffair HQ is set, we'll be transferring from our temporary digs. You can call down there if you need me."

As the men turned for the door, Lawrence stood.

"Um, I don't know if I should say this," the broker offered weakly. "But, um, I can get into a lot of trouble with the SEC if this thing goes south."

Sol's dead-fish eyes were flat. "Cold feet, Larry?"

"No," Lawrence said hastily. "God, no. It's just that the, um, *feds* wouldn't be happy with any of this."

What little spark of light that remained in them drained visibly from Sol Sweet's eyes. "Of course they wouldn't, Larry," the attorney said. "And please don't say feds. It doesn't sit well on your tongue. Besides, neither you nor any of us are gangsters."

Lawrence squirmed. "Well, it's..." He dropped his voice low. "It's just that you mentioned something happening in New Jersey. I heard this morning about some drug raid that went bad. A bunch of federal agents were killed."

It was the closest thing to a direct question Lawrence Fine dared ask. If there was a link, things here at LFB could be a lot worse than he'd imagined.

Sol Sweet's answer was terse.

"That's the price of doing business," the attorney said coldly. "Larry, your personal, ethically questionable Raffair stock has doubled in value in the last three days. If you're having any pangs of conscience, you should take them up with your checkbook."

Their meeting at an end, he offered the LFB employee his back. Without a backward glance, the attorney and his small entourage left the office.

Lawrence sank back into his chair. He closed his eyes.

It was the phone call from Anselmo Scubisci that

had rattled him. If he had been thinking more clearly, he never would have mentioned New Jersey. He shouldn't have said anything to the Mob lawyer. He should have just let it go.

After a long time, Lawrence opened his eyes. He noticed his name plate was ajar. He hadn't seen before that it had been moved. Lawrence picked it up. The brass was cold.

His given name had been crossed out. By the looks of it with a set of keys. In the narrow space above, the name "Larry" had been scratched into the brass.

Larry Fine. For some reason, people loved to call him that. Lawrence had no idea why.

He let the nameplate slip from his fingers. It struck the desk with a thud.

**4**

Remo's flight was an hour away from landing at Boston's Logan International Airport when the commotion began. It came from the back of the plane.

"Whadaya mean no more! Gimme a drink, now!"

Over the past two decades, everyday airfare had been drastically reduced. The practical result was that the sort of people who used to take buses had now taken to the sky, turning commercial planes into Greyhounds with wings. In recent years, the stories of obnoxious and dangerous behavior on airplanes had been multiplying at an alarming rate.

When Remo looked back, he expected to see someone relieving himself on a service cart. Instead, he saw a harried flight attendant standing in the aisle next to a seated passenger.

"I'm sorry, sir," the flight attendant offered with a weak smile, "but don't you think you've had a little too much to drink?" She blew a stray lock of hair from her face.

Fire raged in the man's bloodshot eyes. His mouth opened and closed in silent shock. And as his brain tried to catch up to the words that would not come, Remo found himself studying the man's face with narrowed eyes.

He looked familiar. Then it hit Remo.

On assignment in Africa three months ago, Remo had run into a group of men in an East African restaurant. He'd succeeded in removing all but one of them. In a moment of sudden realization, he knew that he was looking at the one that got away.

"I'm not drunk," Johnny "Books" Fungillo snarled at the flight attendant.

The woman shook her head. "I didn't say you were," she insisted pleasantly. "But we'll be landing soon, and I thought you might like to freshen up a little first."

"I'll freshen up your lunch cart," Johnny belched furiously. Big drunken hands began fumbling at his belt.

With a shriek, the woman tore off down the aisle.

"Eek! Code 9, code 9!" she yelled to the other flight attendants as she ran.

It was the most dreaded distress signal in their entire chosen field, dubbed the midair "Poop Alarm."

The other flight attendants reacted like trained soldiers. Serving carts bounced and rattled as if encountering mad turbulence as they raced them from the danger zone. The entire crew of flight attendants disappeared into the galley.

A worried excitement filled the cabin. In the moment of chattering confusion, Remo slipped up to Johnny Books.

The gangster was still trying to work the buckle on his belt. His clumsy fingers were having a difficult time maneuvering the little silver clip.

"If monkey can't dress himself, monkey shouldn't wear people pants," Remo advised.

The words soaked into the liquor-swamped mind of Johnny Books Fungillo. He looked up with belligerence that quickly faded to confusion. "Hey, I know—"

A gasp. Johnny's confused expression flashed to abject terror. With a lunge, he grabbed underneath his jacket.

Remo could sense by the way he carried himself that there was a weapon there. Somehow, Johnny had smuggled it onto the plane undetected.

"No, no, no. No guns for monkey," Remo warned, quickly pinching Johnny's elbow between two delicate fingers. The big man's darting hand froze in place. "Not until monkey stops throwing feces at the nice lady."

Before Johnny could grab his gun with the other hand, Remo tapped him in the middle of his forehead. All movement stopped as the gangster froze in place.

Johnny Fungillo tried desperately to move. He could not. Sweat beads formed on his forehead as he struggled in vain. Helpless, his wide eyes flitted fearfully to Remo.

Remo wasn't even paying attention to Johnny.

Snaking a hand up under the man's jacket, he found both holster and gun. They came free with a gentle tug that trailed nylon tendrils.

The holster's soft material was strangely frictionless. Using his body to shield himself from other passengers, Remo snapped the gun into two fat halves, which he deposited in the in-flight magazine sleeve. The cloth bulged at the weight.

"How'd you get this on the plane?" Remo asked, genuinely interested.

But when he looked at Johnny, the gangster's unblinking eyes stared helplessly from his frozen face.

"Oh, yeah."

His curiosity wasn't enough to bring Johnny out of it. He tugged the thug's eyelids down. They shut like dark window shades over Johnny's petrified eyes.

Remo stuffed the holster into the sagging seat pocket. He was back in his seat by the time the galley curtain slid open.

A group of flight attendants appeared with buckets and sponges. Each wore a pair of big yellow rubber gloves. Clippy clothespins held their nostrils tightly shut. They seemed surprised to find the unruly passenger still in his seat. Better yet, he appeared to be sound asleep.

Relieved that the passenger had not relieved himself, they decided to let sleeping dogs lie. On silent toes, the entire crew tiptoed back up the aisle.

They hid out in the galley, refusing all passenger

entreaties for peanuts or seat-belt instructions for the rest of the blessedly silent flight to Boston.

TWO HOURS LATER, as baffled Boston paramedics were driving the comatose Johnny Fungillo across the windswept Logan tarmac, Remo's cab was dropping him off in front of the Massachusetts condo he shared with the Master of Sinanju.

The building he called home was an old remodeled church. A decade ago, when a contract negotiation demanded a house, Remo's employer had bought the entire complex, turning it over to the exclusive use of Remo and his teacher.

The building was big, homely and located in a city that was regularly featured on the local Boston news for the daily murders that took place there. It was a far cry from the tidy little home with a picket fence and a loving wife Remo had dreamed of once upon a time.

With a wistful sigh, Remo trudged up the stairs. He was pushing open the front door when he heard the sound.

It was a cry of indescribable pain. And the voice that produced it was unmistakable.

Remo felt his heart catch. *"Chiun,"* he breathed.

The shrill cry had come from far upstairs. From the foyer, Remo took the entire main staircase in two massive strides. He was already running when he hit the second-floor landing.

More screams. They were killing him. *Torturing* him.

Fearing not the force that could harm the Master of Sinanju, Remo flew on, his only thought to aid his teacher.

The next flight of stairs led to a closed door. Remo picked up steam as he rounded to the staircase. He took all the steps in one leap, twisting in air and slamming against the door with the heels of both feet.

The door assembly splintered into a million wooden shards. Daggers of pine ripped across the bell-tower meditation room, impaling themselves in walls and crashing through windows.

Remo soared into the room in the wake of the door remnants. Eyes alert, every muscle tensed, hands raised to ward off whatever danger might be lurking there.

But rather than an unknown enemy, Remo found himself peering into a pair of shocked, familiar eyes. The hazel orbs were set into a delicate face of bone that had been lovingly wrapped in a thin veneer of parchment skin. As Remo swept into the room, a mummified mouth formed a startled O.

Chiun, Reigning Master of the House of Sinanju, raised his wattled neck from out of the collar of his kimono like an angry snapping turtle. Seated in a lotus position on the floor of his meditation room, Chiun appeared completely unharmed. His spine was erect in his red silk kimono, his bony hands folded delicately to his knees. In the room, there was no sign of either torturer or torturer's tools.

"Remo, what is the meaning of this?" the ancient

Korean demanded, incomprehension pinching his singsong voice.

Breathless, Remo relaxed his muscles. "What the hell is going on in here?" he snapped, exhaling tension.

"I asked you first," Chiun accused. "Why have you crashed in here like a demented bovine?"

"I heard screaming," Remo insisted.

"Do not be ridiculous," Chiun huffed, waving a dismissive hand. "I warn you, Remo, if you are going mad again, I refuse to allow it. I have put up with quite enough of that already."

Face stern, the Master of Sinanju rose with silent fluidity from the floor. He clucked as he inspected the fan-shaped debris field.

"Let's get this straight," Remo stressed, coming up beside the old man. "I am not crazy, I have never been crazy and I definitely heard you screaming."

"I will have Emperor Smith prepare a padded room at Fortress Folcroft for you," Chiun droned. "If you are having another nervous breakdown, you may discuss your childhood bed-wetting with one of his quacks rather than vent your anger on my doors."

Harold Smith was their employer. Folcroft Sanitarium was the private mental health institution he ran, which also doubled as home to the secret organization CURE.

"Hah-hah. They're *my* doors, too," Remo said.

Chiun gave him a withering look. A hand lined with ropy veins appeared from the folds of his kimono. With a tapered fingernail, he picked at a large wooden chunk that still clung to the archway. The hinge it was connected to was torn and twisted. When the Master of Sinanju looked back at his pupil, his accusing eyes were hooded.

"I *thought* you were being tortured," Remo explained, scowling at the old man's silent admonishment. It sounded ridiculous to even say such a thing. Chiun obviously agreed.

"Oh, Remo," he said sadly, the harsh light flickering from his eyes. It was replaced with knowing sympathy.

Remo raised a warning finger. "Don't start," he threatened. "I'm as sane as you are. I'm *saner* than you are. I'm the freaking poster child for mental stability."

Chiun's face was a placid pool. "All those present who did not attempt to blow up a foreign nation's capital with nuclear booms, please raise your hand." The Master of Sinanju's hand alone appeared, fluttering high in the air.

"Oh, can the crap," Remo snarled. "There were extenuating circumstances there. Besides, they weren't even my bombs."

With a smile of flickering satisfaction, the old man lowered his arm. "I only consider myself fortunate that, in your madness, you were not more concerned. Had you been, you might have brought a wrecking ball to bear against the walls of Castle Sinanju. Clean up this mess."

With that, the old man turned on a sandaled heel.

He marched back to the center of the room, settling back to the rug. For the first time, Remo noticed the small stack of sleek black equipment piled there.

"What's all that stuff?"

"None of your business," Chiun sniffed.

"It looks like stereo equipment."

Chiun rolled his eyes. "I will tell you, O Nosy One, *after* you remove this mess."

Remo could see there would be no arguing. With a sigh, he began collecting the largest chunks of door. He propped them against the wall. As he worked, Chiun fussed with the equipment on the floor. A long extension cord ran over to a wall outlet. Remo saw a number of plastic boxes stacked in neat piles at the Master of Sinanju's scissored knees.

"You can't blame me for being worried," Remo commented as he hefted the last of the big door slabs. "It sounded like you were raping roosters in here."

"All was joy until you charged in here like a boob in a China shop," Chiun replied, uninterested.

"That's bull," Remo corrected dryly.

"No, it is truth," Chiun maintained. He fixed his pupil with an acid eye. "Less talk, more work."

It took Remo ten minutes to tug all the wooden darts from the wall. With a dustpan and brush, he picked up the shattered glass and smaller wood fragments.

"Finished," he said as he dumped the last dustpan of splinters into a paper shopping bag. "I'll have to pick up a new door at the hardware store tomorrow. Guess I'll have to hire someone for these windows." A thin, cold wind snaked through the shattered panes. Neither man felt the cold. "So what's with the stereo stuff?"

For the past few minutes, the Master of Sinanju's mood had been lightening. With Remo's work finished for the moment, he stood, proudly extending a shiny plastic CD case to his pupil. His wrinkled face beamed.

"Behold!" Chiun announced grandly.

Remo inspected the album. His face fell at once.

On the compact disc, an overweight woman in a cowboy hat sat on a split-rail fence. It was a testament to the skill of the fence's engineers that it didn't splinter beneath her wide derriere. She looked like a hippo on a park bench. At the top of the CD was the name Wylander Jugg.

"Oh, God, no," Remo moaned, his stomach caving in. It was all clear to him now. "That caterwauling I heard was you singing, wasn't it?" he accused weakly.

"I do not know what your demented ears think they heard, but it is possible that I did burst into song. Her voice is infectious."

"So's syphilis. And at least that's fun while you're getting it. Where'd you ever hear of Wylander?"

A brief thundercloud passed over the old Asian's face. "You left on the radio in your car when you went into the video store last week."

Remo remembered. For reasons he hoped would

never be brought up again, Chiun avoided video stores like the plague.

The old man's dark moment passed.

"I chanced to hear her lilting voice as I switched channels. With but one strain, I knew I had found true love." Chiun drew the case to his narrow chest.

"Chiun," Remo said, forcing a reasonable tone, "everybody hates country music. The only thing entertaining about it is George Strait's driving record and the guy who does the Kenny Rogers impersonation on 'Mad TV.'"

Chiun raised a thin eyebrow. "As usual, I have no idea what you are talking about. I will have to remember to thank the gods for this continued blessing before I retire this evening." He turned the CD in his hand, examining Wylander Jugg carefully. "She is lovely." He sighed.

"If 'lovely' is redneck slang for 'fat as a house,' sure."

"She is not fat," Chiun dismissed. "She is simply well proportioned."

"If I was one-tenth that well proportioned, you'd have me doing squat thrusts till my colon dropped out."

"You are jealous of her comeliness." As he glanced rapturously at the photo once more, a contented smile kissed Chiun's dry lips. "Her beauty is on the inside," he insisted.

"So's Jonah, Pinocchio and about a million soggy Big Macs," Remo countered.

With a thin scowl, Chiun shook his head. "Really, Remo, your lack of depth amazes me. At last your nation has produced an art to rival the daytime dramas of old, and you, soulless as you are, deride it.''

''Chiun, let's face facts here. Your tastes and mine have never been quite the same.''

''Another small favor for which I will thank the gods.''

Chiun sank to the floor amid his CD collection.

''Snipe all you want,'' Remo said. ''I like what I like. And I don't like country music.''

''That is because you refuse to evolve,'' Chiun replied. ''You are content to leave things exactly as they are, little realizing that despite your protestations, things change.''

At that, Remo fell silent. He had managed for a time to banish the weighty thoughts that had plagued him of late.

Chiun noticed the heavy silence. As he pretended to fuss with his plastic cases, he turned a half-interested eye on his pupil.

''Have you given any thought to the words of my son, Song?'' he questioned absently.

Remo's head snapped up. ''What? Oh. No, not really.'' His troubled look made clear what was truly on his mind.

Chiun nodded. ''It is a difficult time, this long goodbye between Master and student,'' he said, his voice soft.

The words brought another, greater pause.

The truth was, Chiun was as eager as Remo to

forget that aspect of their shared future. The Master of Sinanju's eventual retirement and Remo's inevitable ascension to Reigning Masterhood. But the old Korean had seen many winters, and so understood better than his pupil what an impossible task it was to hold back the future. It would come whether they wanted it to or not.

"Can we just leave that one alone for a while, Little Father?" Remo asked quietly.

The old man nodded. The wisps of hair that clung to scalp above each of his shell-like ears were cobwebs stirred by cold eddies of air.

"There is always your future pupil," Chiun offered, his tone lightening. "That was the purpose of Song's visit. What thought have you given to that?"

"I haven't run an ad in the Help Wanteds yet," Remo said. A moment's hesitation. "But, yeah, I'm giving it some thought." He felt guilty even admitting it.

Chiun nodded in satisfaction. "Good. We will have to visit Sinanju in the autumn. Most of the winter babies will have been born by then."

Remo frowned. "Can't they just send us their fall-baby catalog?" he said sarcastically. "I told you, Chiun, no wacky breeding rituals and no pulling some Sinanju infant from his crib while mamasan's in the kitchen getting the rice-flavored Similac. We do this, we do it my way. In my own time."

He expected an argument. He expected yelling. He expected every trusted standby for ingrate all the way back to the now never used pale piece of a pig's ear. Instead, he was greeted with calm acceptance.

Chiun's face showed no hint of emotion. "As you wish," the old man said. He returned to his CDs. Popping one open, he removed a silver disc.

"That's it?" Remo asked. "As you wish? Aren't you gonna kvetch?"

At this, Chiun shook his head. "I do not kvetch, I instruct. And it is not my place to instruct in this matter. You have admitted that you are thinking of your protégé. You have accepted fate. The rest will happen as it is meant to." Head bowed, he turned to his stereo.

Remo recognized the truth in his teacher's words. He locked them away in a quiet part of his heart. For another time. Crouching, Remo braced hands on knees.

He scanned the CD titles. In addition to the Wylander CDs, there were a dozen more.

"You have any Nitty Gritty Dirt Band?" Remo asked hopefully. He remembered the group from the 1970s.

"No," Chiun replied as he fed a CD into the player at his elbow. "But in addition to the enchanting Wylander, I have something called a Garth Brooks. I am about to play his music now."

When the old man looked up, he found that he was alone. His hazel eyes caught but a glimpse of his pupil's fleeing back as the younger man flew from the meditation room.

A proud smile crossed the Master of Sinanju's

face. Even departing in haste, his pupil had not upset any of the natural air currents in the room. His loafers made not a sound on their way to the ground floor. Chiun only knew he had fled the building when the front door slammed shut four seconds later.

There was no doubt about it. Remo was a worthy pupil. Who would one day soon make a worthy teacher.

Justifiably proud of his own accomplishment, the tiny Korean reached out a long, sharpened fingernail. When the CD started, Chiun's face became a mask of utter contentment as he allowed the music to wash over him.

5

Commander Darrell Irwin was standing above the radar station aboard the USS *Walker*, a nuclear-powered cruiser patrolling the Windward Passage between Haiti and Cuba, when he noticed the errant blip.

"What's that?" Irwin asked the seaman seated at the screen. He pointed at the phosphorescent dot.

"We thought it was a fishing boat, sir," the young man replied earnestly. His eyes were wide and bright.

Irwin frowned at the eagerness in the sailor's voice.

The kid was practically an infant. His dirty blond hair was shaved to his pink scalp. His eyes tracked the moving boat with eager interest. He was about the same age as Irwin's own son back home in Florida. He still had baby fat, for crying out loud.

There was no doubt about it. The enlisted men these days were joining up straight out of grammar school. That was the only explanation. There was no other way they could look so much younger than Commander Irwin.

"So is it a fishing boat or not?" Irwin demanded.

"Too big, sir," the seaman said. "We're thinking it's one of those big cabin cruisers."

"Heading for land?"

"East of Guantánamo if she holds course."

"Smack dab into Guantánamo if she holds course," Irwin corrected. He noted the blip with a frown.

"It'll be in visual range in ten minutes, sir."

"Let's keep an eye on her."

The boat came close enough for visual inspection in just over seven minutes. When it passed by the nose of the *Walker,* Commander Irwin went out on deck to see it.

Irwin and the two lieutenants who accompanied him had brought binoculars to view the boat. They proved to be unnecessary.

It was a cabin cruiser. Cuban registry. The luxury boat was eighty feet long and traveling at a good sixty knots as it buzzed the prow of the much bigger naval vessel.

"Are they nuts?" one of the lieutenants yelled, gripping the rail in amazement.

The boat came so close it nearly rammed the *Walker.* It slipped off toward land, trailing a wake of angry white foam.

Irwin whipped up his binoculars.

Frantic men ran along the deck. Even more crammed the bridge, screaming and pounding on equipment. When Commander Irwin lowered his glasses, his face was grave.

"She's out of control," he intoned ominously.

As the calm sea churned white in the wake of the runaway luxury cruiser, Commander Darrell Irwin raced to the bridge of the *Walker.* He had to warn Guantánamo.

THE BIG CABIN CRUISER did not veer east at Guantánamo. It continued on, straight through the outer defenses of the island's United States naval base.

By this point, most of the men on the luxury boat had gone out on the deck. Arms raised above their heads, they waved in desperate fear as the ship plowed ahead.

The Navy brass on the Cuban base were unsure what to do.

According to every report, the boat was heading straight into the heart of the Guantánamo base. But if the looks on the faces of the men aboard were any indication, they weren't some kind of suicidal terrorists. Somehow, their boat had gone out of control.

There would be hell to pay if the United States Navy torpedoed a civilian Cuban ship from a base that Cuba had for years wanted off the island.

For the military, it was the most tense moment on the small Caribbean island since October of 1962.

The Navy's paralysis ate up enough time for the situation to resolve itself. With Cuban nationals screaming and leaping from the deck, the cruiser plowed into the broad side of the aircraft carrier USS *Ronald Reagan,* which had been docked at Guantánamo after being towed from the Mideast six months before.

Running full out at the moment of impact, the cabin cruiser's nose was pulverized back to midship. Wood and metal ruptured and splintered, skipping and splashing across the water of the bay.

The men who had remained aboard were thrown forward off the deck, slamming like meat-filled bags against the gunmetal-gray side of the massive aircraft carrier.

Only then did the Navy snap into action.

Smaller ships circled in, fishing battered survivors from the water. Crewmen were quickly deployed to the half-submerged Cuban boat. Medics prepped the bleeding crew of the crippled ship for air transport to medical facilities at Guantánamo.

And as helicopters swooped in from shore to land on the broad flight deck of the nearby carrier, the first square bag floated to the surface.

At first, no one noticed the plastic-wrapped package.

It was quickly joined by another. Then another.

Eventually, a sharp-eyed sailor spotted the yellow bags bobbing gently in the bay waters.

The first helicopter was lifting off for its short hop to land as one of the bags was being fished from the drink. Using a Swiss army knife, a sailor sliced the bundle open. A white crystalline powder dumped through the slit onto the sailor's shoes. The young man looked up in amazement.

As officers and enlisted men exchanged dark glances, bag after bag slowly bobbed like corks to the once more calm blue surface of Guantánamo Bay.

**6**

"Just keep your head down and your mouth shut," the CIA director ordered Mark Howard on the ride over from Virginia. When he spoke, he didn't even glance at the man who shared the back seat of his government sedan.

It was painfully obvious that the CIA director wasn't the one who had requested Howard's presence at this high-level intelligence meeting. He had been hostile to Howard from the moment the younger man got in the car at Langley.

In tense silence, they drove through the early-morning streets of Washington, D.C.

It had snowed the night before. Just an inch was enough to paralyze the nation's capital, which in many ways still considered itself a small Southern town. Luckily, it had just been a dusting. Not that it would have mattered in this of all weeks. With Inauguration Day at week's end, city government was reacting to everything—crime, emergencies, weather—with shocking efficiency. In a month, when the parties were over and the balloons and confetti had all been swept away, the local government would revert to its regular incompetence.

Though it was only a little after 7:00 a.m., the commuter traffic was heavy. It was bumper to bumper all the way to the end of Pennsylvania Avenue. When the White House came into view, Mark Howard felt the flutter of butterflies in his gut.

The Washington Monument rose high to the south as the CIA director's car crossed over to the Fifteenth Street entrance of the most famous address on Earth. A Marine guard stood at attention as they passed through the wrought-iron gates. Driving onto the grounds, they parked near the West Wing in the shadows of twisted hundred-year-old trees. Only when the engine was silent did the CIA director at last look directly at Mark. His gaze was harsh.

"Remember," he warned. "Mouth shut."

He popped the door and headed up the short flight of stairs to the big stone archway.

Mark nodded to himself. "I guarantee it," he grumbled, still not positive why he was even here. Although he had an inkling.

Plastering on a professional face, the young analyst hurried from the car and trotted up the stairs to the Executive Wing of the White House.

MARK HOWARD COULD only assume that this strange turn of events had something to do with the mysterious, unexplained background check. It had all been very thorough, very detailed. More meticulous even than when he had joined the CIA fresh out of college.

Howard assumed it was somehow related to "Black Boris," a deep-cover mole alleged to have been squirreled away at Langley for years. Mark had always suspected that Boris was a myth—the Loch Ness Monster of the spy game.

Since the background check came not long after the well-publicized incidents of Chinese spying at Los Alamos, Mark assumed this was just some new attempt to flush out someone who probably didn't even exist. Until, that is, he learned that he alone was being investigated.

He found out the truth after dropping a casual comment to a fellow analyst at lunch in the cafeteria. Afterward, a few more discreet inquiries confirmed the fact that no one else was being scrutinized like Mark Howard.

The knowledge that he was being singled out for some reason made for a few tense weeks.

Then one day, as abruptly as the investigation had started, it stopped.

Most people would have let the matter drop. Indeed, Mark would have. Gladly. If not for the "feeling."

That was what he had learned to call his special gift. The feeling. It was a strange sense, an intuition he'd had since childhood. Back then, when a ball was lost in the woods, Mark would know precisely where it was, even if he hadn't been playing the game. The other kids would come and find him and bang, there it was.

It worked with animals, too. He'd found lost dogs, cats, even a rabbit that had gotten out of Mr. Grautskeeb's hutch. The saddest day of his childhood back in Iowa was that time when he was six when he'd found Ronnie Marin's missing collie in the weeds out behind the tool shed. She'd been there for two days. No one had bothered to look for her there. No one but little Mark Howard.

As he grew older, he realized that this ability of his could be applied in other ways. At the CIA, it allowed him to draw together meager, disparate facts and assemble them into a whole with remarkable accuracy.

While Mark didn't consider the feeling a psychic thing, he had to admit his brain worked differently than other people's. It was more an ability to intuit on a level greater than the average man on the street. Which was probably why he found himself holding the rewritable CD on that day not long after the unexplained background check ended.

Mark didn't know why he'd fished the silver disc from the back of his drawer. Sitting in his drab little cubicle in the bowels of CIA headquarters in Virginia, he studied the disc. Fluorescent light reflected off its gleaming surface.

He'd made the disc more than six months before.

On a day that would prove to be one of the strangest of his young career, a man who identified himself as General Smith had called looking for an analyst.

Mark had been given the urgent task of locating a ship at sea. A geosynchronous spy satellite over the Atlantic was turned over to him for the task. After Mark had located the ship, General Smith had briefly commandeered Howard's computer to confirm his findings. It should have been impossible, but the lemon-voiced man on the phone was able to access Mark's computer with ease.

When he was through, Smith had thanked Howard for his assistance and had receded into cyberspace, never to be heard from again. All Mark had to show for that weird afternoon was a single CD-ROM of satellite images. And the feeling.

Instinct had compelled him to dig deeper.

Rather than let the matter drop, Mark kept track of the general's ship through surreptitious means. Howard was stunned when, mere hours after it arrived in the Mideast, a previously unknown type of nuclear weapon was detonated in Israel. Chaos had descended on the entire region for several frightening days.

When the situation finally stabilized a week later, Mark learned that the men suspected of deploying the device had been found dead in an oasis in Jordan. The cause of death was listed as "unknown."

Mark didn't know why, but after reading that short report, something clicked. It grew worse a few months later.

The Mideast had largely recovered when a new crisis developed, this time in East Africa. The defense minister of that country had hatched a crazed scheme to turn his country into the crime capital of the world. But although everything seemed to be in place for him to succeed, his plot had somehow miraculously imploded.

It was then Mark knew for certain he was looking at another piece of a larger puzzle. Sifting through the East Africa data, he found one report overlooked by everyone else at the CIA. It mentioned a young white and an elderly Asian who were somehow involved with the native Luzu tribe at the time of the crisis. And in the moment he read that report, it all became clear.

General Smith—who probably wasn't a general at all—was the leader of some secret force. The white and the Asian were his operatives. Mark didn't know for certain how he knew this to be so. He just knew it was true.

Later, when he went back to look at the computer report, he found that all references to the two men on the ground in East Africa had been expunged. Someone had covered their tracks. And that someone was computer literate and could access the CIA's files.

Smith.

The ramifications were huge. When he found the files deleted, Mark had immediately retrieved the CD-ROM from his desk. Deleting its contents, he used a borrowed cigarette lighter to melt the disc into unusability. Once it was warped out of shape, he snapped it into small pieces and flushed them down the toilet.

Woodenly, he returned to his desk.

For Mark, this was the most exciting, frightening moment of realization he'd ever experienced.

The events in the Mideast and Africa had been big. They had each in their own way threatened to destabilize the world as America perceived it. And yet they had not.

There was something big lurking beyond the known fringes of American government. Alone in his cubicle that amazing day, Mark understood with blinding clarity that the clearance it was given pointed like a neon arrow to only one place.

THE OVAL OFFICE WAS bigger than Mark expected.

In the rooms beyond came sounds of packing. Through the door that opened on the office of the President's personal secretary, boxes were stacked high.

A person unseen could be heard gently sobbing. Mark assumed it was someone who didn't want to relinquish the reins of government at the end of the week.

The men in the Oval sat on the two long sofas near the fireplace. In addition to the CIA, there were agents from the FBI, NSC and the Justice Department present. Mark sat quietly off to one side of the senior government officials.

The President came shuffling in ten minutes late.

America's departing chief executive looked as if he'd slept in his clothes. He wore a heavy wool bathrobe, open wide. The belt dangled, lopsided, and dragged on the floor behind him. His green sweat-pants were stained, and his ample belly threatened the seams of his ratty Global Movieland T-shirt. His unlaced sneakers scuffed morosely on the carpet as he made his way to his desk.

On one of his last days in office, the leader of the free world had given barely any attention to his omnipresent makeup. A few thick smears of orange-tinted rouge had been glopped haphazardly on both cheeks. The tiny broken veins in his big nose faded into the wide rosacea blotches that marred his otherwise pasty face.

He didn't acknowledge the chorus of "Good morning, Mr. President" that trailed him to his tidy desk.

There was no sign in the Oval of the move that would take place this weekend. The President had refused to allow anyone—either government or political employees—to touch so much as a single scrap of paper in his office. In this way, he hoped to put off all reminders of the few fleeting hours that remained for him at the White House.

No one said another word as the President took his seat and swiveled away from his guests. He sat quietly for a moment, his bleary eyes trained on the Washington Monument. When at last he spoke, his hoarse voice was faraway.

"Cure," he muttered, the bitter word directed at the bleak January sky.

The men behind him frowned in confusion. No one spoke.

"Cure, my ass," the President grumbled as he looked out the window. His words were directed at the monument, at the sky. At something far, far beyond that famous room. "They didn't cure nothin' for me. Two lousy terms. Wouldn't even help with a third. FDR got *four*, for chrissakes. *Four*. Instead, I get some rigmarole about some Twenty-second Amendment that I never even heard of until I got into office in the first place. That and some lemon-voice technocrat lecturing me on 'operational parameters.'" His tone grew mocking. "'We do not exist to indulge your political whims,'" he growled quietly. "Sanctimonious bastard."

His mumbled words were met with baffled silence. That was, by all but one man.

Alone in his corner, Mark Howard's eyes betrayed intrigue. Although muttered, the President's "lemon-voiced technocrat" comment hadn't gotten past the young analyst. His thoughts flew to the mysterious General Smith.

When the silence in the room at last became intolerable, the NSC man spoke up. "Mr. President, are you all right?" he asked, leaning forward.

After an interminable pause, the President finally spun slowly to face the men in the room. His puffy eyes were flat. "Let's just get on with this," he said gruffly, rubbing the sleep from his face. "What's going on in Cuba?"

They all knew the situation to which he referred. Since the previous day, the runaway boat that had found its way into Guantánamo Bay had become a minicrisis.

"Castro is furious," the CIA director said efficiently. "He claims the boat's Cuban property, that it had medical supplies aboard and that it was seized illegally."

"Blah-blah-blah," the President snapped. He waved away the man's words with a soft white hand that had never seen a single day's work. "What do *you* think about this, Mark?"

Mark Howard assumed he hadn't heard correctly. He had a stack of papers on his lap. When he looked up from them, he found all eyes in the room had turned to him.

The Oval Office had grown deathly quiet. The only sound was the person crying in the next room. For the first time, it sounded like a man.

"Um," Mark Howard said slowly. "Me?"

"Yeah, you," the President said, annoyed. "Didn't you write some memo or something about this?"

Howard was surprised anyone had read it, least of all the President of the United States.

Mark had detected a pattern in organized crime that had been evolving over the past month. Even before the previous week's botched DEA raid in an old New Jersey airplane hangar, Mark had linked the emerging pattern to a company called Raffair. He didn't know why. The feeling again. It hit him while he was going through the NYSE listings in the newspaper. His finger was tapping "Raffair" even before he realized it.

The fact that audiotapes collected from the abandoned DEA van had mentioned prominently the name Raffair merely clinched it for Howard. He had filed a report yesterday.

Since the CIA's responsibilities were to advise the President and NSC on international developments, Mark assumed that his memo would be turned over to the SEC or FBI at best. At worst, it would be ignored completely. The fact that it had been read by the President shocked him.

He could feel the eyes of the other men burning into him. The CIA director seemed particularly agitated.

In the outer room, the sobbing continued.

"There, there," the disembodied voice of the President's secretary consoled. "I know getting a new job's scary, but it must have been even scarier when you were inventing the Internet. Here, let me get you some nice warm cocoa."

The door closed carefully, silencing the crying man.

In the Oval Office, Mark cleared his throat. "The incident in Cuba is part of something larger that's emerged in the last month or so, Mr. President," he began. "I think it's linked to a company called Raffair."

"I know," the president said impatiently. "I read your report. *Why* do you think it's connected?"

Mark glanced at the CIA director. The older man's eyes were locked on his.

Howard knew he'd be laughed out of the room if he mentioned the feeling. He'd spent his entire adult life avoiding explanations for his gift. Fortunately, it wasn't necessary to get into detail here.

"Simple," Mark began, fidgeting uncomfortably. "Raffair was mentioned during a drug raid that went wrong late last week. I happened to check the company's stock price the next day. Turns out it went up a couple of points. After yesterday's screw-up in Cuba, Raffair's stock went down. I thought I smelled a pattern, so I did a little digging. Turns out every time Raffair's stock dips, there's been some kind of action against organized crime the day before. Otherwise, they've had nothing but smooth sailing for the past month, ever since their ISO."

Mark tried not to meet the disapproving gazes of the other men. He kept his eyes focused on the President.

Behind his desk, America's chief executive nodded.

It was as if the others weren't even there. Howard had heard this about the President. The commander in chief had an unerring ability to make a person feel as if they were the only other human being on the face of the planet.

"You sure about all this?" the President asked, biting his lip in thoughtful concentration.

"Yes, sir," Howard said. "Raffair took its biggest hit last Monday when the President-elect mentioned his new drug policy. The stock really took a tumble that day.''

The President's face soured at the mention of his successor. ''That reminds me,'' he grumbled to himself. ''I've got a meeting to set up with him. Betty!'' he shouted.

His secretary's door opened. A middle-aged black woman stuck her face into the room. Behind her, the crying had only gotten worse. The man was blowing his nose loudly.

Although it was barely 7:30 a.m., the President's secretary already looked worn out. ''Yes, Mr. President?'' she asked wearily.

''I need to have a meeting with the incoming President.''

The crying in the outer room grew worse. ''Oh, gawd!'' the man bawled, his voice filled with uncharacteristic emotion.

The secretary rolled her eyes apologetically. ''I'll contact the transition people, Mr. President.'' She nodded. With an exhausted smile, she ducked back into her office.

Behind his desk, the President shook his head. ''Cure,'' he said to himself, his hoarse voice laced with bitterness. ''I'll show him cure.'' He rose to his feet, slapping his hands on his desk. ''That's it. Everybody out.''

The men in the room exchanged baffled glances.

''But…but our briefing,'' the FBI director said, his tone betraying confusion.

''Go brief yourself,'' the President said as he padded to the door. "I've got my own problems. Come next week, I don't even have a place to live. Worse, I could stay in New York. With *her*." He shivered visibly as he left the room.

Behind him, the President's bewildered advisers began gathering up paperwork and briefcases.

Mark Howard didn't even notice the evil glance the CIA director gave him as he collected his own satchel from the floor next to the sofa. His thoughts were somewhere else, far beyond the confines of the Oval Office, a room that now seemed much smaller than it had just a few minutes before.

In the space of this one small meeting, the entire world had collapsed and coalesced into an unrecognizable shape. Numbly, Mark rose from his chair and walked to the door.

Smith, the background check, the President. It was all tied in. Something was very definitely going on. And whatever it was was huge beyond the measure of it.

Mark Howard could feel it.

THE PRESIDENT DID his best to ignore the packing crates stacked in the hallways of the West Wing. In the main mansion, he took the private elevator, getting out at the family quarters.

He closed his eyes in strained patience when he heard the familiar low rumble to his right.

Down the hall, the President's Labrador retriever exposed its teeth, growling menacingly as he passed.

Scraps of shiny paper were spread on the floor around its paws.

His wife had sent the dog for some kind of special obedience training while the chief executive was in Europe the previous year. When the President got back home, the dog's attitude had been completely changed. It now growled and snapped at him whenever he came near. Every White House picture of the current President became a chew toy. He tried to ask his wife what she'd done to the animal, but she only smiled that emasculating smile of hers and flew off for another listening tour of New York.

He left the dog to chew on the state photograph of himself and Israel's Prime Minister Barak. Rounded shoulders sagging, he ducked into the Lincoln Bedroom.

The cherry-red telephone was in the bottom drawer of the nightstand. In another few days, he'd be showing the phone to his successor.

Sitting on the edge of the high bed, the President lifted the receiver. The phone had no dial. It didn't need one. Before it could ring twice, the call was answered.

"Yes, Mr. President?"

Efficient, as usual. The President scowled at the thought of the tart-voiced man on the other end of the line.

"I'm scheduling a meeting with the President-elect," the chief executive said, his voice flat. "Just like you asked."

No hint of emotion. "Thank you, Mr. President."

The President only grunted. "Still don't know why I have to do it. Why don't you just have those people of yours sneak you in here so you can talk to him yourself next week?"

"It has always been done this way, with but one exception. And that was only because of dire circumstances. It is best for the outgoing President to inform the incoming President of our existence. To do it some other way might suggest a rogue intelligence group."

"Yeah," the President said, dabbing at the thick rouge on his cheek. His finger came back orange. "Guess so. Hey, I've got something I'd like you to look into before I'm gone." He rubbed the makeup between thumb and forefinger.

A pause. "Yes?"

That snide tone. Filled with suspicion and condescension.

"It's just a small thing," the President said. "Someone's brought something to my attention about a company called Raffair." He went on to give the broad details as outlined in Mark Howard's report.

"That is not a typical assignment," came the lemony conclusion once the President was through. A moment of thoughtful consideration followed. "However, I will see if there is something larger at work there. Is there anything else?"

"No," the President said. "That's it."

"Goodbye, sir."

The line went dead.

The President replaced the phone, sliding the nightstand drawer closed with his ankle. "Goodbye to you, Smith," he said quietly.

More than anything, this President wanted a legacy. His last year in office had been about nothing but that, with little success. Until now. Although it wouldn't be written in any history books, he was about to get a real legacy.

The old man on the phone was a throwback to another era. It was the dawn of a new century. Time for new thinking. For young blood.

As he was getting up from the bed, there came a growling and scratching at the door. With a beleaguered sigh, the President picked up a book from a stack on the nightstand. There were similar stacks all around the family quarters. His campaign manifesto, *Between God and Man: How Great I Art* had done extremely poorly in stores back in '96. Luckily, the President had recently found a new use for the cases that had been recalled.

He opened the door a crack, waving the cover with his picture through the opening. When the growling reached a fevered pitch, he flung the book down the hallway.

As the frantic trampling of the presidential dog receded in one direction, the President threw the door to the Lincoln Bedroom open and ran like mad in the other.

Remo had walked the streets of Quincy late into the night, returning home in the wee hours of the morning. When he got back, the old church was blessedly silent. It was one-thirty by the time he crawled into bed.

His blissful sleep was shattered at 6:00 a.m. by the full-throated yodeling of the full-figured Wylander.

Apparently, Chiun didn't want to miss a single warbled note. While upstairs, he played the music softly enough, but when he ventured to other areas of the house he turned up the volume. Right now the Master of Sinanju was scouring the basement fish tanks for breakfast, Wylander was threatening to shatter the remaining windows in the bell-tower meditation room and Remo was on his way out the kitchen door. He had his hand on the doorknob when the wall phone rang.

Scooping up the phone, he jammed a finger in his free ear. "Make it quick," he warned.

The familiar voice of Harold W. Smith was as sour as a sack of trampled grapefruit.

"Remo, Smith. I—" the CURE director stopped dead. "What on earth is that din?"

Remo closed his eyes. "It's called a Wylander, Smitty," he said. "And get used to that name, because I have a feeling it's gonna come up during our next contract negotiations. Chiun's got that old Barbra Streisand gleam in his eye." He hopped to a sitting position on the counter. "What's up?"

"Er, yes," Smith said uncertainly. "I was actually calling for two reasons. First, to let you know that the bodies of the MIR terrorists have been discovered and second, to tell you that I have another small assignment for you."

The CURE director went on to tell him of the President's request that they look into Raffair, as well as more detailed background information Smith himself had dredged up following his conversation with the chief executive.

"Why don't we just run out the clock on this guy?" Remo asked once he was through. "He's gone on Saturday. Besides, this sounds like a nothing job."

"Perhaps," Smith said. "However, my relationship with this President has been—" he searched for the right word "—strained. I have decided that it would do no harm to indulge him in this one last matter."

"Leave on a high note, huh," Remo said. "I gotcha. Guess this is your way of apologizing for not crowning him King of North America and Sovereign Ruler of Guam, the Virgin Islands and American

Samoa. Okay, Chiun and I will go rattle a few cages. It'll probably be good to get him out of here anyway. I think the neighbors are already assembling with torches and pitchforks.''

Not wishing to ponder the ramifications of what Remo was saying, the CURE director forged ahead. Smith gave Remo the New York address of Lippincott, Forsythe, Butler.

''An agent for that firm guided the IPO for Raffair. Perhaps he can tell you how a company can do so well without having an apparent owner or generates revenue without producing a clear product. His name is Lawrence Fine.''

Remo raised a skeptical eyebrow. ''You're kidding, right?'' he asked.

''Why?'' Smith asked, puzzled.

Remo opened his mouth to explain. But then he remembered a story Smith had told him about the days when the future director of CURE and his wife were dating. They had gone to see a Marx Brothers movie, and Smith had spent the entire evening complaining about the fact that Groucho's mustache was only painted on and that Chico was obviously not Italian. For Smith, these transgressions shed serious doubt on the notion that Harpo was an actual mute. It was the last movie the Smiths saw together. The cultural vacuum the old man lived in would make an explanation pointless.

''No reason,'' Remo said. ''We'll get right on it.''

As he spoke, he cocked an ear toward the hallway stairs.

The music seemed to have stopped. The silence lasted only a few seconds. Chiun had apparently bought a multi-CD player. Wylander's eardrum-detonating whooping began anew.

"I'm not kidding about Wylander, Smitty," Remo growled into the phone. "You'd better get on the blower to Monster Island, 'cause when the next contract comes due you're gonna need an awfully big cage for country's King Kong."

He slammed down the phone.

CHIUN AGREED to abandon his new lady love to accompany Remo to New York.

The short commuter flight was relatively incident free, with only two wet T-shirt contests and one midair chug-a-lug competition. Two drunken businessmen who threatened to defecate midway through the flight did so to protest the in-flight movie. Since it was an Adam Sandler film, Remo didn't blame them. The flight attendants were hosing down the carpets when he and the Master of Sinanju deplaned.

On the cab ride into the city, the old Korean was a picture of wrinkled contentment. He almost appeared to be in a state of grace. As they crossed the Williamsburg Bridge, Chiun let out a satisfied sigh.

"I know what's going on," Remo said abruptly.

The wizened Asian continued to stare wistfully at the East River. His aged hands were clasped together in his lap, forming a tight knot of bone.

"Remind me to record such an historic moment

in the sacred Sinanju scrolls,'' the Master of Sinanju replied.

Remo ignored the sarcasm. "Country music," he pressed. "I know why you like it so much."

Chiun turned a bland eye on his pupil. "Is there a way I might be spared this?" he asked.

"No, listen. You like Ung poetry, right?

A cloud formed on Chiun's brow. "Of course."

"Right," Remo nodded. "You like it even though it doesn't even rhyme, and everyone in the universe but you thinks it sounds like shit."

Chiun's eyes grew flat. "There are limits, Remo, to how much I will indulge you," he said in a level tone.

"Work with me here," Remo insisted. "Ung sounds awful, it's repetitive and totally devoid of any depth or beauty. Basically, it's Korean country music except with butterflies instead of barflies. *That's* why you like country music."

He nodded, a knowing look on his face.

Chiun's level gaze never wavered. "One day many years from now, Remo, scientists will crack open your granite skull and announce, 'Behold! Here was a being with the aspect of Man, yet possessed with a cavern between his ears!' School children will take field trips to see the hollowed head of Empty-Skulled Man."

He turned his aged face back to the cab window. The looming Manhattan skyline was reflected darkly in the glass.

"Empty head, but full heart," Remo smiled. "And I know I'm right."

"You are never right," Chiun replied without turning. "And you get more not right with every passing day."

LIPPINCOTT, FORSYTHE, Butler occupied most of a somber Wall Street building within shouting distance of Trinity Church. A plaque above the door read, simply, LFB. So celebrated was the firm that no more advertising was needed.

As their cab dropped them off, Remo took note of the police cruisers parked in front of the building.

"Something's up," Remo commented as he and Chiun stepped around the police cars. "Maybe we should use a back door."

"You may climb through an alley window if you wish," Chiun sniffed. "I, however, will use the perfectly serviceable door before me."

Lifting up the hem of his purple kimono, the old man marched across the sidewalk. Eyes on the cop cars, Remo followed. Side by side, the two men strolled into the lobby.

The confusion inside was such that no one stopped them as they crossed to the elevators. They accompanied a pair of police officers up to the fourteenth floor.

The doors opened on the sedate LFB logo. It was etched into a small bronze plate that was secured to the wall above a vacant receptionist's desk.

The cops walked from the elevator area down past several lobby desks, Remo and Chiun trailing.

"Remember, Little Father," Remo whispered. "We're looking for a guy named Larry Fine."

"Yes," Chiun droned. "I don't know why you trusted that that was not some new manifestation of Smith's madness."

"Let's give Smitty a break, okay?" Remo said as they walked. "He's been living a waking nightmare these past few years. We're only here so he can make nice with the President before he leaves office."

"Then this is truly a waste of all our time," the Master of Sinanju muttered. "For Smith has already told us that we will visit the Corpulent Pretender in but a few day's time to administer the Emptying Basin."

This was the Sinanju selective-amnesia technique used to erase all memory of Smith, CURE and Sinanju from the minds of departing Presidents.

"Too bad we can't use that technique on 270 million more Americans," Remo said. "Make them forget the last eight years ever happened."

They followed the policemen through a wide archway and into a large, drab room filled with small cubicles. Coming toward them up the long gray aisle was a sheet-draped gurney.

"Uh-oh," Remo said. "I hope that's not who I think it is."

While the gurney was still at a distance, Remo stopped near a group of LFB employees. They were watching the approaching covered gurney with sick fascination.

"I'm looking for Larry Fine," Remo announced.

Judging by the looks he received, his instinct about the gurney's occupant was correct.

*"Lawrence,"* a sniffling woman corrected. She dabbed her mascara-smeared eyes with a sopped Kleenex. "His name was Lawrence. Those thugs murdered him in his own office."

All of a sudden, it wasn't funny to make fun of his name. That happened not long after Fine's body was discovered, his neck nearly sawed through with a garrote wire.

Chiun fell in with the passing coroner's office procession. An unseen fingernail bounced the gurney's wheels over Remo's loafers on its trip out of the office. The Master of Sinanju continued with the rest out into the hall.

One of the office workers lowered his voice to a conspiratorial whisper. "I hate to say it, but I'm just glad LFB didn't assign me to work with those racketeers."

"*I* knew something was wrong the moment I laid eyes on them," the weeping woman said. "Poor, poor Larry. I mean Lawrence." She blew her nose into her dripping tissue.

"Does all this have anything to do with Raffair?" Remo asked as she picked bits of tissue from her moist fingers.

All eyes turned to him. The crying woman took

sudden notice of Remo's too casual attire. She froze in midsniffle.

"Are you with the police?" she asked suspiciously. "What's your name? Where's your identification?"

He rolled his eyes as he reached into his pocket for his phony ID. "My name's Remo—" he began.

A shocked intake of air. Before he knew what was going on, the woman before him let out a blood-curdling scream.

"What the hell's wrong with you?" Remo asked as she shrieked bloody murder.

The other LFB employees dove for their cubicles. Cops spun Remo's way. Some were already running toward him.

"He's one of the killers!" the woman screeched.

"What?" Remo said, stunned. "No, I'm not."

By this time, he was surrounded by police, their guns drawn.

"Let me see some ID," one of the officers demanded. *"Slowly."*

Remo reached back into his pocket. When he searched his wallet, he came up empty. He checked his other pocket. The only things there were a small figure carved from stone and a crucifix he'd been carrying around as good-luck charms for the past few months. He suddenly remembered leaving Smith's newly issued IDs on his bureau back at Castle Sinanju.

"Oops," he said sheepishly. He eyed the many

guns. "I'm out of practice. Is this a good time to offer a bribe?"

The woman screamed once more before jumping behind a cubicle wall.

"Face on the floor!" an officer commanded.

"No," Remo corrected. "Feet on floor. See feet go. Go, feet, go."

And before the cops knew what was happening, he was gone from their midst. When they spun, they saw him flying up the aisle toward the main entrance.

Gunfire erupted in Remo's wake. He flew into the hallway amid a hail of bullets.

The Master of Sinanju was with the coroner's men near the elevators. He frowned deep displeasure as Remo raced up to him.

"What have you done now?" Chiun demanded as Remo slid to a stop beside him.

"Nothing," Remo said. "Told somebody my name. The rest's a blur."

Chiun's wrinkled furrows grew deeper. "If you must say something stupid, do not say anything at all."

Police officers began spilling into the distant hall. When they yelled for Remo to stop, the two men from the coroner's office immediately leaped behind the broad receptionist's desk beneath the LFB plaque.

"I like my name," Remo challenged, hurt, just as the police opened fire.

Standing before the closed elevator doors, the two

Masters of Sinanju weaved and dodged around the incoming volley of bullets. Several screaming shards of hot lead thudded into the sheet-draped corpse beside them.

"By all means, then, remain here and like your name to your heart's content," the Master of Sinanju began. With a ping, the doors slid open. "I, however, like my life more."

As bullets whizzed by his parchment-draped skull, the old man ducked aboard the elevator car.

Remo shot a final glance at the still-firing police. Arranged at the end of the hall, they were frustrated by their inability to sight down on their quarry. They continued shooting as Remo jumped inside the elevator car. He stabbed the button for the first floor.

"Can they not halt our descent?" Chiun asked as the doors slid shut. He tucked his hands inside his voluminous kimono sleeves as the elevator began its swift slide downward.

"You've seen too many movies. By the time they figure out how to shut it down, we'll be long gone."

"How?" Chiun asked skeptically.

Remo smiled. "I've seen a lot of movies, too."

Reaching up, he pulled down the cheap suspended ceiling. Behind it was a small trapdoor. He gave it a push, and the door slapped against the roof of the car.

"Rock, paper, scissors for who goes first?"

Chiun was peering up through the hole. "Hurry up, retard," he said peevishly.

"Guess I volunteer," Remo muttered.

Hopping up, Remo snagged the open mouth of the trapdoor with both hands and slid his thin frame easily through the narrow opening. In a flash, he was on the roof. The grimy dark walls of the elevator shaft were close.

They were already closing in on the eighth floor.

"Get the lead out, Little Father," he called down into the car.

"Do not rush me," Chiun complained.

Through the opening, Remo saw the old Korean carefully gathering up the hems of his purple kimono into a tight ball.

They were approaching the sixth floor.

In the elevator car, Chiun's exposed ankles tensed. The instant they did, it seemed as if he were locked in place as the elevator continued to descend. The hole closed down around him. For a moment, as the trapdoor slid down around his shoulders, his flowing robes made him look like a wrinkled jack-in-the-box. A second later, he cleared the door and joined Remo on the roof of the car.

"What now?" the Master of Sinanju asked, releasing his bunched kimono.

"We make like all of Wylander Jugg's high-school blind dates and jump for the nearest available door," Remo replied.

They were passing the second-floor doors.

Remo's feet left the roof of the car. Chiun's sandals hopped away a split second after his pupil. They landed simultaneously on the narrow ledge before the closed doors.

Behind them, the empty car continued its descent. Even as it was stopping one floor below them, Remo and Chiun were prying open the second-floor doors. They stepped out into the corridor. As they did so, shouted voices began echoing up from the depths of the elevator shaft.

They quickly found a fire exit. Before the police figured out what had happened, they'd taken the stairs down to the street. As sirens of the first backup police cruisers rose over the snarl of Wall Street traffic, they were walking briskly away from the Lippincott, Forsythe, Butler building.

The two Masters of Sinanju melted in with the foot traffic near Trinity Church.

"I suppose this means we hit a dead end with Larry Fine," Remo commented as they strolled down the street.

Chiun shook his head. "Our trip was not wasted," he replied. "In spite of your best efforts to make it so."

Remo raised a curious eyebrow. "Why? You get a chance to sneak a peek at the body before the fireworks started?"

The Master of Sinanju nodded.

"And?" Remo pressed.

As they walked, Chiun stroked his thread of beard thoughtfully. "In days gone by, it was common for emperors to slay the builders of their palaces to keep secret any hidden treasure rooms or escape passages."

"I know that," Remo frowned. "Why, was there a secret passage back there?"

When he craned his neck back to see the LFB building, he found it hopelessly out of sight.

Beside him, Chiun's impatience at his pupil's persistent obtuseness manifested itself with a weary drooping of his bald head. With a single delicate nail against Remo's chin, he guided the younger man's gaze away from the vanished LFB building.

"Please, Remo, make an attempt to focus your thoughts." The Master of Sinanju sighed. "If not for your sake, for the sake of our village. Smith's dead stooge built a house of finance," the old man explained. "He was removed because his services were no longer required by the Romans."

Remo blinked. "Romans?"

"Or whatever ugly name they go by now," Chiun waved dismissively.

The notch in Remo's brow deepened. "Larry Fine probably wasn't Italian, Little Father," he said slowly.

"That would not prevent him from working for Nero's sons," Chiun said. "If you need further proof, when did the constables begin shooting at you?"

"After I told that ditzy woman my name," Remo said.

"Which is a *Roman* name," Chiun stressed. "She probably took one look at you and mistook you for one of them." He dropped his voice low. "Given the mongrel soup out of which you flopped, I really cannot blame her for her error, Remo. In the right light, you can pass for nearly everything that walks, crawls or swings by its tail from a banana tree.''

"Don't knock my roots," Remo warned thinly. "When I shook my family tree, a Master of Sinanju fell out."

Chiun couldn't argue with that. He therefore ignored it. "The woman feared the Romans because she knew the stooge was in league with them," he said.

"So how do *you* know?"

Chiun raised himself to his full height. "The smell of death is strong," he intoned. "The smell of boiled tomatoes, even stronger. At least two mashed-tomato eaters were involved in this killing."

"Even if you're right, I don't know that it means anything," Remo said. "I'll give Smitty a call and let him know what happened to Fine."

"Be sure to tell the emperor to direct his oracles to search for those of Roman descent," Chiun instructed.

"I'll tell him your theory," Remo agreed. "But his computers look for criminal stuff, not people's ancestry. Unless they're in the Mob or something, we've hit a dead end. Of course, I'm keeping a good thought that maybe these guys who are following us can tell us."

He'd sensed the two sets of eyes focused on his back almost since they'd left the LFB building. As he spoke, the car that had been slowly following them through the Wall Street traffic screeched to a stop.

Two men were springing from the front seat when Remo and Chiun turned. They wore fatigue pants, camouflage jackets and heavy boots. Black ski masks obscured all but their eyes and mouths.

"We need one of them alive, Little Father," Remo said.

"Do whatever you wish," Chiun sniffed. "They are interested in you, not me."

It was true. All their attention appeared to be focused entirely on Remo.

At the front of their car, both men drew long knives from their jackets. Bringing their hands back expertly to their shoulders, they swept their arms downward. With twin hums, the knives sailed at Remo's chest.

He caught one blade with a broad sidestroke, batting it harmlessly to the sidewalk. The second he smacked sharply by the handle, twisting it in midair. The knife had not fully stopped flying in one direction before a firm nudge from Remo sent it zipping back from whence it had come.

The blade buried itself deep in the nearer man's face. His mask seemed to sprout an extralong snout, and he dropped to the sidewalk, dead.

A frightened shudder rose palpably among the throng of pedestrians. Remo ignored the scattering crowd, moving directly for the second masked man.

When he saw Remo coming at him, the second man's eyes went wide inside his ski mask. He had apparently thought two knives would do the trick, for as he searched his khaki jacket for another weapon he came up empty.

There was only one thing left for him to do.

Turning, the man flung himself onto his belly out in the street. He skidded directly under the wheels of a passing New York Transit Authority bus. His body made a sickening crunching sound before being dragged up into the slush-encased wheel well of the big bus.

"So much for getting answers from them," Remo grumbled as the bus rolled to a ponderous, squeaking stop.

He hurried back to where his first attacker had fallen. Chiun stood above the body.

"I do not recognize this symbol," the old man said when Remo stopped beside him. He pointed to the dead man's coat.

There was a simple white button pinned to his chest. On it, what looked like a pair of wavy black parentheses enclosed a plain black oval. Remo pulled it loose.

"Me, either," he said. "But we better let Smitty know we've made some new friends." He pocketed the button.

As a crowd began to form around the two fallen bodies, the two Masters of Sinanju melted back into the crush of onlookers. They were long gone before the fresh sound of sirens rose in the cold city air.

**8**

With his arms stretched out wide to either side, Sol Sweet resembled a tidy little scarecrow. A long wand bent in a U-shape was passed up and down both sides of his body. He had gone through the same drill many times in the drab room.

He took in his surroundings with an impatient eye.

The cinder-block walls were painted green. Bare white recessed ceiling bulbs glared out through wire mesh. A desk was bolted to one wall. It was fashioned from the same metal as the door. Both door and desk were starting to rust.

That was all. The U.S. government hadn't spent much on upkeep for Missouri's Ogdenburg Federal Penitentiary. Most of the budget these days went for color TV, cable, gym equipment and other vital human necessities people on a limited budget in the outside world couldn't afford.

"You're taking an excessive amount of time," Sweet accused, his nasal voice clipped. In his head, he was already sketching out his formal complaint.

The nearest prison guard didn't seem to even hear him.

"He's clean," he announced to his partner. He pulled the wand away.

"It's about time," Sol whined angrily.

The second guard had been going through the attorney's briefcase at the desk. He passed it back to Sweet.

Briefcase clutched tightly, Sweet followed one of the guards to the interior steel door. Once they'd been buzzed through, Sweet preceded the guard into a narrow hallway. They passed into another, larger room.

There was a long table inside, bolted to the floor. Two chairs were arranged on each of the two longest sides.

"It'll be a couple more minutes," the guard said. He backed into the hallway and closed the door.

The wait was shorter than usual. Five minutes later, the door opened once more. A new guard ushered a prisoner into the visitor's room.

The media reports of the strain prison had put on Don Anselmo Scubisci had been accurate.

The Manhattan Mafia Don had lost a considerable amount of weight. His shoulders were narrower, his face more angular and his protruding belly all but absent. Sol Sweet was amazed every time he saw this thinner Anselmo Scubisci. Put a paper bag of greasy peppers in his hand, and he'd be the spitting image of his father, the late Don Pietro.

The Dandy Don had at least retained the fastidious sense of style he'd always been famous for. His gray prison slacks were sharply creased, his shoes were polished and his shirt was clean and starched.

Anselmo Scubisci smiled at the sight of his lawyer.

"Solly, you're looking well," he said, wrapping his arms around the smaller man in a paternal hug.

Sol Sweet didn't like to be touched, so he was relieved when the guard spoke up.

"Mr. Scubisci," the man warned.

"What? Oh, yes. Yes, of course. I'm sorry," Don Scubisci said, releasing Sweet. He sat at the table.

"Could we have some privacy, please?" Sol asked the guard.

The young man glanced into the hallway. "Make it quick, okay?" he suggested. He stepped from the room, pulling the door closed behind him.

"Nice kid," Scubisci confided when the door clanged shut. His voice had a faint rasp due to a brush with throat cancer two years before. "Maybe we can find a better-paying job for him when I get out."

Sol's face was serious. "No new news as far as that's concerned, I'm afraid," he said, sitting across from his client. "The appeal process has been very slow."

Don Anselmo scowled. "I'm a businessman, Solly, that's all. Why are they even wasting time on me when they should be going after real criminals?"

"Mr. Scubisci," Sweet said reasonably, "the charges against you, while totally without merit, are nonetheless very serious."

"Serious," Scubisci mocked, waving a contemptuous hand. He shook his head in disgust. "Let's just get on with this."

The lawyer nodded. Thumbing the hasps on his soft leather briefcase, he reached inside. "Another letter arrived. As per your standing order, I brought it to you at once."

Sweet pulled a business-size envelope from a larger yellow envelope. He slid it halfway across the table. Anselmo Scubisci placed a delicate hand flat over the airmail stamp.

"Did anyone else see this?" he said, his voice level.

"Just the usual person."

Scubisci nodded. He swept the letter over to his side of the table.

The first thing he checked was the seal. As usual, it had been stamped over the flap. The mark was still intact. The legend "A.S. c/o A. Scubisci" had been printed carefully in bright red ink on the front. The address was a special postal drop set up by Scubisci's lawyer.

Nodding his satisfaction, Don Scubisci left the letter near his elbow. He wouldn't tear the seal until he returned to the privacy of his cell.

"I also have another reason for this visit," Sol said somberly. "Some unfortunate news about a business associate of yours. Larry Fine. Apparently, he was murdered. A terrible, brutal crime, I'm told."

Scubisci buried the glimmer of a smile. His first in a long time. "When did this tragedy take place?"

"This morning," Sweet replied efficiently.

Don Anselmo nodded thoughtfully. "The world

has gotten very dangerous. I hate to say this, Solly, but when I hear of all that's happening on the outside, I sometimes feel safer in here.''

As he was speaking, the door opened. The young guard reappeared, his face nervous.

''I don't want to rush you, Mr. Scubisci, but if you're gonna take much longer, I'll have to stay in here.''

Anselmo Scubisci's eyes were flat as he pushed up from the table. ''It's okay,'' he rasped. ''We're through.''

He didn't bother to shake hands with Sweet. Collecting his airmail letter, he nodded crisply to his lawyer. ''Keep in touch, Sol,'' he said. It was a command. Letter in hand, Don Scubisci was ushered from the room.

As he waited for the guard who would take him back outside, Sol Sweet gave only a passing thought to the strange envelope. It was just the latest of many Scubisci had received in recent months.

As usual, Sol wondered what was in the envelopes. Not that he'd ever try to check. He valued his life too greatly to be so foolish.

When the guard came to collect him, he banished all thoughts of the mysterious letters. Sol followed the man out into the hallway, grateful for the parking lot and his rented car and the miles of empty highway that waited for him beyond the high prison walls.

## 9

The walls that enclosed the sprawling, snow-covered grounds of Folcroft Sanitarium were a prison to but one man. The others who passed through the high gates with their attendant stone lions—be they staff, visitors or patients—all left in their time. There was only one individual who had been committed to Folcroft for life.

Dr. Harold W. Smith would not have considered himself a prisoner. After all, he could come and go as he pleased. And yet most of the time he did not go. Most days and for much of the day, Harold Smith could be found in the same place he had been the day, the week, the year before.

As director of CURE, which operated in secret from behind the high stone walls of this exclusive mental-health facility and convalescent home in Rye, New York, Harold W. Smith was as much a prisoner as any man with a life sentence. It was only the cell that was different.

In his Spartan administrator's office, Smith sat behind his broad onyx desk. Through the one-way picture window at his back could be seen the churning black waters of Long Island Sound. Whitecaps formed on the wintry surface like Poseidon's grasping claws. Smith failed to notice.

His arthritic fingers moved with swift resolve across the edge of the desk. Below the surface, an illuminated keyboard tracked his sure path with bursts of soothing amber. A buried monitor reflected a constant data stream in the owlish glasses perched on Smith's patrician nose.

The CURE director had spent hours attempting to unravel the complicated finances of Raffair, with little success. As a corporation, Raffair was a mess. But it was clear that it was a mess with a purpose: to thwart an investigation such as the one Smith was attempting.

Still, in spite of the roadblocks he'd encountered, some rough outline of the beast had begun to take shape. Raffair was big and popular. Like a lot of high-technology stocks that had fueled the economic boom of the nineties, there seemed to be not enough revenue generated by the company to justify the inflated price of its stock. Yet like those high-tech stocks, ordinary people were eager to invest. Interest in Raffair's stock had further driven up the price, rewarding handsomely those who had bought into the company in the month since its initial offering.

The pattern was the same one that had developed of late for on-line bookstores, auction houses or Internet service providers. Yet in those cases, though greatly inflated, there was a clear product or service provided. With Raffair, there was none. Individuals were sinking their money into a ghost of a corporation that seemed on the surface to do little more than accept the influx of capital.

To Smith, it was clear that Raffair was nothing but a massive front for something. But for what, he had no idea.

With a troubled sigh, he rubbed his tired eyes. Sinking back into his cracked leather chair, he spun to face Long Island Sound.

Winter's wind attacked the rolling waves. Frothy foam collected at the shore near the rotted boat dock that extended into the Sound from Folcroft's back lawn.

Smith removed his rimless glasses, dropping his hand down beside his chair. The days when he could stare at his computer for hours on end without a break were long gone.

A thin UV coating on his glasses, as well as in his desk just above his monitor, was meant to shield his eyes from damage. If it worked, he was lucky to have the protection, for at this point in his life the years he'd spent sifting through cyberspace had caused an enlargement of his optic nerve. Possibly a precursor to glaucoma. Another sign of the march of time.

The signs had been there for some time now. There was no denying it. Smith was old. His body was beginning the inevitable betrayal visited on all living things.

At first, it had been small things. Tired eyes, creaking bones. Silly things that could be dismissed or ignored. But like a snowball rolled down a steep hill, the small things had begun to grow large.

His hands ached.

Understandable, of course. After all, he'd spent forty years pounding day after day on a computer keyboard. But an understanding of the reason didn't lessen the pain.

The worsening arthritis in his gnarled fingers made it difficult to type. Some mornings, it took him a full hour before he could work out all the overnight kinks.

The creaking bones had given way to aches in nearly all his joints. His right knee in particular was giving him problems lately. Some mornings, it was as if there were nothing beneath the skin but bone on bone.

These were problems of the flesh, however, and could be easily ignored. Indeed, Smith had put the minor aches and pains to one side even as they grew to distractions. Most troubling to him of late were his lapses in concentration.

It was not yet a memory problem, nor did it seem to be developing into one. Yet. But there were moments when weariness combined with age would take hold and Smith would find himself lost in a gray fog. They were not technically daydreams, for Harold Smith did not dream. But they were instances of lapsed consciousness during which his tired brain seemed to close itself off from the world.

Smith had always prided himself on his sharp mind. Even that seemed to be betraying him of late.

And a man in his position could not afford to lose his faculties.

It was fitting that his daydreams should be filled with clouds of gray, for Smith himself was cast in shades of gray. From his grayish skin, to his flinty gray eyes, to his three-piece gray suit, he was an emotionless figure from the age of black-and-white. A gaunt representative of the World War II generation, he was a man out of time. An anachronistic throwback to an era that an increasing number of Americans were beginning to view as ancient history.

In truth, all was not gray for Harold Smith. In his vest pocket was a small pill—not gray, but white. Fashioned in the shape of a coffin, it held a special place near his heart, not emotionally but literally. On his last day as head of CURE, Smith would remove the pill and swallow it. The fast-acting poison would kill him in a matter of minutes.

He had considered taking the pill several times over the past few years.

The current President had placed a strain on Smith like none of his predecessors had. He seemed unwilling to see CURE for what it was, an emergency firewall to deal with threats both domestic and foreign. There had been a number of instances where the President had wanted to use the resources of CURE for personal or political gain. The most recent was his less than subtle suggestion that Smith help him to remain in office beyond his constitutionally mandated two terms.

Of course Smith had refused. The President had withdrawn into silence broken by occasional bouts of surliness. Smith fully expected that the change of power would come in Washington this weekend without his ever having to speak to the President again. He was surprised when the chief executive called. Even more surprised to learn what it was he wanted Smith to do.

Investigate Raffair. It seemed like such a minor thing—something that shouldn't interest the outgoing leader of the free world. More for the office he held than for the man himself had Smith agreed. A final act of professional courtesy for a man who would almost certainly be one of the last Presidents Harold Smith would serve.

Beyond his picture window, the Sound continued to churn white. Smith blinked the water away. Replacing his spotless glasses, he turned back to his desk. His hands had not yet brushed the keyboard when the blue contact phone on his desk jangled to life.

"Smith," he said crisply.

"Only me, Smitty," Remo's voice announced. "I've got some bad news and some weird news out of New York."

"I have seen the preliminary police report," Smith said. "Fine was murdered in his office."

"That's the bad. By the sounds of it, in broad daylight in a building full of people," Remo said. "We didn't have much time to ask around, so you're gonna have to keep your eyes peeled for police reports if you want us to follow up.''

"Why?" Smith frowned. "Did you have difficulty there?''

"We had difficulty everywhere," Remo said. "As far as the inside-the-building part goes, there was screaming, shooting, running. You know, the usual.''

Smith pursed his lips. "Remo, I have a report here of two men who eluded police capture at the LFB building this morning," he began cautiously.

"Did they baffle their pursuers by effecting an amazing escape from a moving elevator car?" Remo asked proudly.

Shutting his eyes, Smith pinched the bridge of his nose. "That was you and Chiun," he said dully.

"Escaping, yes," Remo agreed. "But it was my idea to use the trapdoor.''

"It was also his idea to get us shot at, Emperor Smith," the Master of Sinanju's squeaky voice called from the nearby background.

"Technically, that was more the cops' idea than it was mine, Little Father," Remo said.

"Remo," Smith interrupted wearily, "I should not have to remind you to exercise discretion.''

"Discretion had nothing to do with this one, Smitty," Remo said. "The folks there were already wired about Larry Fine's Raffair business partners long before we even showed up. Chiun's thinking it's some kind of Mob hit.''

"I said nothing of the kind," the Master of Sinanju called. "I merely correctly observed that the stooge's killers were sons of the Tiber."

"Tiber?" Smith sounded puzzled. "Does he mean they were Italians?"

"At the risk of getting picketed by the antidefamation league, yeah," Remo said. "At least that's the vibe he got from sniffing around the body."

"Hmm," Smith mused. "The Mafia angle might fit with what little I have learned of Raffair so far. They seem marginally connected to trucking, construction, waste removal and the like. However, on the surface, Raffair's activities appear to be legal."

"Yeah? Well, dig deeper," Remo said. "Because by the looks of it, they've got roving hit squads out trying to stab innocent pedestrians."

"What are you talking about?" Smith asked.

Remo quickly told him about the two masked men he and Chiun had encountered on Wall Street.

"That does not make sense," Smith said once he was through. "If you are telling me everything, you did nothing at LFB to provoke such an attack."

"I'm glad you're with me on this one, Smitty," Remo said. "All we were doing was minding our own business. Oh, and the guys with the knives were wearing some kind of button. I never saw the design before. I gave a cabbie a couple hundred bucks to drive it out there."

Smith's brow was troubled. "I am curious to see it," he admitted. "I would have to say, however, that this attack—whatever the reason—is unrelated to your visit to LFB. Perhaps it was a simple assault.''

''I don't know,'' Remo said uncertainly. ''They seemed to be targeting me specifically.''

''Nonetheless, I doubt we need be concerned that it has anything to do with Raffair.'' Smith's voice remained troubled.

''If you say so,'' Remo grumbled. ''I have my doubts, though. And while we're on the subject, what the hell kind of name is Raffair?''

This was something that had vexed Smith from the start. ''It strikes me as somewhat familiar,'' he admitted. ''Although I have no idea from where I would know it.'' His brow wrinkled above his tired eyes. ''No matter. After the events in Fine's office, as well as your encounter in the street, it would be best for you and Chiun to return home. I will do further research on this end.''

''You're doing a lot of work for a guy who's gonna be out of office in a couple of days, Smitty,'' Remo suggested. ''Just in case you forgot, Chiun and I are due to make him forget all about our little quilting bee this Friday night.''

Alone in his Folcroft office, Smith's spine stiffened at Remo's reminder. His thoughts turned to his earlier concerns for his own memory.

''I had not forgotten,'' the CURE director replied tightly. He moved to his keyboard. ''Raffair has established several offices around the country,'' he said as he typed. ''When you arrive in Boston, perhaps you should check the one there before going home."

He read Remo the address from his monitor.

"Can do," Remo agreed. "And we'll do our best to keep from getting shot at. Scout's honor."

With that, the buzz of a dial tone replaced Remo's voice. Smith hung up the phone.

He sat there for a moment, staring off into space.

Remo's flippant attitude toward the events in and outside the LFB building had become the norm. There was a time when even he would have recognized what a potentially serious breach of security his and Chiun's actions of this morning represented. Not anymore. That Remo was long gone. In a lot of ways, his attitude was now Chiun's.

Perhaps it was Smith's own fault. Maybe he had been too forgiving of these lapses. It just seemed that there was no way to rein in Remo and Chiun.

A muted ringing shook him from his reverie.

It was the special White House line. The President was no doubt looking for another update.

For the first time in a long time, Smith let the phone go to two rings. Finally, with an exhausted groan, he stretched his gnarled hand to his bottom desk drawer.

**10**

Mark Howard scanned the Associated Press report for the third time.

The news story out of New York was short. A junior executive at Lippincott, Forsythe, Butler had been murdered. Mark wouldn't have given the story a second look if not for the connection to Raffair.

As it was, he studied the terse text carefully. His green eyes—flecked at pupils' edges with creeping brown—were alert, straining to see something he might have missed.

There was nothing.

No feelings came to him as he exited the report. There was no need. It didn't take any weird supernatural instinct to tell him that somebody was covering their tracks.

In the privacy of his drab cubicle, recycled basement air hissing through rusted vents, Mark leaned back in his cheap blue swivel chair.

He'd picked up the chair himself at an office supply store after his last one had broken. The way the CIA's budget had been going these past few years, he would have been lucky if they'd requisitioned him an orange crate to sit on.

He had been trying to put that morning's White House meeting out of his mind. There was something extralegal going on at the highest level of American government. And somehow—at least peripherally—Mark Howard was involved. Since he had no control over it, he'd opted to ignore it.

On his desk sat a manila folder. He'd begun assembling a file on Raffair after the botched DEA raid the previous week.

There had been a lot to sift through. Mark had spent many monotonous hours collating the material, most of it on his own time. Still leaning back, he stretched out a hand, pulling the folder into his lap. Absently, he flipped open the cover.

The alphabetized listing of Raffair's offices was on top. The first was Boston, followed by Chicago, Houston, Los Angeles, Miami, New Orleans and New York.

For some reason, his eyes strayed to the short paragraph he'd assembled on the Boston office.

The building had been recently purchased by a Paul Petito. Mark found the transaction listed in the real-estate transfer section of the *Boston Blade*. According to public company records, Petito was Raffair's Boston branch manager.

Mark was surprised to learn after digging only a little further that Raffair wasn't that particular about whom they hired.

Petito had a criminal history dating back to his

teens. Although he seemed to have dabbled in everything from extortion to burglary, apparently his real passion lay in counterfeiting. According to Mark's information, Petito had been released from his most recent prison sentence two months ago. He had bought the Boston Raffair building one month later.

Earlier in the day, Mark had printed the phrase "funny money?" in the margin beside Petito's name. Picking up a pen from his desk, he underlined the words.

Doodling absently on the paper, Mark allowed his thoughts to stray back to his early-morning meeting in the Oval Office.

The President had been deeply angry about something. Part of Mark's special gift allowed him to sense very strong emotions. Although it didn't take a mind reader to know that the President was unhappy about something, Mark alone had sensed how embittered the chief executive truly was. The well of resentment he wallowed in was deep and wide. And by the sound of what he'd muttered, a good chunk of his anger was directed at Mark's own General Smith.

How this involved him, Mark had no idea.

With a sigh, he pulled himself out of his thoughts. When he looked back down at his notes, he was surprised to see that his wandering pen had written something.

The words "Asian" and "white" were now written in the margin next to his other notation. An arrow beside the sloppily printed words steered directly to the word "Boston."

Shocked, Mark looked down at his fingers. It was as if someone else's hand had taken root at the end of his arm.

He had long grown used to the strange episodes that had been with him all his life. They were all easily identifiable, falling into the same neat categories. But this...

This was new.

Mark glanced back down at the paper.

Another word was written beside the others. It was this one that had caused him the most concern. The word was "death."

In the cool of Langley's basement, Mark felt a shiver of fear. Standing woodenly from his chair, he took the single doodle-filled sheet from the top of the slender Raffair file.

Somewhere in the CIA headquarters, there had to be a shredder that wasn't broken. Paper in hand, Mark Howard went off in search of it.

**11**

Seymour Botz had just about had it with the constant talking. Not that he'd ever dare say so. Under ordinary circumstances, Seymour didn't have much of a spine, but when dealing with Louis DiGrotti, the timid accountant from Boston's Whitehall and Marx was without vertebrae, spinal cord and most of the musculature in his upper and lower back.

"I ain't seen one walrus since I got here," Louis DiGrotti snarled. Even with his tough Bronx accent, every word he uttered sounded like a whining complaint.

"Walrus?" Seymour asked, trying to sound interested.

"Yeah," DiGrotti nodded. "Them's the ones what got them big teeth in the front." He demonstrated with a pair of pencils from his desk. "I thought I seen one yesterday," he said, spitting out the pencils, "but it was just a dog."

It had been like this ever since Louis DiGrotti had shown up at Boston's Raffair office from New York. The big man—who, according to reputation, was adept at mangling much more than just the English language—knew Boston was north of his regular haunts. Geography not being one of his strong suits, DiGrotti had assumed it was somewhere roughly between the wilds of untamed Canada and Santa's magic workshop.

Even though he'd been in town for two weeks without getting run down by an advancing glacier, he still hadn't been disabused of his preconceived notions.

"I tooked a pitcher of it just in case," DiGrotti continued. On his desk was a small disposable camera. He had a drawerful. Louis was going to make a photo album of all the amazing animals he encountered while in exile in the Boston tundra.

"I guess it coulda been a walrus," he mused. "It was real small, though. Maybe it was a baby walrus. Or a cat."

Across the room at his own desk, Seymour did his best to tune out the other man's voice.

DiGrotti had already taken dozens of snapshots of a moose that was actually a shrub, a fire-hydrant penguin and a sleeping polar bear that was really a snow-covered Volvo.

"Youse know what really pisses me off?" DiGrotti said. "Dem reindeer. I been up every night till two since I got here and I ain't seen one. My neck's killin' me."

He rubbed at the back of his neck with a massive hand. Both hand and neck were covered with hair. So was the rest of his hulking body.

Back home in New York, he was known as Louis

the Bear. Some said that he bathed in Rogaine. Of course, they had sense enough to say this behind his furry back. In addition to his physical resemblance to his animal namesake, Louis the Bear had a temper as great as the average grizzly and the strength to back it up.

Seymour Botz was aware enough of Louis Di-Grotti's intimidating size to not test his temper. The accountant continued to work as the big man talked.

"I figured the reindeer would be the easy ones to find what with all that sky up there," Louis complained. "They must be hidin' out with all the walruses."

Frowning deeply, he picked up his camera. He was picking at the lens when the bell above the front door suddenly jingled to life.

Louis glanced up, a hopeful expression tugging at his five-o'clock shadow. But instead of a wayward reindeer, it was two men who had just entered Raffair's Boston offices. Face sagging once more, Louis tossed his camera to his desk.

"Damn Rudolphs," he growled.

The two men didn't seem to hear him. As they crossed to the desks, they continued an argument that had started outside.

"I'm not saying you can't listen to her," the young white guy was saying.

"You are absolutely not saying that," the old Chinaman interrupted icily.

"I'm just saying that the neighbors might appreciate it if you didn't turn it up so loud when you're not in the room. At least until I can replace the broken windows," Remo said.

"And who broke the windows?" Chiun replied frostily. "Besides, our neighbors are Vietnamese. If I can get used to the sounds of cats being strangled every night at dinnertime, they certainly cannot complain about the lovely Wylander."

"Wylander gives the cats a run for their money," Remo muttered. "Let's just try to keep the volume down, okay?"

"Absolutely not," Chiun sniffed. "Will you next muzzle the nightingale or whippoorwill? Where will your callous attacks on beauty end? I must draw a line in the sand."

At his desk, Seymour Botz eyed the new arrivals with concern. "Can I help you gentlemen with something?" he asked, his eyes bouncing from one man to the other.

"Just a sec," Remo said. "The only birds you can link to Wylander Jugg are the three hundred that give up their lives every week to fill her buckets of extra crispy."

Seymour cast a confused eye at Louis DiGrotti.

The big man was reacting to the two visitors not with bemusement but with concern. Eyeing Remo and Chiun, he was slowly sliding a furry hand beneath his jacket.

Seymour shot to his feet as if his chair were on fire.

"You want stock!" he sang, hoping to cut off any violence. "I can give you a list of Boston brokers!"

Fumbling at the papers on his desk, he held a sheet out to Remo.

Remo turned a bland eye on the computer printout.

"Not interested," he said. "I believe in gold, not stock."

"Don't think you can get around me that way," Chiun cautioned.

Remo ignored the old man. "Look," he said to Seymour Botz, "I just wasted a whole day flying to New York to visit a dead man and I've apparently got a night of Grand Ole Opry and angry phone calls to deal with, so why don't we just make this easy for everybody concerned and tell me who's pulling the strings on Raffair."

Botz tensed. "I don't know what you mean," he sniffed.

"Well, first off, I'm gonna go out on a limb and say it's dirty," Remo suggested. "Otherwise, the office Furby wouldn't be pointing that gun at us."

"He is pointing it at *you,* not us," Chiun corrected. "People must be instinctively drawn to your negative energy."

Botz spun to Louis DiGrotti. When he saw the gun in his huge hand, his eyes went wide. "What do you think you're doing?" the accountant cried.

"Friggin' reindeer," DiGrotti growled. "If them and the walruses ain't gonna help me do what I wanna do, I'm at least gonna do what I was sent here to do."

With that pronouncement, he squeezed the trigger.

A sound like a sharp thunderclap exploded in the small office. It was followed nearly simultaneously by the meaty thwack of lead against forehead.

As the smoke cleared, Louis the Bear blinked. And frowned.

Remo still stood before Seymour Botz's desk. Behind the desk, Seymour's mouth was open wide. For some reason, a thick maroon dent dotted the center of his forehead.

When the accountant lurched forward onto his blotter, the spray of brain and bone from the back of his blown-out head could be seen decorating the office wall.

"Wha...?" Louis questioned, unable to wrap his tiny brain around what had just transpired.

A clamping pain on his wrist drew his attention.

When he looked down, he found himself staring into the upturned face of the Master of Sinanju.

Chiun squeezed, and Louis DiGrotti's hand sprang obediently open. His gun thudded to the floor.

"Tell me, Remo, have you ever met someone who did not shoot at you?" Chiun said blandly as Remo stepped over.

"Never happened till I met you," Remo replied. He turned to DiGrotti. "Okay, spill it, fuzzy. What's the deal with Raffair? And make it snappy before you start shedding all over my pants."

"Raffair?" DiGrotti said, blinking. He was coming out of it. One eye glanced down at his gun. It was lying on the floor near the leg of his desk.

"Okay," Remo declared. "Let's remove all distractions."

He bent and scooped up Louis's gun, handing it back to the thug.

Louis would have used the handgun on his assailants had something strange not happened to the weapon on the way up from the floor. It had apparently disintegrated.

Woodenly, Louis looked at the fragments of scrap metal in his hand. They rattled. When he looked back up, Remo was slapping a cloud of metal dust from his palms.

"Your teeth are next," Remo said flatly.

Feeling true fear for the first time in his life, Louis "The Bear" DiGrotti offered a wide, agreeable smile. Thinking better of it, he slapped a hand over his mouth protectively.

"Whatever you wanna know, I'll tell you," he promised, his voice muffled by his big furry palm.

Remo opened his mouth to speak, but the Master of Sinanju suddenly forced his way in front of his pupil.

"*I* have a question," he announced imperiously.

"Chiun, can we get this over with?" Remo griped.

"Silence, hater of beauty," the old Korean snapped. He trained a steely hazel eye on Louis DiGrotti. "You will speak truth, hairy one?" he demanded.

Both hands now clamped over his mouth, Di-Grotti nodded. "Uh-huh," he mumbled.

"Then tell my loutish son who has two tin ears how much you enjoy the singing of the lilting siren Wylander."

Behind a faceful of overlapping hands, DiGrotti's brow dropped low. "Wylander?" he asked from between his fingers. "Ain't she dat heifer country star? She's awful, ain't she?"

His guileless eyes stared hopefully down at the old man as he nodded at the truth of his own words.

DiGrotti continued nodding even as he saw the faint rustle of fabric at the old man's kimono sleeve. He thought he was nodding even as he felt the sudden pressure against his neck. He was only marginally certain he'd stopped nodding when his head slipped off his shoulders and the floor came racing up to meet him. He hit, rolled, stopped nodding and stopped processing all conscious thought at the exact same moment.

Remo jumped forward even as Chiun's hands were returning to his sides.

"What the hell did you do that for?" he demanded as DiGrotti's headless corpse toppled backward to the floor.

"I was merely saving you from wasting any more precious time," the old man said. "If this shaggy thing would lie about the comely Wylander, he would lie about anything."

He flicked a single droplet of blood from one tapered fingernail before replacing his hands in his kimono sleeves.

"Next time, could you check with me before doing me a favor?" Remo had to take a step back to avoid the widening pool of blood.

"It was not only for you," the Master of Sinanju sniffed. "By insulting the fair Wylander with his words of hate, he offended all of what it means to be truly American. Such a slur could not be allowed to pass unpunished on this most solemn and holy week for your fledgling nation. I was merely doing my patriotic duty."

"Why don't you let me worry about the national honor and you worry about not getting filmed lopping people's heads off," Remo said sourly. "Or didn't you notice that?" He aimed a finger ceilingward.

In the far corner of the room, a single motionless video camera peered out across the office.

"Of course I noticed," the Master of Sinanju replied blandly. "Now go and collect the tape. You may use it as an educational tool when we return to Castle Sinanju. I will be in the car."

With that, the old man spun on one sandaled heel and marched from the building.

Alone, Remo shook his head. "Old buzzard," he muttered.

He ducked into a back room. At the ceiling, the camera wires ran in from the front. When he followed them to a supply shelf, Remo expected to find a VCR.

The wires continued out into a back hallway.

He began to worry when he found that the cable wire ran up a dark stairwell.

Three flights up, the cable snaked out onto the roof. Remo's stomach sank when he saw where it led.

A squat white satellite dish was affixed to the icy roof ledge. Tilted up, it was aimed in a southerly direction. The fat black cable was connected to the back of the dish.

With troubled eyes, Remo looked up at the night sky. The city lights dulled the diamonds of the stars.

A cold breeze blew up, tousling his short hair and flapping his chinos. When he spoke, Remo's voice was small.

"Uh-oh," he said to the desolate wind.

There wasn't even a hint of movement. Maybe a tiny flutter of purple. If you looked hard enough.

Louis "The Bear" DiGrotti was just standing there one minute, hands over his mouth, scared—Louis the Bear actually *scared*—and the next minute, he was in pieces on the floor.

"Damn, his head just up and drops off," one of the men in the small bedroom said, his gruff voice amazed.

Behind him came a terrified peep. It was the tenth time they'd watched the video, and it still shocked Paul Petito.

"Maybe it was already loose," Mikey "Skunks" Falcone suggested. "Like a tooth."

"Heads don't just come loose," Petito insisted.

"I had a toenail that did once," Mikey Skunks said. "And toenails ain't supposed to come off. Maybe Bear's head's like my toenail."

"No," Petito stated firmly. "That old Chinese guy chopped it off."

On the TV screen for the tenth time that evening,

Chiun flicked a dollop of blood from the tip of his index nail.

Although the three men in that room had seen the tape multiple times, the man they had beamed it to in New York was viewing it for the very first time. Apparently, he hadn't expected so grisly a scene.

"Oh, my God," Sol Sweet's nasal voice gasped over the speakerphone.

For several long seconds afterward, Anselmo Scubisci's lawyer could be heard retching over the crisp line.

Paul Petito couldn't blame him. He'd had the same reaction the first few times they'd watched the images that had been beamed into his Massachusetts home. Fingers stained black with old ink wiped sweat from his forehead.

"My God, he just—" Sweet's voice finally managed to say. "How did he *do* that?"

"I guess with them fingernails," Mikey Skunks suggested. "They're pretty long. Maybe he's got, I don't know, razors or something taped to the backs."

Sol Sweet seemed to not even hear the speculation. "This isn't—" he began. "I mean, it can't... *Who are they?*"

"I don't know, Mr. Sweet. Coupla guys, I guess. Hey, you want us to do 'em?"

Paul Petito's eyes went wide. He wheeled around.

Mikey Skunks was calmly watching the screen. Along with the other New York import, he sat on the edge of Paul's bed, a bored look on his face.

There was a pause on the line as Sol Sweet collected his thoughts. "Yes," he ventured finally. "Now, let me think. I'm not sure I heard the last thing you said, but I think our mutual employer would want you to do what *he'd* do under these same circumstances." He didn't want to get roped into giving any direct orders. These days, there was no telling who might be listening in on private conversations.

Mikey Skunks scratched his cheek thoughtfully. "I'm pretty sure Don Anselmo would want us to kill them, Mr. Sweet," he suggested.

There was another gasp from the speaker, this one panicked. The line abruptly went dead.

"Yeah," Skunks nodded. "He wants us to kill them." Tongue jutting between his broad lips, he thumbed the VCR remote, rolling back the tape once more.

"So how do we find them?" Petito asked.

He sounded ill. This business at the Boston Raffair office was like some awful dream. Paul Petito was just a counterfeiter. He'd been roped into this for selfish reasons that had nothing to do with killing or being killed.

"We get a picture from here," Skunks said, waving at the image of Remo and Chiun on the screen. "Then I guess we circulate it, start asking around. Can you get their pictures from the TV?"

Petito nodded. "I know a guy who can do it digitally," he said weakly. As he spoke, he was vaguely aware of the front door opening.

Skunks heard the sound, too. "It's about time," he snarled. "We're in here!" he hollered.

By now, the tape had rolled back to the start. Remo and Chiun were standing at the desks in the Boston Raffair office when Paul Petito's bedroom door opened. A fourth man entered the room, lugging two big paper bags. The warm smells of greasy sausage and tomato sauce poured from the bags.

"What, we eating in here?" he asked with a scowl.

"Shh!" Skunks snapped at the new arrival. *"Here,"* he said, pointing at the TV.

On the screen, Louis DiGrotti's head was just rolling off his neck.

"What the hell?" The new man gaped. "Was that the Bear?"

Skunks and the others nodded.

"How did he—?" The man with the bags froze midsentence.

On the screen, Remo had just stepped forward. He was plainly visible now, standing next to the Master of Sinanju.

Two shopping bags dropped to the worn carpet. White foam containers split open, spilling red sauce all over the floor. Flecks of red splattered on shoes, wall and bed.

As the others jumped angrily away from the mess, the latest arrival remained rooted in place. He continued to stare in shock at the satellite-fed taped image on the crystal-clear screen.

Remo's cruel face remained in sharp focus.

The man standing in the puddle of sauce shook his head in uncomprehending shock. In the center of his forehead, between his wide-open eyes, was a large purple bruise.

When he at last spoke, his voice was small.

"Oh, shit, not him again," gasped Johnny "Books" Fungillo.

**13**

"This is inexcusable," Harold Smith accused, struggling to control his anger. "How could you allow yourself to be filmed? I thought that you and Master Chiun could avoid cameras."

"Avoid, yes," Remo said aridly. "When we need to. But I didn't think we had to here. I figured this was just some other dumb-ass stop that didn't matter. Besides, I thought I could just snag the tape. How was I supposed to know it'd be hooked up to a satellite dish?"

When Smith exhaled, a rusty noise escaped like a wounded genie from the mouthpiece of the pay phone.

Chiun glanced up, his wrinkled face puckering with displeasure at the sound.

"Your enemies will quake in fear when they behold the terrifying wrath of the Master of Sinanju, Emperor Smith!" he called loudly. Dropping his voice low, he said to Remo, "Remind me to do something to aid his breathing the next time we see him. Those wheezing jackass brays are becoming depressing."

"Please tell Master Chiun that I am less concerned about my enemies than I am about the organization," Smith said tersely.

Remo cupped the phone. "Smitty says—"

"I heard," Chiun said thinly.

The old Korean stood near the curb a few feet away from Remo's sidewalk phone. Hands clasped behind his back, he turned his gaze back to the street where he'd been watching Boston traffic, leaving Remo and Smith to discuss their white nonsense.

"Anyway, I didn't know what I should do, Smitty," Remo said, "so I figured I'd better call."

"What you should have done was avoid the camera in the first place," Smith said tartly.

Remo's brow darkened. "Hey, I didn't want to schlepp off on this harebrained assignment for Captain Diddlepants in the first place," he warned. "So take the snot somewhere else or Chiun and I are outta here."

Smith sighed again. "I'm sorry," he said. "I suppose recriminations are pointless anyway until we find out what it is we are dealing with." He gave a thoughtful hum. "You're certain it was a satellite dish?" he asked abruptly.

"Yeah, I think," Remo replied. "It was one of those cockamamie Frisbee-looking things."

"And you're sure there was no video equipment on the premises?"

"The cable went right from the camera to the dish. I might not be too good with gadgets, but I can follow a wire."

"Perhaps it is a private security company," Smith mused.

"Great," Remo said. "Gimme an address and I'll get the tape from them."

"One minute, please."

A few seconds of gentle tapping on his special keyboard, and the older man was back on the line.

"This is strange," the CURE director said. "I checked to see if there was a local security firm in the employ of Raffair, Boston. When I found none, I checked nationally. There is no record of any security company anywhere doing business in any way at all with Raffair."

"So what?" Remo said. "Maybe they're just a little too trusting."

An impatient hiss came from the curb.

"They do not need hirelings, for they are guarded by their own reputation," the Master of Sinanju called over his shoulder. He was now studying the parked cars that lined the side of the road. A black Mercedes had caught his eye.

Smith had heard the old Asian's words. "It *is* strange for an operation that spans the country to not have at least some outside security," he agreed. "But if Raffair is inspiring fear, it must be purely by word of mouth, for there is no electronic record."

"Not word of mouth alone, Smitty," Remo disagreed. "If they've got a guy at every office like the one whose head Chiun lopped off here, most people'd have sense enough to tread lightly."

Smith's tone grew strained. "He decapitated him?" he asked wearily.

"Oh. Didn't I mention that?"

Ignoring Remo's sheepish tone, the CURE director plowed on. "I will attempt to find out where the signal might have been sent," he said. "Until I uncover a lead, you and Chiun may return home."

"Raise a flag," a squeaky voice volunteered behind Remo. It was followed by a piercing metallic scratching sound, like fingernails on a blackboard.

When Remo glanced back, he found that the Master of Sinanju had taken more than a passing interest in the parked Mercedes. Bored, the old man was drawing the edge of one long fingernail across the door panel. In the nail's wake, a shiny line of exposed silver glinted in the streetlights. A slender corkscrew of peeled paint curled down into the curbside snow pile.

"Knock it off, Chiun," Remo groused. Apparently, the noise was such that only sensitive eardrums were bothered by it. Somewhere distant, a pair of dogs howled.

The wizened Korean ignored his pupil.

"Didn't you say there were other offices, Smitty?" Remo asked. He scowled as he plugged his free ear. "Maybe we could find out who saw us from them."

"Unwise," Smith said, unmindful of the persistent noise on Remo's end. "We do not need another compromising incident today. Your images could have been sent to them by now. If this is the case, were you to show up at another Raffair office at this point, it is likely they would shoot first.''

''It is more likely that they would hold their manhood and run, Emperor,'' Chiun proclaimed as he continued etching the door. ''Any blackguard with designs on your throne would be cowed by my demonstration. Thanks to Sinanju, you may rest your regal head on silken pillows, confident in the knowledge that Fortress Folcroft is safe.''

''Please inform Master Chiun that it is not Folcroft that concerns me,'' Smith said seriously. ''The Boston Raffair office is very close to your own home. It is the two of you who could be in danger.''

At that did Chiun raise his head. His weathered face was astonished.

''Just when I think the lunatic can't get more insane,'' he said. Shaking his head in amazement, he returned to his work. A trapezoid shape familiar to Remo had begun to form on the car's door panel.

''I don't think Chiun's sweating this one too much, Smitty,'' Remo informed the CURE director.

''Nevertheless, please remain cautious, Remo. We still don't know who it is we are dealing with. And it's a good rule of thumb for the two of you to keep a low profile whenever you are in Massachusetts.''

''Point taken,'' Remo said. ''And speaking of risks to life and limb, did you find out anything from that button I sent you?''

''Oh, I had forgotten,'' Smith admitted. He seemed irritated with himself for the lapse. ''I searched several iconography databases. The design on the button was unknown to all of them. Since it appears on the surface to be meaningless, we can assume that the two men who attacked you were nothing more than common street criminals."

"They weren't decked out for mugging, Smitty," Remo said. "My money still says they're with Raffair."

"And I assume not, but I will keep an open mind," Smith said. "According to the New York coroner's office, neither man carried identification, so we may never know. However, I will continue to monitor that situation, as well as Raffair. If anything new turns up in either case, I will call you at home." With that, Smith terminated the call.

Turning from the phone booth, Remo joined the Master of Sinanju at the curb. Chiun was etching a final, bisecting line through the center of his silver trapezoid.

"He seems more on edge than usual," Remo commented as the last thread of curling paint fell to the snow.

"Water cannot be more wet than wet," Chiun observed, uninterested. "There," he proclaimed, extending a palm to the simple trapezoid design he had engraved on the car door. "The symbol of our House, engraved as it should be. With the Knives of Eternity and not with some silly machete."

Remo glanced at the old man, dark surprise clouding his face. "The Luzu blabbed, didn't they?" he accused.

Chiun shrugged as he clasped opposing wrists.

"Do not blame the messenger," he said. "It is you who must resort to tools because you refuse to grow your nails to their proper length. My only hope now is that your own student will be more traditional."

Turning from his pupil, he began padding down the sidewalk. Although sand had been spread liberally on the path to provide traction on the ice, his soles made not a single scuffing mark or sound.

Remo trotted up beside him, a thoughtful expression on his face. "Speaking of the Luzu, how traditional are they—I mean with succession and all? Like for king, for instance."

Chiun raised a thin eyebrow. "The eldest son succeeds the father," he replied.

"Hmm," Remo said. "And that big fat chief they've got now, is Bubu his eldest son or his only son?"

They had met the tribal chief and his offspring while in Africa on their last assignment.

"Chief Batubizee is fortunate to have five sons other than the one you met," Chiun replied cautiously. "Each is in line to succeed the other. Why do you ask?"

"Oh," Remo shrugged. "No reason. The sign of Sinanju." He jerked his head back in the direction from whence they'd come. "You just reminded me of all that nonsense back in East Africa is all." Dodging the suspicious slits that were the Master of Sinanju's eyes, he quickly changed the subject. "You know, Smitty might be right, by the way. Until he finds out where our faces were beamed, it might be smart for us to lay low for a while.''

The tiny Korean gave him a baleful look. ''A Master of Sinanju does not scurry down a hole like a frightened rabbit. Smith forces us to lurk in shadows too much as it is.''

''Different world than it used to be, Little Father,'' Remo pointed out. ''No more pharaohs' courts and royal assassins. Gotta adapt to the times.''

''Do not remind me,'' Chiun droned. ''What I would not give for another Herod or Attila. Even a Borgia or two. But cruel fate has given me a Smith, and so Smith I must endure.''

Beside the tiny Asian, Remo's face was pensive. He seemed lost in private thoughts.

''We all have our crosses to bear, Little Father,'' he said softly.

**14**

When the President of the United States trudged into his secretary's office from the hallway, he did his best to ignore the large plastic storage totes and cheap collapsible cardboard boxes that were stacked four-high around the room.

"That package arrive from CIA yet, Betty?" he asked.

His frazzled secretary nodded. "Yes, Mr. President," she said, handing him an envelope from the top of the mess on her desk. It was embossed with the emblem of the Central Intelligence Agency. "You've got an 11:00 p.m. meeting with the incoming President this Friday night, like you asked."

"Mmm," the President said absently as he headed for the nearby door to the Oval Office.

With one pudgy pale finger, he broke the seal on the envelope. He tapped the contents into his free hand as he shouldered the door open. The President took only two steps into the room before he froze in midstep.

"Betty!" he thundered hoarsely.

His secretary stuck her head into the room. "Sir?"

"Where the hell's my desk?" he demanded. He waved the envelope toward the spot where his desk had sat for the past eight years. It was the same desk JFK had used.

The desk was gone. Brilliant yellow light from the floor-to-ceiling windows on the wall behind cascaded over the vacant area, shining brightly on the permanent indentation the heavy desk had made in the carpet, as well as emphasizing the many spots and stains on the rug.

"Oh," his secretary said worriedly. "It was gone when I came in this morning. I assumed you asked the GS staff to move it."

"No," he answered flatly. "I didn't."

"Oh," she said again. "Do you want me to look for it?"

He shook his head with quiet anger. "Don't bother," he grumbled. "I'll be upstairs."

CIA documents in hand, he left the Oval Office.

Things had been turning up missing at the White House for the past year or so. Since they'd never owned a real home of their own, the only furniture the President and First Lady had in storage during their years in Washington was a few torn beanbag chairs and a couple of broken lava lamps.

His wife needed furnishings for the house she'd acquired in New York and so had been helping herself to odds and ends around the Washington mansion for months. Lately, however, the items had been getting larger.

An entire set of Bellange chairs was gone from the Blue Room, and someone had pried the carved marble mantel from around the fireplace in the Green Room. The chandelier and table had gone missing from the State Dining Room, and nearly the entire collection of antique books dating back to President Fillmore had slowly disappeared from the library. The Smithsonian had just gotten word that the Steinway grand piano had somehow vanished from the East Room late last week.

The President had hoped to blame the strange disappearances on a bureaucratic snafu at the Smithsonian Institution. But now with his own desk among the missing, he wasn't sure if he shouldn't just blame the White House staff, sic the FBI on them and sneak away in the confusion. After all, it had worked for two straight presidential terms.

On top of the stolen-furniture problem, his wife had dropped yet another doozy of a dilemma in the President's lap right after he'd gotten off the phone with Smith yesterday. Her ambition was always getting him in trouble. He had no idea how this new mess was going to play out.

He was still wondering what exactly he should do when he entered the family quarters.

He was greatly relieved to find the First Dog nowhere in sight. As the elevator doors closed behind him, the only sound he could hear was the meowing of the unseen First Cat. Documents in hand, he hurried down the hall to a small study.

This room was as cluttered as most in the White House these days. He found a clear spot on the sofa and settled down to read the documents.

The President had called Mark Howard personally and asked the young man to send over the information. To cover the trail, he'd had Howard courier them through the CIA director's office.

Though obviously curious, Howard had accepted the unusual orders without question. The kid was intelligent, quiet and obedient. With any luck, he'd be loyal to boot.

The President quickly went through the information. There wasn't anything of any great interest. Still, he had to find something. He'd made a promise, after all, to the one person in the world he couldn't betray.

Taking but one sheet of paper, the President stood.

There were a number of paper shredders plugged in in perpetuity in this room. Some were battery operated just in case the regular power sources and emergency backup systems ever went out. Most of the shredders were battered and wobbly from overuse.

Selecting a big workhorse model that had been an anniversary gift from an order of Buddhist nuns, he ran the bulk of the papers and the CIA envelope through the machine.

With his lone piece of paper in hand, the President

left the disordered study and headed down the hall toward the Lincoln Bedroom.

IT WAS ONLY 9:00 a.m. and Harold Smith was ready to call it a day. He had spent the previous long night attempting to learn where Remo and Chiun's satellite images had been beamed. He'd had no luck. Morning's light found fatigue and anxiety etched deep in the gray lines of his face.

In days gone by, many a sleepless night had Smith remained at his desk. He had been finding out these past few years that at his age it wasn't as easy as it had once been.

But he could not leave. He was right to be concerned.

What should have been a simple visit to the Boston offices of Raffair had turned into a security threat to CURE.

More than anything else, Smith worried about secrecy. The very existence of CURE was an admission that America and her Constitution had failed. If the organization were ever to become known beyond the tight inner circle of Smith, Remo, Chiun and the President, the consequences would be dire.

The rooftop satellite could have beamed Remo and Chiun's images anywhere. Some unknown entity had a glimpse of CURE's enforcement arm in action.

For Smith, the one silver lining in all this had been the thought that Raffair wasn't likely to involve the authorities in the events at their Boston offices.

To do so would be to invite the sort of scrutiny they obviously shied away from. However, the bodies had been discovered by a customer who had entered the building after Remo and Chiun. Word of the deaths had gotten out. Still, as long as the company held on to the tape, there was hope.

Raffair itself continued to be a dead end. Smith had connected a number of small-time criminals to the company, but a larger corporate structure had yet to emerge. Given events in Boston, he would prefer to go after the Hydra's main head rather than send Remo and Chiun up the chain of command.

Beneath the onyx surface of Smith's desk, the word "Raffair" was printed in ghostly fashion on his buried computer screen. The patient cursor blinked methodically, partially obscuring the first *R* with every strobelike flash.

As usual, the name sparked something in the deepest recesses of Smith's mind. He had begun to assume that it was just his tired brain playing tricks on him.

Surrendering for a moment to his weariness, Smith turned to face the picture window.

The wind was not as severe today. The black waters of Long Island Sound rolled to shore in soothing waves. The old boat dock rose and fell in time with the water. It was by way of that very dock that a much younger Harold Smith had first entered the grounds of Folcroft Sanitarium.

Farther out across the sound, a few boats bobbed in the wan winter light. Smith had seen many such boaters while ensconced in his Spartan office. Decades' worth.

For Harold Smith, this view had always had a calming effect. Someday it would belong to someone else. Either a new head of CURE or the next director of Folcroft. In a brief moment of introspection, Smith wondered if his replacement in that lonely chair would find pleasure in the view. And in that moment, the telephone rang.

"Yes, Mr. President," Smith said once he'd pulled the red phone from his desk drawer.

"Any progress, Smith?" the hoarse voice of the President of the United States demanded.

"None of any significance," Smith admitted, leaning back in his chair. "My people went to New York to check with the firm that helped launch Raffair as a public company. However, the lead there had been severed before they arrived. Beyond that, the financial structure has not been easy to unravel. There are various trusts and offshore banks to which the money is being funneled. It is clearly an illegal venture, but it has been created by an as-yet-unknown agent."

"Hmm," the President said. His voice had taken on a vague, distant tone. "I understand there are regional offices. Why not try going through one of them?"

Smith frowned. "That has already been attempted," he said carefully. "There was some difficulty at the Boston office. My people were put in a compromising position."

"I know what that's like," the President muttered bitterly. "Were they injured?"

"It would take extraordinary circumstances for them to sustain injury," Smith said. "However, without going into great detail, the situation was less than ideal. I am attempting to use the resources at my disposal to minimize the security risk to CURE."

"You do that," the President said. "In the meantime, what about your people? They still in the Boston area?"

"Yes," Smith admitted. He deliberately did not mention that Remo and Chiun called the Commonwealth of Massachusetts home.

On the other end of the line, Smith heard the faint sound of paper rattling.

"Have them check into someone while they're there. Could help you out. It's a counterfeiter named Paul Petito."

Smith pursed his lips. "I know of him," he said slowly.

The name had turned up in his own research. Though curious as to how the President of the United States would know of a man like Petito, the CURE director held his tongue.

"Yeah, I got a source that says he's linked to Raffair. Might be a good idea to check him out. Move up the chain of command from there." The President's voice suddenly grew more cheerful. "Here, kitty-kitty," he said off the phone.

Smith assumed that the presidential cat had just

wandered into the Lincoln Bedroom. A moment later, he heard the sound of contented purring close to the phone.

"At least *someone* in this town hasn't abandoned me," the President said warmly.

"Mr. President, I'm not sure how much more I can do in this matter," Smith said, trying to steer the chief executive back to the topic at hand. "However, I will see what can be done with Mr. Petito."

"Thanks, Smith," the President said, the warmth still lingering in his tone. "You know, man's best friend ain't a dog," he added knowingly. "Those fickle fleabags'll turn on you faster than a drunken ex-press secretary. Cats are the pets that are the real loyal ones. Nice pussy." This last phrase was uttered lovingly off the phone.

As soon as the President had said it, there came a violent hissing from nearby. It was followed by a yelp of pain from the chief executive.

"Dammit!" the President snapped into the receiver. "She even had the damn cat brainwashed for voice commands."

Smith sat up straighter in his chair. "Is everything all right, Mr. President?" he asked, concerned.

"No," the President said sourly. "Who knew you could have a cat reclawed? Just keep looking into that stuff, Smith. I've gotta go find some Bactine."

With a final angry huff, the chief executive severed the connection.

Smith slowly replaced the red phone. The frown

on his gaunt face had only deepened during their conversation.

While Presidents often informed Smith of wrongdoing, in the nearly forty-year history of CURE, not one chief executive had ever been interested in something so small.

A counterfeiter. Why would the commander in chief be concerned with something so trivial?

Smith glanced down at his computer screen. The word "Raffair" blinked up from the sinister depths of his desk.

Wondering what could be going through the President's mind, Smith stretched a hand for the blue contact phone.

FOR THE SECOND MORNING in a row, Remo's peace was shattered by the full-throated yapping of Wylander Jugg. Rather than get into another argument, he'd ducked outside, ignoring the nasty looks given him by two women pushing baby carriages down the sidewalk in front of Castle Sinanju. He spent the bulk of the day hiding out at the dollar movie theater, returning home as the setting sun was just beginning to touch the tops of the nearest buildings.

The condominium complex was brightly lit and blessedly silent. As he walked inside, the Master of Sinanju was floating down the main staircase.

"Why's it so quiet in here?" Remo asked. "Wylander take eating breaks in midrecord? Not that I think that'd be very quiet."

"I am resting my ears," Chiun said. "A handful of flowers is a bouquet—a field is hay fever."

He turned abruptly away from his pupil, rounding the base of the stairway. Remo trailed the old Korean down the hallway to the kitchen.

"A guy I never met before just stopped me outside to ask us to keep it down in here. His newborn's got colic, and Wylander's keeping her awake."

"Impossible," Chiun sniffed. "If anything, she should be lulled to sleep. Tell this whoever-he-is that his disagreeable offspring will only cause some man grief later in life. He should drown her in Quincy Bay at once and spare her poor future husband."

In the kitchen, Chiun began poking through the cupboards. He crinkled his nose in displeasure.

"Good way to make friends," Remo groused, leaning against the counter.

"I do not need friends. I have you."

Although he smelled a scam a mile away, Remo still felt his heart lighten. "Okay, what do you want?"

"Duck," the old man answered. "Preferably ruddy duck."

"Aw, c'mon, Chiun," Remo said, the beginnings of a smile evaporating. "You've got a hundred fish tanks in the cellar."

"I do not feel like fish."

"Okay." Remo sighed, pushing away from the counter. "There's duck in the freezer."

The Master of Sinanju shook his head. "No," he

insisted. "You thaw it improperly. I want fresh duck."

"Frozen or fresh tastes the same to me."

"Your barbarian's palate goes well with your Philistine's ears," Chiun droned. "We will go out to eat."

"But I've been out all day," Remo complained. "I had to put up with two hours' worth of that wet-eyed moping that Tom Hanks calls acting, not to mention some sci-fi mess with Jann Revolta in dreadlocks that made me want to start a freaking crusade against that dipwaddle Hollywood cult of his. Can't we just spend a quiet—stress *quiet*—night at home?"

Chiun waited until he was finished. The old Asian wore a deeply thoughtful expression. "I wonder if the restaurant will have ruddy duck?" he mused. "Oh, well. Whatever the house duck is will suffice."

Remo opened his mouth to speak when the phone squawked abruptly to life.

"Oh, and Smith called," the Master of Sinanju offered absently as his pupil reached for the telephone.

"Hello," Remo said into the receiver as he gave the old Asian a peeved glance.

"Remo, it is about time." Smith sounded more agitated than normal. "I have tried to call a dozen times today."

"I spent the afternoon in exile," Remo said

aridly. "What's up? You find out where our faces got beamed?"

"Not yet," Smith replied. "The biggest impediment to that search is the easy acquisition of such technology by private individuals. One need no longer hire a service to set up a system like the one you encountered."

"Okay, so we go to question B. What about the guys who attacked me?"

"Nothing on that front, either, I'm afraid," Smith said. "But there is something else you can look into. The man who purchased the building you were filmed in lives near you. Perhaps he can offer a lead, if not to Raffair itself at least to where the satellite image was directed."

Remo scrunched up his face. "I thought we were gonna give the small fries a rest until we could go after the big kahuna."

"There are no small matters where you are concerned, O Emperor," Chiun called. "For anything that gives your soul a moment's distress is an enemy of tranquillity that must be dealt with harshly by your humble servants. Point us to he who vexes your thoughts, and Sinanju will make him rue the day he had the temerity to trouble your sweet mind."

Remo cupped the phone. "You're still angling to go out to eat," he accused.

Chiun's face was bland. "We *are* going out," he said firmly. "As long as we are, we might as well humor His Royal Grayness. Plus I am tired of his phone calls disturbing my peace every five minutes.''

Frowning, Remo took his hand off the phone. "Okay," he sighed. "Looks like we're going out. Who is this guy?''

Smith gave him the name and address of Paul Petito. Remo jotted it down on a pad next to the phone.

"Got it," he said once the CURE director was through. "Although I still don't know why we're wasting our time with all this. I was sure you'd get tired of this whole 'let the President leave with a smile on his face' thing after last night's fiasco. Plus aren't there any maniacs with weather machines or neo-Nazis bent on world conquest out there yet?''

"Yes, it is small," Smith admitted with a tired sigh. "But Petito is a counterfeiter. According to my information, it is likely he has started up his operation again since his release from prison.''

"Like I said," Remo insisted. "You're sending the A-Team out after something even the FBI could handle." He quickly rethought his own words. "Well, maybe not the FBI. But the Cub Scouts or Brownies'd probably be up for it.''

Smith was silent for a long moment.

In the privacy of his Folcroft office, the CURE director was settled back in his chair, his weary eyes closed on the darkening room.

How could he explain to Remo the reverence he felt for America and its institutions? Even the poor, beleaguered presidency. Although possessed with some latent patriotism, CURE's enforcement arm had never had very high regard for most politicians. He disdained Presidents in general, this current one in particular. Yet Smith was of a different generation, a dying breed. And if the President of the United States—*any* President—begged a reasonable favor of Harold W. Smith, the rock-ribbed New Englander with the heart of a patriot felt it his duty to honor that request.

"Please, Remo," Smith said at last. His tart voice was strained.

In the kitchen of his condo, Remo frowned at the effort in the old man's voice. It held an intense world-weariness.

Remo paused but a moment.

"Okay, Smitty," he said softly. "But let's get this straight. I'm doing this for you. No one else."

Without waiting for a reply, he slipped the receiver back into its cradle. His expression was darkly thoughtful as he turned to the Master of Sinanju.

"You ready to roll?" he asked.

"One moment," the wizened Asian commanded.

Kimono sleeves flapping, Chiun flounced from the room. He returned a moment later, a small plastic case gripped tightly in one bony hand.

"What's that?" Remo asked warily. By his tone, it was clear he already had his suspicions.

"Oh, merely something to make our ride more enjoyable," the Master of Sinanju replied airily.

"Bring the keys. The taping device in the car will not work without them."

He bounded out the kitchen door.

"Give me strength," Remo muttered softly.

Praying for some mechanical defect in his leased car's tape player, Remo followed Chiun outside.

UNFORTUNATELY FOR REMO, the car stereo system worked perfectly. The speakers vibrated to Wylander's twangy voice as they drove out of the big parking lot next to the old converted church.

On their way out of town, they passed a slow-moving car driving in the opposite direction. Remo was so distracted by Wylander that he didn't notice a familiar face in the back seat. A black-and-purple bruise decorated a spot dead center in the man's forehead.

In the other car, the worried eyes of Johnny "Books" Fungillo scanned sidewalk and building. So focused was he on the street that he failed to see Remo pass by.

Both cars separated and slowly withdrew, fading to invisibility in the frosty January night air.

**15**

Paul Petito was an artist in a world of heathens.

This troubling thought weighed on him even as he inspected the first bills to run off his newest press.

Petito had a jeweler's loupe jammed into one eye. The bills were clipped to three clotheslines in his basement workshop. A fluorescent light glared down over them.

The crisp lines of Alexander Hamilton's face looked back at him in magnified perfection. Hair, eyes, girlish smile—even the shadow beneath the nose. All perfect.

Flashing his own satisfied smile, Petito dropped the loupe into the pocket of his ink-stained smock.

The bills had been run through the drier before he'd hung them up, so there was no danger of smearing the ink. With grubby fingers, he plucked them one at a time, depositing them in a plastic laundry basket. Once they were all harvested, he brought them over to the chimney. Grabbing them by the handful, he stuffed them past the small flue door at the chimney's base. They formed a crumpled bluish pile.

Petito took a book of matches he'd filched from a restaurant the night before and set the bills alight.

The chimney grate was a fine wire mesh. Even if a wispy, incriminating ember made it to the top, it wouldn't escape into the neighborhood. When the flames had consumed the bills completely, he closed the chimney door.

These first ones had only been a test. He hadn't even tried to get the color right yet, let alone the paper.

As he pulled himself to his feet, Paul Petito wished briefly for it to be as easy for him in this modern age as it had been for the counterfeiters of old. Twenty years ago, it was a cakewalk. Now everything was tougher.

The Federal Reserve had begun to issue new multicolored bills with larger pictures, watermarks, special paper grains and identifying emblems visible only under certain light.

For Paul Petito, government meddling had become an almost unbearable nuisance. To make matters worse, the new wave of funny-money manufacturers working with computers and scanners were crowding the traditionalists off the field.

Feeling the pressure when he'd gotten out of prison two months before, Paul had approached several local crime figures in the hope of striking up a business partnership. Unfortunately, everyone was either tapped out, locked away or not even interested. Without someone to pony up the start-up costs, Petito was out of luck. Then strange fortune struck.

One afternoon as he was lying on his elderly mother's plaid sofa watching *Court TV,* the old rotary phone rang.

"Mr. Petito?" the voice on the phone had asked. "You don't know me, but I represent a party who is interested in helping you with the business difficulties you're having."

He spoke in a patronizing nasal whine, overpronouncing words in a vain attempt to smooth his New York accent.

Paul picked some gunk from his ear as he talked. "Pal, the only difficulty I got is that I don't have a business."

"And I understand it's not from lack of trying."

The caller was cool and efficient and wasted no time in telling Paul that his employer would gladly send him the cash he'd need to get his presses rolling. There was only one small favor he would have to do in return.

"I'll do anything short of murder," Petito enthused.

"Please don't say such things," the man he would come to know as Mr. Sweet said. "Not even in jest. *Ever.* As for the rest, I'll be in touch."

Sweet was true to his word. Within two days, the money was sent to Paul. Per his instructions, he used some of it to buy the Boston Raffair building; the balance he kept. The arrangement was perfect except for one thing. The people Mr. Sweet sent up from New York to guard his building.

From the start, they were always hovering around. They hadn't left him alone in weeks. Until last night.

Paul didn't know whether or not he should be relieved for those two men from the surveillance tape. Because of them, Sweet's thugs had finally left him to work in peace.

They had stopped back briefly to say they'd tracked the young one as far as Quincy. A cabbie who'd driven him from the airport wasn't quite sure where exactly he'd dropped his fare. Somewhere near a church.

Johnny Fungillo had been nervous that evening when they'd gone back out. He kept warning the others that the young one was something special even as he brushed at his bruised forehead with his shaking fingertips.

Petito didn't need to be told that they were dangerous. He'd seen with his own eyes what the old one had done to Bear DiGrotti. As he worked, Paul tried to put all of the unpleasantness out of his mind.

There were still a few of the blue-tinged bills lying on a table near his photocopying machine. He had only just begun to sweep them up when he heard the noise. A popping crack of wood followed by the scattering tinkle of metal.

It had come from upstairs.

For Paul Petito, the panic grabbed hold at once. Someone had just broken down his door.

The bills were still clutched in his hands. No time

to burn them. He looked left, then right, then down. Before he even knew what he was doing, he did the first thing that his frightened instinct commanded.

Hands flashing in desperation, he began stuffing the bills into his mouth. He was chewing frantically even as the cellar door opened. He almost choked when he saw who came floating down the stairs.

It was the two men from the surveillance camera at the Boston Raffair office. In real life, the old one's fingernails looked even sharper than they did on video. Petito's eyes bugged even as he continued chewing on the vile-tasting wad of paper.

"It smells funny down here," Chiun complained as he and Remo glided across the basement floor.

"You could have waited in the car," Remo replied.

"And allow you to sneak away on foot?" Chiun said blandly. "Oh, wipe that look of innocence off your face. You are as predictable as a two-year-old."

Remo's expression grew glumly guilty. "I would've left you the keys," he grumbled.

Before them, Paul Petito was rooted in place by fear. Dark blue saliva was dribbling down his chin when the two intruders stopped before him.

Remo stood toe to toe with Petito. "You gonna eat your printing press next?" he asked.

This bit of incriminating evidence hadn't occurred to Petito. His eyes grew wider above his puffed-out cheeks.

"Mmggmmm," Petito said, shaking his head as he chewed.

"Mommy forgot to tell you not to talk with your mouth full. Probably was too busy teaching you not to steal."

Reaching over, he cuffed Petito in the back of the head.

A fat wad of pulpy blue paper launched like a soggy cannonball from between his stained lips. It flattened with a wet splat against the cellar wall.

"Don't kill me!" Petito begged. His frightened mouth was a dark blue cave. It grew wider as Chiun swept forward. "Ahhhh!" the counterfeiter screeched, flinging his hands protectively in front of his face.

But instead of a decapitating pressure at his neck, he felt a gentle tugging at his hands. Before he knew what was happening, the remaining counterfeit bills he hadn't had a chance to chew were being pulled from his knotted fingers.

"Chiun, what are you doing?" the young one said wearily.

"Hush," the old one admonished. "I am counting."

Petito peeked out from behind his hands. The Master of Sinanju was laying out the bogus bills in one wrinkled palm.

"That stuff won't even buy a hotel on Baltic Avenue," Remo warned.

"Do not think you can trick me into giving you

half,'' Chiun replied as he carefully flattened the bills.

Remo turned to Petito. "Okay, what's with that building you bought? And the first lie I smell gets you a one-way ticket through that." He pointed to the printing press.

Petito couldn't talk fast enough. "They mailed me the money from New York. I was the front so who-ever really owns everything wouldn't show up on paper. Guy who contacted me was Mr. Sweet. I don't know his first name, uh, uh…" His mouth and brain struggled to keep pace. "Oh, some of the New York guys stay here. They saw him kill that guy at the office yesterday." He pointed to the Master of Sinanju.

Chiun had one bill loose and was examining it in the light. He seemed oblivious to the quivering counterfeiter.

Remo's face soured at the mention of the events at Boston Raffair. "Where'd that satellite dish go?" he demanded.

"The picture came here. They rigged it to a re-ceiver in the yard. I've got the tape upstairs. Oh, and they sent a copy to Mr. Sweet back in New York. That's it."

Remo was about to ask more when Chiun broke in. "These bills are flawed," the old Asian an-nounced, his brow creased.

Terrified eyes darted to Chiun. "I don't think so," Petito apologized. "They took months to engrave."

"The engraving is adequate." Chiun frowned unhappily. "Although there are many errors, most white eyes would be blind to them. It is the color. These ugly paper things are supposed to be green."

"I think he knows that," Remo said impatiently.

Petito nodded. "I was just testing them," he explained.

Chiun's eyes narrowed slyly. "You can make them in the proper color?"

"It's not easy nowadays, but it's doable," Petito said.

Chiun folded his arms imperiously over his chest. In the process, the bills somehow disappeared inside his kimono.

"Do it," he commanded.

"Knock it off, Chiun," Remo said. "We're not helping this nit screw the United States government."

Chiun's hooded eyes were flat. "What has the government done for *me* lately?" he queried.

"Pay you a king's ransom in gold every year, for one."

Chiun erased Remo's words from the air with one flapping hand. "There is no reason why the one should have anything to do with the other," he dismissed. "If you hope your future Masterhood to be anything more than a footnote in the annals of Sinanju, you must be aware of opportunities when they present themselves."

"Chiun, I am not shackling this numbnut to the furnace back home, and I'm sure as hell not hauling all this crap out into the car."

"Not even if I make it worth your while?" Chiun asked craftily. A pair of blue ten-dollar bills appeared from the folds of his kimono. Thinking better, he pocketed one and offered Remo the other.

Remo shook his head wearily. Turning from the Master of Sinanju, he focused his attention back on Paul Petito.

"Before he's got you stashed in the hold of some freighter bound for North Korea, that's everything you know?"

The counterfeiter racked his brain. While there was certainly more, he couldn't seem to get it out in time.

"Uh, oh, um…" he began.

"Time's up, Gutenberg," Remo pronounced.

Hand moving in a blur too fast for Paul Petito's eyes to even follow, Remo sank a single hardened index finger into the man's ink-soaked occipital lobe.

Petito's mouth formed a blue circle. He slipped from Remo's receding finger and toppled onto the stained floor.

When Remo turned back to the Master of Sinanju, the old man wore an angry scowl.

"You are a hateful man, Remo Williams," he accused.

"Just keeping you honest," Remo said. "Besides, the golden rule of Sinanju says paper is just the promise of real money. I've gotta call Smith." He headed for the stairs.

"Do not lecture me on the rules of our House, engraver killer," Chiun said, following unhappily.

"I did us all a favor," Remo said absently. He had suddenly noted a sound upstairs. "Sure, you wanted to bring him home today, but I know who'd end up having to feed him and walk him." His eyes were trained upward.

Chiun aimed a stern finger at his pupil. "*You* can explain to my grandchildren why they will not be receiving birthday gifts this year."

Bullying past his pupil, he had placed but one sandal on the bottom cellar stair when the darkened figure appeared at the top of the staircase.

Both of them had been aware of the man skulking across the floor above them, but Remo hadn't prepared himself for what the latest arrival would be wearing. Head to toe, he was dressed in the same commando outfit as the two men who had attacked him on the street in New York. The white button with its circle-in-parentheses design was affixed to his camouflage jacket. Through the holes of his ski mask, his eyes peered down the stairwell.

"What the hell?" was all Remo had time to ask before the man let a small object slip from his fingers.

A hand grenade clunked down the cellar stairs. Above, the masked man darted away.

With a puff of impatience, Remo scooped up the grenade, slapping both hands around it. When the grenade went off an instant later, Remo had softened his hands to relax his muscles, meeting the explosive force with an equal containing force. The grenade made a little clicking noise and died.

Remo tossed the still intact but now useless hand grenade to the floor.

"Let's see what's what with the khaki downhill set," Remo announced.

He and Chiun flew upstairs, racing out into the backyard where they'd heard the commando's boots clomp. The man was crouching in the snow near a squat brick wall, his index fingers tucking mask material into his ears to ward off the sound of the expected explosion. When he saw Remo and Chiun exit into the yard, his mouth and eyes widened in his mask.

"Okay, lodge bunny," Remo announced as they crossed over to him, "who are you guys and why are you trying to kill me?"

For a moment, the commando didn't seem certain what he should do. But as Remo and Chiun continued to walk toward him, he seemed to reach some inner conclusion.

Pulling another grenade from the pocket of his camouflage jacket, he wrenched the pin loose. Remo fully expected him to lob it at them, but the man did something completely unexpected. With a grunt, he thrust the grenade up under his own ski mask. For a moment, it looked as if his head had sprouted a particularly grotesque tumor. Then he was gone.

The commando flipped over the brick backyard wall. There was an explosion from the other side, and the sky began to rain little flecks of red-streaked slush.

"Dammit," Remo growled, "not again."

When they looked over the wall, they found a corpse with a crater where a head used to be. The little white button was streaked with black.

"And I am not very fond of the type of boys you are playing with these days," Chiun sniffed beside him.

Twirling, he marched back through the snow toward the house.

WHEN THE PHONE RANG, Smith was dozing in his chair, the dull light of his desk lamp the only illumination in his shadowy office. Blinking sleep from his eyes, he picked up.

"I'll give you three guesses who was just attacked by another button-wearing commando," Remo announced.

Smith's brain snapped instantly alert. "Like the ones in New York?" he asked worriedly.

"Right down to the suicide-before-capture work ethic. Looks like I was right. They work for Raffair."

Smith was still trying to absorb the information. "No," he said. "It does not add up. You were not a risk when they went after you in New York. I have been thinking that they could be associated with MIR."

"The Puerto Rican terrorists?" Remo asked. "No way, Smitty. They'd have no way to find me unless they followed me from San Juan. And I didn't sense any beady little revolutionary eyes watching me on the plane home. Anyway, I've gotta keep this short, seeing as how I'm using that counterfeiter's phone and right now there's a blown-up commando sleeping in his neighbor's petunia bed. The guy's boss is named Sweet. No front name, but he's in New York.''

Smith adjusted his rimless glasses. ''That limits the search parameters. Anything else?''

''There was more than just the one guy Chiun kacked back at the office. Sounds like there's a whole goon squad out looking for us right now.''

Smith's lips thinned. ''I was afraid of that.''

''Still no bigee,'' Remo assured him. ''They've got a needle in a haystack's chance of tracking us down. And you don't have to worry about us ending up on 'Bloopers, Boners and Beheadings.' This is where the video was fed. That Sweet guy got the only other copy, so it looks okay on that front.''

In Boston, Remo glanced at the floor from where he sat at the edge of Paul Petito's bed. Spools of videotape coiled like silvery serpents on the worn carpet.

''Very good,'' Smith said. ''I will commence the search for Sweet. In the meantime, the two of you may return home. I will contact you when I learn more.''

''Check,'' Remo said. ''But don't call for a while. We're going out to eat first.''

When he glanced at the Master of Sinanju, he saw

that the old Korean was standing just inside the bedroom door. He was once more examining one of his blue ten-dollar bills.

"*I'm* paying," Remo added firmly as he hung up the phone.

**16**

The information was damning enough to topple the United States government.

Mark Howard hunched behind his desk in the bowels of CIA headquarters. Although he stared at the swirling screen saver on his computer monitor, his thoughts were miles away.

All was quiet save the soft background hum of equipment. The murmuring voices were gone for the day. Few people haunted this part of the building so late at night.

The overhead lights had been dimmed. They'd been encouraging such penny-saving measures at the CIA for much of the past decade. The money saved could be redirected to buying field agents actual bullets for their guns.

In the shadows of his cubicle, Mark had read the report out of Boston twenty minutes before. Even though he'd been looking specifically for it, he hadn't expected to see it.

The feeling again.

Paul Petito was dead. Local authorities had found him on the floor of his basement. At first, they'd said the counterfeiter had died from a single gunshot wound to the head. That had soon been amended. Now they were saying his skull had been pierced by an object unknown.

To Mark, the details of Petito's death were irrelevant.

He'd couriered his Raffair dossier to the President this morning, after a personal phone call from the chief executive. In those documents was a fresh printout with Paul Petito's name. To replace the one Mark had doodled on.

Death. That's what he'd written next to Petito's name. And Petito was now dead. A secret arm of the executive branch, sanctioned to kill.

Anyone who knew about this was at risk. And now Mark Howard knew. Knew for *certain*.

For some reason, the President was involving him in this. Though he had tried to figure out why, no feelings came to him. The sense of dread swamped all else.

For a long time, Mark merely sat. A shadow among shadows. At long last, a leaden hand reached out and shut off his computer. The internal fan hummed to silence.

He thought of Petito. A hole pierced in his skull.

Of Smith and his unknown agents.

His cubicle was eerily quiet. The dark walls, close.

He wouldn't be trapped. Couldn't allow thoughts of defeat. Fate was coming for him. He had to be ready when it arrived.

As he rose to his feet, the first hint of determination clenched his jaw. Mark Howard gathered up his topcoat. It was winter, after all. He didn't want to catch a cold on the way to meet his destiny.

**17**

Johnny Fungillo knew enough to be scared. The others hadn't a clue. They had only seen the old one in action, and even so, they still thought he'd used some simple sleight of hand to take down Bear DiGrotti. But Johnny Books alone had seen the young one up close and personal. Twice.

In East Africa, he'd managed to take down two of Johnny's oldest and dearest friends in the blink of an eye. If Johnny's guess was right, he was even faster than the old man. The second time he'd met the skinny guy with the thick wrists had been a complete shock.

Back in Africa, most of New Jersey's Renaldi Family had been wiped out by a bunch of crazy natives with spears. Johnny had been forced to scrape up this current gig from Sol Sweet, attorney to the wrongly incarcerated Don Anselmo Scubisci. He had been absolutely stunned when on the plane ride up to Boston he'd found himself staring into those dark, dead eyes again.

He couldn't move fast enough to avoid the man's

darting hand. Before he knew it, the guy's finger was pressing his forehead.

That simple touch had completely paralyzed Johnny. While he wanted to scream at the doctors who stared down at him after he'd been transferred by ambulance to Boston's St. Eligius Hospital, Johnny couldn't budge an inch. Some were saying that he'd be stuck like this for the rest of his life. And he might have been, if not for a fluke.

His first and only night in the hospital, the nurses on his floor had ordered ice-cream takeout from Friendly's. The portly RN who was checking in on Johnny had been in a hurry to get out to her melting cookies-'n'-cream sundae. While struggling to reset his IV with one hand, the impatient woman had banged him on the forehead with the full bedpan she'd been clutching in her other hand.

It was a one-in-a-billion shot, but apparently the edge of the bedpan had hit him just right. The woman almost had heart failure when Johnny sat bolt upright in bed and demanded his pants.

When Johnny had showed up at Paul Petito's house twelve hours late and with a big swelling bruise on his head, no one had even bothered to ask what had happened to him. Such was the nature of their business. And Johnny Fungillo would have been happy to never, ever mention that skinny, dead-eyed stranger with the lightning-fast hands—if not for the damn surveillance pictures.

Johnny was new to the Scubisci Family. He couldn't risk not telling when he saw that face again.

Yet even when he and the others had set off in search of the young guy and the old Chinaman, Johnny had kept a low profile. He'd stayed in the car at Logan while the others circulated the pictures they'd gotten from the video; he'd hunkered down in the back seat after they'd learned their quarry had gotten a cab to Quincy; and he had said a silent prayer to the Madonna when the angry neighbor with the crying baby had pointed out the big ugly stone church on the corner.

Luckily, the occupants of the building weren't home. When the two men he had driven with came out to collect him from the floor of the car, Johnny had to first thank the Virgin Mary for not dropping him in the path of his antagonist again. He doubted he would have survived a third encounter.

Inside looked like a bunch of small apartment units that had never been used. Only a few of the rooms in the whole complex looked lived-in.

"Should we wait for them?" one of the Scubisci regulars had asked once the three of them had done another sweep and had turned up empty.

They were in one of the ground-floor kitchens. It looked to be the only one used in the whole building. A table that was set so close to the floor it looked as if someone had stolen the legs was pushed neatly against one of the walls.

"No way," Johnny Books insisted. He was sweating near the door. "Didja see all those fish tanks downstairs? These guys are heavy-duty weird. Can't we just—I don't know—leave them a nasty note or something?'' He gave a hopeful, lopsided smile.

''That old guy was pretty fast,'' agreed the first man who'd spoken.

The third man in their party, Mikey Skunks, considered. Although he would never admit it, he was a little concerned about the old codger, too.

''Sweet never told us what to do 'xactly,'' he mused. ''Maybe we just gotsta show 'em not to mess wit us no more.''

Johnny felt a weight lift from his shoulders. ''I'll look for a pen and paper,'' he enthused. He spotted some on a shelf near the phone and jumped on them.

''No,'' Skunks insisted as Johnny grabbed up the notebook. Skunks Falcone was examining the gas stove. ''It's gotta be a stronger message.''

When they finished their work ten minutes later, Johnny Fungillo was still wishing that they'd opted to leave a note. Something with a lot of very cross underlines and angry exclamation points. He was thinking this even as he ran with the others through the downstairs hall of the old church.

All three men were breathing through the tails of their untucked shirts. They passed through the main kitchen and hurried out the side door. The stove in the main kitchen hissed ominously as they ran by.

While Johnny and the other man caught their breath in the parking lot, Skunks went to the trunk of the car. He returned a minute later clutching a Coke can in his big paw. A gasoline-soaked rag hung from the open end.

The two others were climbing in the car even as Mikey Skunks was hauling back. He heaved the gas-filled can through the open door of the kitchen. When flame met hissing gas, the explosion was instantaneous. With a rumbling burst, the entire kitchen erupted in a ball of brilliant fire.

Windows exploded into the parking lot, spraying sparkling shards across their parked car. A wave of heat and flame belched through the open door even as Skunks was jumping into the front seat.

Shocks sank in protest to his weight. Another explosion sounded from deeper inside the church. More breaking windows. Up the short flight of stairs, flames curled up from the open door.

The fire ate a voracious path through the big building. When Skunks slammed his door, the entire first floor was already engulfed in flame.

"*Dat's* a message." Mikey Skunks nodded surely. His face was cast in weird shadows by the dancing flames.

In the back seat, Johnny Fungillo felt his stomach liquify. Even as the car backed up to turn, he was wishing they'd left a simple note.

Reflected on the back window pane of the accelerating car, lethal licking fingers of flame sought the cold second story of Castle Sinanju.

ONE MINUTE BEFORE Mikey Skunks lobbed his fatal soda can, Remo and Chiun were driving up the long road home.

"You're lucky they didn't call the cops," Remo was complaining.

In the passenger seat, Chiun's face was blandly innocent. "Is generosity now a crime?"

"It is when you try to tip the waitress with blue counterfeit bills."

"I fail to see the difference between my currency and the scraps of green you use," Chiun sniffed. "In fact, mine are superior, for as art they are worth much more than their face value. And by killing their creator, you have made them collector's items."

"You would've had a better time bartering with a six-pack of Billy Beer or an Action Comics number one, Little Father," Remo said. "Next time just leave the check to me."

The old Korean's face was a dark scowl of incomprehension. He was thinking unpleasant thoughts about what constituted art in the Western world when the first small rumble reached their car.

An explosion. Amplified to their highly tuned senses through the compressed air of the moving car's tires.

"You think the city's working on the roads this late at night?" Remo asked, puzzled.

Morose on the seat beside him, Chiun shook his bald head. "Do not ask me," he replied. "I am but a visitor to this backward land."

A succession of soft booms. All from a very specific direction. Behind the wheel, Remo began to feel the first soft knot of concern form deep in his belly.

He saw the reflection of orange flame on the snow-lined street before they'd even reached the corner.

"Oh, no," Remo said, his voice soft with shock.

Beside him, the Master of Sinanju's weathered face flashed to instant horror.

"Our home!" the old man cried.

The entire first floor of the remodeled church was already ablaze. Flames threatened the second story.

Remo squealed to a stop in front of the building.

The Master of Sinanju shot from the front seat like a bullet from a chamber. Arms and legs pumping in furious unison, he attacked the main stairs. Remo sprang around the car, flying in his teacher's wake up the staircase.

"My possessions!" the old man cried.

The front door was closed. One sandaled foot sent it crackling into the foyer. A vicious wall of fire and impenetrable black smoke burst out into the chill night.

Remo ducked back from the flames.

The hallway beyond was completely engulfed. Walls, floor and ceiling formed a hellish path to the staircase. The stairs themselves crackled and burned.

Despite the inferno, the Master of Sinanju pulled in a deep breath.

Remo grabbed him by one bony arm.

"Are you nuts?" he yelled. "You can't go in there!"

"Unhand me!" Chiun shrieked in a voice that was not his own. The old man twisted and pulled, slipping from Remo's grip. Before the younger man could stop him, he'd bounded through the door.

Across the wall of flame, Remo could see the wizened Asian leaping from one burning stair to the next. In a heartbeat, he was gone.

Remo was about to go in after him when he heard the sound of a car door slamming out beside the building. It was followed by a squeal of tires.

Twisting from the burning doorway, Remo sprang down the stairs like a demented grasshopper. He was running before his loafers brushed the icy sidewalk.

Legs pumping in perfect, furious rhythm, he ate up the distance between front and side of the building just in time to see the car speeding across the parking lot.

He was shocked to see a familiar face in the back seat.

Johnny Fungillo was slouched in the shadows, a half-dollar-size bruise decorating his forehead.

Sinanju had long ago trained Remo away from anger. Yet in that moment it was not even simple anger, but pure unbridled rage that descended like a pouncing primal thing on Remo Williams.

It came fast and furious. Exploding in heart and mind.

Propelled by rage, Remo flew at the car.

It was racing out into the street. He'd intercept it easily. Make Johnny Fungillo pay.

Running. The car twenty feet away. Ten.

A sudden voice behind him. High. Frantic in the crystalline night air.

*"Remo!"*

Stopping, spinning.

Chiun was framed in an upper-story window, small and frail against the burning backdrop.

*"Help me!"* he pleaded. He flapped his kimono sleeves at the smoke that was curling up from the lower story.

Remo hesitated. Behind him, the car bounced over the sidewalk and out into the street, speeding away. Fungillo hadn't even seen him.

He could still catch them. Even with the vehicle driving full out, he could outpace the rapidly accelerating car.

But he couldn't abandon Chiun. Ever.

Remo let the men who'd set fire to his home go.

He flew back across the parking lot. Sliding to a stop beneath the open window, he threw out his arms.

"Jump, Little Father!" Remo yelled up through the roar of flames. "I got you!"

A scowl formed on the old man's soot-streaked face. "Don't be stupid!" Chiun snapped down through the choking smoke.

The old Korean's head disappeared back inside the upper-story window. A moment later, Remo saw the sharp contours of a steamer trunk peek like a timid child over the windowsill.

It didn't linger on the window ledge for long. As soon as it had cleared the frame, the trunk rocketed downward at a speed far greater than the simple pull of gravity. When it reached his level, Remo reached out and snagged the trunk from the air as easily as if he were picking a ripe plum from a tree. He set it on the ground.

Chiun hadn't been in trouble. The Master of Sinanju only wanted Remo to stand below the window and catch every one of his fourteen lacquered steamer trunks.

Chiun's worried face appeared once more. Some relief came when he saw the trunk on the asphalt at Remo's feet.

"*This* is why you stopped me?" Remo snarled.

In the distance came the first sound of fire trucks.

"Less chat, more catch," Chiun snapped.

Wisps of hair above his ears quivered in the smoke. His head vanished once more.

A second trunk followed the first.

As he was stacking the third trunk atop the first two, Remo glanced angrily down the street. The car was long gone. Red streaks of light sliced the night as the first fire trucks raced into view.

Yet another trunk peeked over the sill.

"Pay attention, imbecile!" Chiun's voice commanded as he launched the latest trunk downward.

Remo snapped the luggage from the air.

The fire engines, followed by two ambulances, tore into the parking lot. Lights continued to flash all around the street, stabbing crazed patterns across snow and tar. Running firemen quickly hooked hoses to a nearby hydrant.

By now the ground floor and most of the second story were engulfed in flame. Windows shattered, sending shards of glass out across the sidewalk and parking lot.

A fireman raced through the falling glass, helmet tipped low to keep the shards off his face.

"Get out of here!" he yelled angrily at Remo.

"In a sec," Remo insisted tensely.

"We almost done here?" he yelled up.

Another of Chiun's trunks appeared. It flew at supersonic speed to the ground below. Remo snatched it before it crushed the fireman to jelly.

"My God!" the man gasped, stumbling back. "There's someone *in* there?"

"Yeah, but don't worry. He'll be through in a minute."

The fireman wasn't listening. "Get the life net!" he screamed out to his companions.

As the firemen scrambled around one of the trucks, Remo took a rapid count of the trunks.

Twelve. Only two more left.

"Get the lead out, Little Father!" Remo shouted.

Another trunk appeared, flying down at him.

As Remo was piling it with the others, he noticed a hint of yellow silk sticking out of one side.

Although some of the trunks remained packed in perpetuity, others had been emptied over the years. Chiun was racing around, collecting his belongings.

From this angle, Remo could see that the flames had reached the Master of Sinanju's room. Flickers of orange light played along the visible walls and ceiling. Through it all, Chiun was packing.

Fear and concern formed a tight ball in Remo's stomach.

"Forget it, Chiun!" he yelled up to the open window.

Eight firemen ran through the parking lot from the street. They carried a collapsible aluminum device that they quickly folded open. It snapped into a rigid circle. A fireproof mesh was strung across the interior of the hollow metal tubes.

"Stand back!" a fireman bellowed at Remo.

Remo ignored him. "Hurry, Chiun!"

A hand took his bicep. Glancing over, he found a Quincy police officer at his elbow.

"Move!" the cop ordered, yanking.

Remo didn't. The cop's hand sprang loose and he went into free fall, landing on his rump in a puddle of melting snow.

At last Chiun appeared at the window.

The sill was ablaze. The old man had to battle flames as he wrestled the last of his precious trunks out into the open air. It dropped like a stone.

Remo snatched the trunk before it hit the life net. He put it with the rest.

The roof was going now. A section collapsed inward.

"*Now*, Chiun!" Remo begged.

Before he'd even finished the shouted plea, the old man sprang into view. He flew through the open window like a genie from a lamp, kimono hems tucked modestly between his ankles. Once he'd cleared the wall of flame, Chiun tightened himself into a ball and allowed gravity to take hold.

A delicate collection of frail bone and flesh, he fell the two stories to the life net, hitting with no more force than a dropped feather. Tipping the net, the firemen rolled him to his feet.

A few men grabbed out for him. The old man slapped their helping hands away.

He hurried to Remo's side.

"Remo, our home!" Chiun cried.

Remo's grim face was reflected in the tiny Asian's moist eyes. "I know, Little Father," he nodded, his voice soft.

The life net was dragged to one side. Nearby, men were running a hose to the open kitchen door. Pressurized water and searing flame fought a battle, the outcome of which was known already to all.

The fireman who had gotten the life net was at Chiun's side. "Oxygen!" he called to his men.

"I am fine," Chiun snapped. Sadness laced his anger. His hazel eyes were fixed on the collapsing building. His and Remo's home for a decade.

"We've got to get you to a hospital," the man insisted.

"Dammit, he's fine," Remo growled.

Through the choke of nearby smoke, the fireman inspected the old man for the first time. He was surprised that Remo appeared to be correct. There was hardly a spot of black on his robin's-egg-blue kimono.

No time to argue. He stabbed a finger at Remo.

"Is there anyone else in there?" he demanded.

Remo shook his head. "No," he volunteered quietly.

Satisfied, the fireman hurried off.

The Master of Sinanju's trunks were dangerously close to the burning building. Remo grabbed two of them, carting them quickly to the far side of the parking lot. He was stunned on his return trip to find Chiun carrying two toward him. Chiun never, ever carried his own trunks. But they'd never been in immediate peril like this before.

Without exchanging a single word, the two men passed each other, Remo to grab two more trunks, Chiun to place his with the others before hurrying back for more.

They were finished in a matter of minutes. Standing amid the pile of steamer trunks, Remo and Chiun both turned to the condominium complex.

By this time it was blazing out of control. All the firefighters could do was wet it down and try to keep the embers from sparking other fires in the nearby houses.

The roof of the former church collapsed completely, bringing down with it the glass-enclosed turret that was the entire third floor.

Chiun's meditation room. For ten years, he had welcomed the morning sun in the former bell tower.

Crowds had gathered along the street. Men and women in nightclothes gawked and pointed.

Through it all, Remo and Chiun stood, silently watching.

Remo had always insisted that he hated that building. When it became their home, it had been Chiun's doing, not his. But as the old structure collapsed in on itself, he felt as if a piece of him were dying, as well.

He glanced down at the Master of Sinanju.

Chiun said nothing. Chin jutting firmly in the air, he viewed the nightmarish scene through damp hazel eyes.

He seemed so old and frail. So lost.

Remo put a gentle arm around Chiun's shoulders.

Before both Masters of Sinanju, the fire raged, uncontrolled; consuming utterly the place that they called home. And as the spit of sparks took flight in the cold night sky like January fireflies, the hellish conflagration was reflected in the single salty tear that rolled down the old Korean's weathered cheek.

**18**

The morning breeze that blew in from the Tyrrhenian Sea hinted at a mild Naples winter's day.

It was a good wind. Not warm, but certainly not cold. It came from the east. From the direction of Corsica and Sardinia. Intolerable was the breeze from farther south; from hated Sicily.

That air was always foul. Even if he were blindfolded and lost in the vineyards, the old man sitting on the tidy stone patio, wrapped in a thick wool sweater, would have been able to know if he was smelling that vile Sicilian air.

The island of Sicily rested like a mound of shit at the toe of Italy's boot. Its people were filthy to a man. Its women had no virtue. Its children were cradle-bred thieves. When that wind blew, he would hide inside like the sons of Moses waiting for the Angel of Death to pass by.

But this was not Sicilian air, thank God. It was good, fresh air from far north of that hated den of cutthroats and brigands.

The old man took a deep, cleansing breath.

White early-morning sunlight showered brilliantly

over the vines below his terrace. Men already worked amid the tidy rows of dormant plants. Pruning and tying the vines in preparation for the next growing season.

Although the big house behind him cast a gloomy shade over the patio, he still wore sunglasses. The sun would peek around the house by nine, and at his age he liked to be prepared. For anything.

Through tinted lenses, he looked up at the man who had just arrived on his glass-enclosed terrace.

"Nothing yet?" the old man asked.

"Silence so far," the younger man replied apologetically. He was dressed for the Italian winter, a black woolen cardigan beneath his thin jacket.

The old man frowned thoughtfully.

A glass of red Aglianico sat on the wrought iron table before him, pressed from his own vineyards. Picking up the glass by the stem, he took a thoughtful sip.

"Perhaps we were too clever," he said, replacing the wine to the table. It touched the metal with a click.

"Don't worry, sir," the younger man said. "It's only been a few days since New Jersey. Less time since Cuba. Someone has to recognize it soon."

The old man smiled wistfully, exposing a row of corn-yellow teeth.

"I am impatient, I know. It has been a long time. I suppose a few more days will do no more harm than the last eighty years. *Avanti*," he said, shooing the man away.

Alone once more, he took another sip of wine.

The wine was as disappointing as the news from America.

He'd been a young man during World War II, back when the tanks of the Allies had rolled into Italy to crush the hated Il Duce once and for all. The old man had met many Americans then. Most had seemed quite clever.

They had returned home from their great victory in Europe only to raise dullards for children.

He had been certain they would have figured it out by now. It really wasn't even that clever. In fact, it had been designed to be obvious.

Below him in the vineyards, men continued to snip and tie.

The gently blowing breeze died down. The death of the wind brought fresh warmth to the Campania region.

It was going to be a warm day. Maybe it would break a winter record. Pondering the weather, the old man reached for his crystal wineglass.

## 19

For some reason, Remo had left his phone off the hook. Smith had called steadily until one o'clock in the morning. After that he had given up.

Bone tired, the CURE director had dragged himself home for a few hours of sleep. By six the following morning, he was back in his office.

With practiced fingers, Smith located the recessed switch beneath the edge of his desk. The light from his buried computer screen swelled within the black depths of the desk.

The preamble to the United States Constitution appeared on the start-up screen. As he did every morning, Smith read the words carefully before getting to work.

He pulled up the Raffair file.

The information on Sol Sweet was there. Graduate of Harvard. Attorney in New York. One notable client.

Smith frowned as he read the client's name. He had hoped to never see it again.

Scubisci.

CURE had had several run-ins with the New York

crime family in the past. Most notably with the deceased patriarch, Don Pietro. Remo had eliminated the old Don a decade ago. After his death, his son had taken control of the Family's interests. But Anselmo Scubisci was in prison now. If it was he who was running Raffair, he was doing so while a guest of the federal prison system.

They would know more once Remo had interrogated Sweet.

Smith picked up the blue contact phone. Without looking at the old-fashioned dial, he quickly entered Remo's number.

Still busy.

Frowning, Smith replaced the phone.

The Master of Sinanju might have been disturbed by a telemarketer. Sometimes when this happened, he took out his anger on every phone in their condo.

It still might just be off the hook. Smith decided to try back in a little while. If it was still busy, he would have to consider alternate ways to get in touch with Remo.

He turned his attention back to his computer screen.

Raffair.

Smith looked at the word with fresh eyes.

The dawning of a new day had not changed the feeling that there was something to the word itself. On some unknown level, it was still somehow familiar to him.

With both hands, the CURE director drew open

the middle desk drawer. He pulled a notebook and pencil out onto the flat onyx surface of his desk.

Sometimes when high-tech equipment failed, it was best to go back to the basics.

He carefully spelled out RAFFAIR in neat block letters. Once he was finished, he looked at what he'd written.

"Raffair," Smith said aloud.

Still, no secret was revealed by speaking the word.

Smith was sure that it was no acronym—either civilian or governmental—that he had ever encountered before.

The word *affair* was obvious. It had occurred to him many times over the past few days. But the letter *R* at the beginning changed it completely.

"*R*," Smith said.

He placed a gnarled hand over the letter.

"Affair."

Lifting his hand, he placed it over the last six letters of the word.

"*R*," he repeated out loud.

All at once, the light dawned.

"*Affair*," Smith said excitedly, his voice loud in his tomb-silent office.

With a thrill of discovery, he pulled his hand away.

The CURE director was amazed when he looked down on those simple seven letters. It was so obvious he was angry at himself for not having seen it before. They had spelled it out for anyone to see.

*R.* Affair. *Our* Affair. Or in Italian, Cosa Nostra. The Mafia was behind Raffair after all.

So brazen were they, the name appeared in the stock market listings of newspapers across the country and around the world. Organized crime was trading on Wall Street. With remarkable, frightening success.

This was too important to wait. If he was unable to contact Remo through familiar means, he would have to place a call to Western Union.

Smith grabbed up the contact phone. He was in the process of dialing when his office door sprang open.

Frozen in middial, Smith glanced up.

He was surprised to see Remo and Chiun stepping in from his secretary's office.

Both men appeared disheveled. The Master of Sinanju in particular was dotted with a few small streaks of soot. The old man wore a funereal expression. Beside his teacher, Remo managed a weak smile.

"Mind if we camp out here for a couple of nights, Smitty?" he asked tiredly.

**20**

"What is wrong?" Smith asked as he cast a narrowed eye over the two men standing inside his closed office door. The CURE director calmly replaced the phone.

Remo shot a glance at Chiun. The Master of Sinanju's expression was stoical. "Something happened to our house."

"What?" Smith pressed.

Eyes downcast, Remo struggled to get the words out. "It sort of...burned down."

Alarm tightened Smith's stomach. "What? When?"

"A few hours ago," Remo exhaled. It all spilled out at once. "We were gonna go to a hotel, but then I figured you might want to talk to me, and I didn't feel like calling and waking you up in the middle of the night to tell you what happened so, well, here we are."

Remo looked shell-shocked. Smith couldn't remember ever seeing such a lost expression on the face of CURE's enforcement arm.

Smith leaned back in his chair, his fingertips gripping the edge of his desk as he attempted to sort through this alarming information. He willed himself calm.

"What caused the fire?" he asked.

The Master of Sinanju answered for Remo. "Vandals," Chiun supplied. The word was a soft lament. The old man hadn't taken his customary seat on Smith's floor. He stood quietly beside Remo, his face a wrinkled mask of sorrow.

"I saw a bunch of guys driving away," Remo said. "They must have tracked us with that videotape. They weren't those guys with the masks." His tone was vague.

"I was afraid of this," Smith said. "Still, they found you more easily than I would have thought. Given the other attacks against you, I hope this doesn't mean there is some greater risk to exposure at work here."

Remo shifted uncomfortably. "Look, it's the tape, okay?" he sighed, exhausted. "It's not some big conspiracy that threatens your precious security. Now, can we please give it a rest? We've just been through hell."

When he looked at Chiun, the old man didn't return his glance.

"I am sorry for your loss," Smith said, shaking his head, "but this could be of concern for CURE."

"It's not, okay?" Remo snapped, his cheeks flushing red. "We just need a place to stay, that's all."

There was something beneath his hot response.

Smith didn't press it. "Your old quarters are available—" he began.

Remo's face sank with tired relief. "I knew we could count on you, Smitty."

"—but I do not think it's wise for you to stay here," the CURE director finished.

Remo's face steeled. "Why the hell not?"

"You said yourself that you believe the men from Raffair, Boston found you. They could do so again."

"Using what? A freaking crystal ball?"

"By employing whatever means they used to find you the first time," the CURE director replied. "Perhaps they even followed you down from Massachusetts."

"We were not followed," Remo insisted.

"Perhaps not. Nonetheless, I still don't believe it is a good idea for the two of you to stay here."

"Too bad," Remo said heatedly, "'cause we're staying."

"Remo, I retain your quarters for our own private security reasons. There have been times over the past decade that have required short stays at Folcroft. However, if your house is a lost cause—I am presuming it is?"

"It's a smoking foundation," Remo said bitterly.

"In that event, you will want more permanent accommodations. I cannot supply them for you here."

"We just need two goddamn rooms," Remo said, cold anger swelling his level tone.

Smith offered a knowing nod. "I worry that you

would think this a permanent solution to your problem.''

Remo shook his head in stunned amazement. "You know something, Smith, you're all heart. The Quincy fire department is still hosing down the pile of glowing embers that used to be our home, and you're already accusing us of overstaying our welcome."

"I am being realistic," Smith said.

"You're being a heartless bastard," Remo accused. "And I've got news for you. We're staying, so you better get used to the idea." He nodded sharply to Chiun. "I'll start bringing your trunks in, Little Father."

Not giving Smith another chance for argument, he spun on his heel and flung open the office door. When Remo prowled out of the room, Chiun remained behind.

The old Asian's gaze was tired and forlorn. Standing on that threadbare rug, the tiny little man looked every day of his hundred-plus years.

Shifting in his chair, the CURE director cleared his throat. "I, er, trust you are all right, Master Chiun?"

The wispy thunderclouds above the Korean's ears rustled. "I am not, Emperor," he said in a soft voice rich with the sorrow of loss. "I have had something dear taken from me." Through all his grief was a whisper of underlying menace.

"I am sorry," Smith offered.

"It is not for you to apologize. That is for he who

directed the Roman hordes to raze Castle Sinanju. Woe to him and his minions, for they will atone for this vile deed with their lifeblood.''

Smith blinked sharply.

*Romans.* He had forgotten all about his Raffair-Cosa Nostra discovery.

''I believe you were right about Lawrence Fine's killers,'' he announced, refocusing attention on his computer. ''There is every indication now that this is Mafia related.''

''I will avenge myself against these sons of Rome,'' the Master of Sinanju said. Though the words were harsh, his tone was lifeless.

Smith had become more animated. Lost in cyber-space, it was as if he had already forgotten about the Asian's loss.

''Chiun, could you please send Remo in here when he is through with your luggage?'' he asked as he typed.

Across the room, a long, plaintive exhalation of air escaped the tiny Korean's wrinkled lips. ''I live to do your bidding, Emperor,'' he said. ''For it is all that remains for me in this hateful land.''

Without bothering to give even an informal bow, the Master of Sinanju padded from the office.

THE WHITE TIP of Sol Sweet's nervous tongue brushed across his dry lips. Cold sweat had begun to break out across his back as he listened to the voice on the phone.

''So that's the story, Mr. Sweet,'' Mikey Skunks

finished gruffly. "It was real lucky Johnny Books knew the guy, or we wouldn'ta even found the place."

Sweet's hand tightened white around his phone. "Lucky?" he questioned, aghast. "Do you idiots have any idea what you've done?"

Mikey had told him about the search for Remo and Chiun, right up to the destruction of their house. Of course, he'd had to relate it in the vaguest possible terms, which was a struggle for a man who had a tendency to blurt out the most incriminating things with the innocence of sheer stupidity.

"Sure, Mr. Sweet," Mikey said, puzzled. "We torched their house."

"Stop it!" Sweet yelled. "And stop calling me by that name. I don't even know who that person is."

Closing his eyes, he gripped his entire forehead with one delicate hand. He was trying to think how to tell Don Scubisci about this disaster.

"Okay," the lawyer said, his hand still clutched to his face. "Here's what you do. Don't go back to the office. Don't go back to your *friend's* house to get your things. Go to the bank, get as much cash as you can. You don't want to leave any kind of traceable trail for a month. Just come back home and lay lower than you've ever laid low before."

"Sure thing, Mr., uh, Mr...."

"Just come back here," Sweet snapped. "And bring those other two morons with you."

"Okay," Mikey Skunks offered, struggling to

mask the confusion in his voice. "But you heard me before when I told you that we didn't kill those two guys, right?"

Fumbling in a dead panic, Sol Sweet slammed down the phone as if it were a living thing.

Sitting in his soft leather chair, he could feel his heart thudding in his chest. A congenital heart murmur gave him a fluttering double-beat at moments of high anxiety. Right now it was flapping like a hummingbird.

They'd gotten Paul Petito. Skunks said that the street was filled with cops when they'd tried to go back there.

Time for damage control. They'd shut the Boston office for now. Thanks to Internet trading, the satellite offices were redundant anyway. Ideally, they would move entirely into the electronic realm within the next five years. But there was a monkey wrench thrown into the whole plan now.

Those two men who had entered the picture had first confused and now threatened everything. Including Sol Sweet's life if Don Scubisci was found to be in a less than forgiving mood. And now the idiot hirelings had made matters worse by antagonizing the two men instead of killing them.

Breathing deeply to calm his skipping heart, Sol opened his squeezed-shut eyes.

Don Anselmo Scubisci's newly remodeled office swirled around him in deep mahogany and fresh white paint. One piece of furniture in particular caught Sol's eye.

Fumbling up out of his chair, Sol held his throbbing chest as he stumbled over to the well-stocked bar.

REMO HAULED the Master of Sinanju's trunks from his car to their Folcroft quarters.

Not all of Chiun's luggage had fit in Remo's car. They had been forced to leave some of the trunks in a rented hotel room up in Massachusetts.

"You want it with the rest, Little Father?" Remo asked as he carted the fourth and final trunk into the Master of Sinanju's room.

"Wherever you leave it does not matter," Chiun answered morosely.

The old Korean sat in the middle of the floor, his despondent eyes trained on the painted cinder-block wall. He hadn't even chosen the trunks his pupil was bringing into the room. Before they'd left Quincy, he'd allowed Remo to pick four at random.

Remo put the fourth trunk with the others. They seemed lost without the rest.

"I'll get the other ten shipped down quick as I can," Remo promised.

Chiun's smile was wan. "You are a good son, Remo," he said.

Clenching his jaw, Remo cast his eyes downward. "Yeah," he said guiltily. "You want anything? Tea, maybe?"

"I am not thirsty," the Master of Sinanju. "Besides, I told you that Smith wishes to see you."

Remo's expression darkened. "Screw Smith. The

bastard was about to turn us out in the snow. You're more important than anything he has to say."

Chiun accepted his pupil's warm tone. "Thank you, Remo," he said. Reaching up, he patted the younger man's hand. "But your presence is not balm enough for me this day. Go, serve your emperor." Chiun cast an eye around the room. "This is a familiar environment."

"Okay," Remo said. "I guess." At the bedroom door, he paused. He couldn't believe what he was about to say. "You want me to run out and pick you up some replacement country CDs?" he offered.

When the fire struck, Chiun's entire collection had been up in his meditation tower.

The old man shook his aged head. "No," he answered. "There will by no joy until vengeance is served. Smith was babbling when I left. I believe he is using his oracles to locate he who commands the Romans who destroyed Castle Sinanju."

Another guilty cloud passed over Remo's face. Saying nothing, he stepped out into the main room. As he closed the door, he cast a final glance at his teacher.

Sitting cross-legged on his tatami mat, Chiun looked old and frail. He made no move to unpack his things. Remo had even had to roll out the mat for him. Around the Master of Sinanju were his four precious lacquered trunks.

Remo closed the door. Alone in the common room, the guilty breath fled his collapsing lungs.

Eyes downcast, he trudged away from the closed door.

REMO'S GUILT HAD ONLY GROWN by the time he reached Folcroft's administrative wing.

It was 7:00 a.m. and Smith's secretary was now at work. Eileen Mikulka looked up as Remo entered the outer room.

"Oh, good morning," she smiled. "Dr. Smith asked me to see you right in."

As the matronly woman stood, Remo wordlessly waved her back to her seat. She gave him a slightly disapproving look for his rudeness as he pushed his way into the Folcroft director's office.

Still at his computer, Smith looked up over the tops of his rimless glasses when the door opened.

Remo closed the door with a click.

"Okay, here's the deal," Remo blurted. "Remember those guys I killed in that East African restaurant a couple of months back? Well, I didn't kill all of them. Flash forward to a couple of days ago, and who do I run into on my connector flight back from Puerto Rico but the goon that got away. I thought I took him out of action without killing him this time, but I guess something went wrong 'cause the same thick-neck was in the car last night with the other two guys who burned down our house. I don't know what happened or how he got loose after I put the whammy on him, but the fact is he did and he led the rest of them right to me. So it's all my fault. Me, me, me. *I* led them to us. And before you ask, no, Chiun doesn't know.''

He had hoped the confession would make him feel better. It didn't. And the critical look the CURE director was giving him didn't help matters.

Smith sat motionless behind his desk. Only when Remo was finished did he place his hands to the onyx slab, fingers intertwined.

"You are certain it was the same man?" Smith asked.

"I wish I wasn't," Remo said, the life seeming to drain from him. He dropped onto the sofa near Smith's door. "I figure he must have tracked me from the plane somehow. I took a cab that day."

Smith nodded agreement. "Do you plan to tell Chiun?"

"Eventually. Someday. You know how he is, Smitty. He carps at me when the cable goes out or when it rains more than two days in a row. I don't even want to think about what he's gonna put me through for something that's actually my fault. Especially something this big.''

Smith raised a single eyebrow. "This individual you encountered before," he said. "You met him on the New York to Boston leg of your flight?" His hands moved to his keyboard.

"Yeah," Remo said glumly.

As Smith began typing, Remo stuffed his hands gloomily into his pockets. He was reaching for his small stone-carved good-luck charm when his fingers brushed something else.

"Oh, by the way, here's another one for your collection," he said.

He flung the object across the office. It landed between Smith's outstretched hands with a tiny click. The CURE director picked it up.

It was another one of the small white buttons that Remo's attackers had worn. This one was streaked with smears of black.

"I pulled it off the guy who went kerblooey at that counterfeiter's house," Remo told him.

Smith inspected the button. Like the first, the O at the center was bracketed by twin waving lines that nearly met at top and bottom.

"I have had no luck tracing this symbol," he frowned.

"Well, it obviously means something to those guys," Remo said, "because they're blowing off their own heads to protect whoever's behind it."

Remo had the small stone figure in his hand now. His fingertips traced the carved lines of the small Korean face.

"Or to protect themselves *from* whoever is behind it," the CURE director pointed out. Smith swept the button into an open desk drawer where it joined the first. "I will continue to research the design," he promised.

He returned his attention to his computer.

Sitting forward on the sofa, Remo pressed his face into one palm. "Why did I just knock him out, Smitty?" he moaned. "I should have ripped off his arms."

Smith didn't look up from his monitor. "Remo, now is not the time for self-indulgence."

Remo peered at the CURE director through half-open eyes. "You sure? 'Cause it really feels right just about now."

Smith's thin lips pinched unhappily. "Did Chiun mention to you that the Mafia was involved with Raffair after all?" he asked as he worked.

"No." Remo sighed.

"I have deduced that Raffair is verbal shorthand for Our Affair."

"That sounds familiar."

"It should. That is its English translation from the Italian 'Cosa Nostra.' Thanks to the counterfeiter's information, I was able to backtrack to a Manhattan attorney by the name of Sol Sweet. He has several criminal clients. I would guess that he is acting as a go-between for one of them." Before he could give out the name of Sweet's most prominent client, Smith let out a hiss of satisfaction. "Your arsonist is one John Fungillo," he announced.

This brought Remo to his feet. "You sure?" he asked, his voice suddenly even. He pocketed the stone carving.

"He was the only individual removed from your flight by ambulance. According to the records, he was suffering from a mysterious form of temporary paralysis that reversed itself several hours after he was admitted to the hospital. He checked himself out."

"Where can I find him, Smitty?" Remo asked coldly.

"His legal residence is the home of his mother in Jersey City." Smith was reading the scant information available on Johnny Books. "Interesting," he said with a puzzled frown. "He is not a known member of the Scubisci crime Family."

Remo thought after the previous night that he'd reached his quota of fresh surprises. But at Smith's mention of the famous Mafia Family, his hard face relaxed to confusion.

"Scubisci? What've they got to do with this?"

Smith looked up. "Sweet's most prominent client is Anselmo Scubisci."

Remo had briefly encountered the Dandy Don once before. "Isn't he in jail?"

"Yes," Smith said. "But it's possible that he is still running his illegal empire from behind bars. It has been done by criminals before. Even so, the connection is tenuous. I suppose we need something more concrete to implicate Anselmo Scubisci."

"*You* need something concrete," Remo said. "I've got what I want. Gimme that Fungus guy's address."

Smith shook his head. "There is no guarantee that he will be there. If you act rashly now, you could scare off Fungillo as well as his two accomplices. Better to learn who all three are so that we can plan a stratagem against all of them."

Before Remo could argue, an electronic beep sounded from the depths of Smith's desk. The

CURE mainframes deep in the bowels of Folcroft's basement had pulled some new data from the Net. Smith brought up the latest information.

"Raffair has finally established a corporate headquarters," Smith said as he read the report the computers had flagged. "It opened in New York this morning."

"Wasn't that place you sent me and Chiun to their HQ?"

"No," Smith said. "Lippincott, Forsythe, Butler merely coordinated Raffair's start-up. Until now, it has been an entity without a visible head, which was why I've had such a difficult time tracking ownership."

"Okay, so now that we've got a home base, we can find out for certain who's behind it."

Smith was staring down at his desk, a sober expression on his gray face. His fingers were resting on his buried keyboard. "We know now," he said evenly.

"Why?" Remo asked. "What've you got?"

The CURE director looked up, his flinty eyes flat. "I know this address," he replied tersely.

From the outside, the Neighborhood Improvement Association in Manhattan's Little Italy appeared largely as Remo remembered it. After parking his car farther down the block, he and Chiun stopped on the sidewalk in front of the Mott Street entrance. Around them, Chinatown continued to encroach on what had formally been exclusive Italian-American territory.

"Did you not slay the Roman lord who ruled from this ugly castle?" the Master of Sinanju asked. There was little enthusiasm in his voice.

"That was Don Pietro," Remo replied. "Thanks to good old-fashioned Mafia nepotism, his kid took over where he left off. Although Smith says he doesn't technically own the joint anymore. He had to sell it to some dummy corporation for legal expenses or something. Come on."

They mounted the stairs and passed beneath the shiny new Raffair sign on their way through the front door.

They found that the real change had taken place within.

The aroma of tomato sauce and the ancient fuzzy wallpaper were both gone, as was the Old World gloom. Stylish artwork now hung from whitewashed walls.

Several of the downstairs rooms had been opened up. This one big room was filled with fresh-faced young men in long-sleeved dress shirts. They were performing a frantic dance from computer terminals to telephones. To Remo, they looked as if they'd been transplanted to Little Italy from some sterile Wall Street office.

"I don't like it," Remo complained as they passed through the foyer. He looked as if he'd smelled a particularly foul odor. "It had a kind of *Untouchables* charm before. Look, they even got rid of the guys who used to shoot at you when you walked in," he said, sounding like a kid who'd gone all the way to Disney World only to find that Space Mountain was closed for renovations.

They were past the empty receptionist's desk and had reached the end of the hall where old Don Pietro used to have a private office. Remo was reaching for the door when he felt a bony hand press his forearm. When he looked down at the Master of Sinanju, there was a hard glint in the old man's eyes.

"We are not here for Smith's nonsense," Chiun warned. "We are here to learn who it was that burned Castle Sinanju."

The pang of guilt that had rested in the pit of Remo's stomach since the previous night swelled larger. "I know, Little Father," he said quietly.

His pupil's tone brought the first hint of suspicion to the old Korean's face. He squinted one eye as he examined the younger man. "What is wrong?" he queried.

"Huh?" Remo asked, suddenly alert. "Nothing. Nothing's wrong. What makes you think there's anything wrong?" He quickly changed the subject. "Anyway, our goals mesh with Smith's here. He just wants us to find out who's running the show."

Chiun's expression did not change. "Just as long as you know which is more important."

Remo nodded. Turning from the old man's penetrating hazel eyes, he reached for the closed office door.

The old walnut door had been lovingly sanded and refinished. When Remo's palm touched the surface, the beautiful antique door cracked viciously along one side. A fragmented chunk of wood held the dead bolt and knob in place as the rest of the door screamed around on its twisting hinges. It slammed with a thunderous slap against the interior office wall.

Inside, a harried little man with slicked-back hair sat at a polished oak desk. When he saw Remo and Chiun glide into his office a split second after the door, the tumbler of Scotch whiskey he'd been lifting to his lips slipped from his shaking hand. It struck the desk's surface in echo to the crashing door.

Sol Sweet jumped to his feet, backing against the wall. His gelled hair bumped a picture frame.

"Oh, God, no," Anselmo Scubisci's lawyer breathed.

"No introductions in order, I see," Remo said. His face brightened when he saw the two other men in the office. "Now, *they're* more like it," he mentioned to Chiun, pointing.

Sweet's two huge bodyguards were lumbering up out of their chairs. Chiun stood between them and Remo.

"Why don't you have them out front?" Remo chastised the lawyer. "Give them some frayed lawn chairs, maybe a couple of muscle shirts. You know, if he knew what you'd done to this place, Don Pietro would be spinning in his grave right about now." He advanced on the lawyer.

"Stay back!" Sweet ordered, his forehead already breaking out with sweat. "You're trespassing here! I can use force against you!"

"Sounds serious," Remo said. "More force than that?" He jerked his thumb to one side.

Sweet heard two soft thuds hit the wall-to-wall carpet even before his eyes darted right. When he saw what Remo was pointing to, he had to slap a hand over his mouth to keep the alcohol in his stomach.

Chiun stood between Sweet's two bodyguards, his arms upraised. Suspended from each of his extended index fingers was a guard. The Master of Sinanju had snagged each man with a long talon in the soft tissue beneath his chin.

To Sweet, it was obvious that those nails were

even longer than they'd seemed on videotape, for neither of his two bodyguards appeared to be doing much in the way of living. Their eyes were already growing glassy. Blood dribbled from their tightly closed lips, splattering the beige carpet.

The sound Sweet had heard was that of their guns striking the floor. The weapons sat useless below their dead, dangling toes.

Like a demented orchestra conductor holding a note too long, Chiun bore the men aloft. When his nails at last withdrew, the two behemoths collapsed into a six-hundred-pound pile of limp Sears poly-ester-blend suits.

Chiun's hands retreated to his kimono sleeves.

Sol Sweet felt his mild arrhythmia knot into the first fluttering fist of a full-fledged seizure.

*"Anselmo Scubisci!"* he gasped, panic dancing across his wide-open eyes. "He tells me what to do. He's serving three consecutive life sentences at Ogdenburg Federal Penitentiary in Missouri. I can drive you to the airport." He tore holes in his pants in his desperation to remove his car keys.

When he held the jangling key ring aloft, he felt a bony hand slap against his own. The keys screamed across the room, embedding deeply in the wallboard.

Sweet was clutching his chest when he looked down.

Chiun had circled the desk and was standing below him.

"Did you or he order the destruction of our

home?'' the Master of Sinanju demanded in a tone that chilled the very air around them.

Despite the cold frisson up his spine, Sol Sweet's chest still burned. ''Neither one of us did,'' he panted. He was becoming light-headed. Blood pounded in his ears. ''Those men acted entirely on their own. Well, for the house-burning part. Not the killing-you part. They were sent to do that. But that was obviously before I knew what wonderful, caring, dangerous people you both are. May I take a nitroglycerine capsule?''

''No,'' Remo and Chiun said in unison.

''Splendid,'' Sweet enthused. He pulled his left arm close to his chest. If he held it tightly enough, he almost could dull the horrific pain that was shooting up it.

''Are you the one who's sending all these lunatic hit men in ski masks after me?'' Remo asked.

Through the pain, Sol Sweet grew confused. ''Hit men?'' he asked. ''No. Just the ones who burned down your house. Did I mention how terrible I feel about that?''

On the other side of the desk, Remo frowned. The lawyer wasn't lying. Remo had been sure the attacks of the past few days had been the work of whoever was behind Raffair.

Chiun steered them back to the most important topic. ''Where are your lackeys, that they might pay for their wicked deed?'' His eyes were truth-detecting lasers, boring twin holes into Sol Sweet's whirling brain.

"Here," he gasped, "lemme..." He staggered to his desk. With a shaking hand, he wrote down three names on a yellow legal pad. "They're hiding," Sweet wheezed as he handed Chiun the sheet. "Don't know where they are. But that's them, I swear."

The old Korean accepted the paper. Sweet felt a pinch of relief when Chiun retreated to the other side of the desk.

"Well, if that's all the business we have, I think I'll just call up an ambulance." He forced a weak smile on his suddenly very pale face.

"Not all," Remo said, shaking his head. "What the hell is this Raffair thing all about?"

"Oh, that," Sweet said. Reluctantly, he took his hand off the phone, grabbing again at his burning chest. "Mr. Scubisci has opened up the business opportunities of organized crime to the masses."

Remo looked to Chiun. The old man was interested only in the scrap of paper in his hand. He turned back to Sweet.

"You're doing what with the what now?" he asked.

Sweet leaned back against the wall, closing his eyes weakly. "Lot of people have a lot of money to invest these days. More regular folks are building portfolios. Scubisci is giving the common man the opportunity to invest in what's historically been a very lucrative field."

Remo blinked. He didn't like the sound of where this was heading. Evidently, Smith had been right.

Sweet had his eyes closed tightly now. His face was ashen and his lips were turning blue. Hands pressed over his heart in a mockery of penitence, he panted out the words in labored spurts.

"Raffair exists as a public cover for the Scubisci crime Family, as well as several others. Money generated by stock purchases goes to developing company infrastructure. Raffair expands, investors reap dividends, company grows, new investors come aboard, Raffair expands more." Sweet's too-white tongue brushed his cold lips. "Is this room spinning?"

"No," Remo answered.

"Oh," the lawyer whimpered. "Anyway, with the money we've made already, we've been able to invest in better methods for narcotics distribution, which feeds a host of other ventures, like gambling, prostitution and bribery. Our great success has been passed on to our stockholders."

Remo couldn't believe what he was hearing. "You're telling me ordinary people are buying stock in the Mob?"

"An archaic term," Sweet said weakly. He opened his eyes. "Is someone gonna shut off that damn alarm?"

"How do people even know about all this?" Remo asked. "It's not like you could take out an ad in the *Wall Street Journal*."

"When the stock's hot enough, word gets around," Sweet said. His ears pricked up as he strained to listen to a sound only he could hear.

"Ah," he sighed, relieved. "They finally shut it off." Eyes rolling back in his head, he collapsed face first on his desk.

"Are you done?" Chiun asked impatiently. He stood near the door, anxious to leave.

"Yeah." Remo nodded. He was turning from Sweet's twitching body when a sudden thought occurred to him. "Oh, crud," he groused.

Quickly flipping the lawyer onto his back, he drummed his fingertips hard on his chest just above the heart. Catching the rhythm of the fluttering attack, he established a counterrhythm that he forced the muscle to follow. The arrhythmia caught, slowed and tripped to a normal pace.

Sol Sweet's eyes rolled open.

"Sorry to interrupt," Remo said, "but I forgot to ask. They said in Boston you got a copy of that tape with us on it."

Sweet nodded numbly. "There." He pointed to a corner closet.

As Remo went over and popped the door, the attorney sat up. The pain was gone in his chest and arm. Even the light-headedness had vanished. His face was flushed as his color returned.

Remo found but one videotape in the closet. Turning, he held it out to Sweet. "This it?" he asked.

Sitting on the edge of his desk, the lawyer nodded. "It's the only copy," he promised. "I took it from the direct satellite feed."

"Great," Remo said. "Off you go."

The hard look in the intruder's eyes told Sweet precisely what Remo meant.

"Wait!" he begged. He leaped from desk to chair, away from Remo. "Where's Anselmo getting the cash for all this?" He waved an index finger all around. "The Scubisci Family's been broke for years. Anselmo's been spending it like water these past few months. Believe me, I don't come cheap, either. I think there's someone behind—" He stopped in midsentence.

An odd sensation had just flitted under his rib cage. Different from anything he'd ever experienced before.

"Oh, my," Sweet said, inhaling sharply.

"Someone other than the Dippy Don's behind this?" Remo asked. He was thinking of the men who'd attacked him. If Anselmo Scubisci wasn't responsible, maybe this other individual was.

Still squatting on his chair, Sweet fumbled in his pocket, producing a small business card. He flung it at Remo. "Scubisci...24A...answer...questions..." His voice grew more labored as he looked down in utter confusion at his own chest. The pain was back, worse than ever. "What's happening?" he gasped.

"Hmm?" Remo asked, glancing at the card. "Oh, that," he said as he pocketed it. "That's just your heart exploding."

Sweet looked up in abject horror. At that precise moment, the struggling muscle in his chest swelled and burst, flooding his thoracic cavity.

Face contorting in a rictus of excruciating death,

he fell backward. His chair rolled into the wall, and his head smashed into the heavy Monet print that hung over the desk. Lawyer, picture and chair crashed to the floor. The glass shattered, and the frame settled about the rounded shoulders of Sol Sweet.

Remo tipped his head as he examined the attorney, conjoined in death with the French countryside. "I don't know much about art, but I know what I like," he said dully.

"Can we go *now?*" the Master of Sinanju complained.

"Yes. No, wait." Remo glanced around the room. "A fire for a fire," he said in a low voice.

Remo found a wastebasket next to the desk. He filled it with computer paper from an idle printer. Pushing the wooden desk against a wall, he sat the wastebasket on the floor in the desk's foot well. He lit the paper with a lighter collected from one of the dead bodyguards. Once the fire had started, he smashed the lighter on the desk's surface.

As an afterthought, he tossed the incriminating video into the burning basket.

"Now I'm ready," he said coldly.

When they left the office, the surface of the desk had already flashed to life, igniting the wall behind it.

Smoke and flames were spitting out the door as they crossed the foyer. The young men in starched white shirts continued to race around the open room, oblivious to the fire that was rapidly engulfing the small back office.

"Let's get them out of here," Remo said.

"Why?" Chiun sniffed. "If they are in league with the villains who burned our home, let them also blister on the pyre that will consume those malefactors."

"If we can get them out of here, maybe they'll jam the street enough that this place'll burn to the ground before the fire trucks can get through." Bracketing his mouth with his hands, he took a deep breath. "Fire!" he yelled into the bustling room.

Although he was certain many of the men had heard, there was no reaction. They continued to switch from computer to phone, lost in the electronic roller coaster of day trading.

Remo tried yelling again, louder this time. Still no reaction. By now, the flames were licking out of Don Pietro's old office and up the hallway.

"I have been through one inferno already," Chiun said, peeved. "If you want this one, you may have it." The old man spun and darted out the front door.

Smoke was pouring in from the hall, hovering in ominous clouds beneath the fluorescent lights of the big room. Obviously, the men knew now that something was wrong, yet their adrenaline-fueled greed held them in place. Remo decided that he needed to find something that would motivate them even more than fear for their lives.

Fishing in his pocket, he pulled out a fat roll of

hundred-dollar bills. He flapped the cash in the rolling clouds of smoke.

At first, there was no reaction. But all at once, a face turned his way. It was followed by another, then another.

Like a herd of gazelles on a scent, the entire crew of traders soon had heads in the air, sniffing the aroma in the smoke. The room grew very still. All was silence save the crackle of flame at Remo's back.

Remo moved the bills to the right.

All eyes followed.

Remo brought the bills to the left. The pack tracked the movement with their eyes. Some of the men were starting to drool. Continuing leftward, Remo moved over to a front window. With a flick of his wrist, he popped it open. The window shot up, burying deeply in the wooden frame.

He flapped the wad of bills one last time before throwing them out the open window. They caught the breeze like autumn leaves.

"Fetch!" Remo yelled.

Chaos erupted in the Neighborhood Improvement Association. Men shoved and screamed on their way to the exits. Some jumped out the one open window while others smashed the sealed windows with chairs and computer monitors. Screeching brakes and honking horns rose up from Mott Street.

Remo turned from the suddenly empty room. He cast one last glance at the growing wall of flame.

Thinking dark thoughts about the men who had set fire to his own home, Remo slipped out the front door into the growing commotion on the street.

## 22

Remo caught up with Chiun on the sidewalk down the street from the Neighborhood Improvement Association. Behind them, men dashed for cash, clogging traffic. The first thread of black smoke was curling into the cold sky.

"Finally," the Master of Sinanju said as Remo trotted up beside him. "Smith can aid us in our quest. Let us hie to his stronghold."

"As long as we're in the neighborhood, let's check out the address Sweet gave up first. It's supposed to be right here on Mott Street."

"If it is not the address of the grape-stompers who burned down my home, then it is irrelevant," Chiun replied.

"We'll get to them, Little Father. Promise," Remo said. "But we're here now, so wouldn't it be easier to get this out of the way now than have to come back?"

A scowl of impatience crossed Chiun's weathered face. "Very well," he relented. "But be quick about it."

Remo used the business card Sweet had given

him to steer them to the right address. As they strolled down the sidewalk, the Master of Sinanju glanced at his pupil several times. His brow finally sank low.

"You are hiding something," Chiun announced abruptly.

Remo felt every joint stiffen at once. "What do you mean?" he asked with forced innocence.

"Please, Remo," Chiun droned. "As an actor, you make a truly great assassin."

The guilt was more than Remo could bear. Since there was no good time for this, he decided to get it out of the way.

"You know when you went up to get your trunks?" he began, his shoulders sinking. "That car that drove away?" A deep breath. "I knew one of the guys," he exhaled.

Chiun stopped dead. When he looked up at his pupil, his hazel eyes were narrow slits. "Explain yourself."

For the first time since his earliest Sinanju training, Remo's palms felt sweaty. He wiped them on his chinos.

"Remember how I told you about that guy I met on the plane? The guy I'd seen when we were in East Africa?"

"Spare me your tedious antics," Chiun clucked impatiently. "I did not listen then, and I am not interested now."

Remo took another deep breath. "Turns out the

guy from East Africa was one of the guys who burned down our house," he blurted.

The Master of Sinanju's eyes split wide. Stunned white orbs grew large beyond vellum lids. "*You* led him to us," the old man hissed.

"I guess," Remo confessed. "He must've helped them track me from that video." He hung his head in shame. "I'm sorry, Little Father."

He waited to be screamed at. To be told he was an idiot and a blunderer. Instead, he was met with silence. For Remo, it was far worse than all the other alternatives combined.

When he glanced up, the Master of Sinanju was still staring at him. The Korean's face had grown utterly flat.

"Aren't you gonna say something?" Remo questioned awkwardly.

Chiun's head began an ominous low roll from side to side. "Words elude me," he intoned thinly.

Remo thought he'd braced himself for anything. But the Master of Sinanju's troubling stillness caught him off guard.

"*Do* something, then," Remo prodded.

"Like what? You are too old to spank and too important to my village to slay."

"I don't know," Remo said. "Maybe a punch in the arm or something. I mean, *anything.*"

Chiun stroked his wispy beard thoughtfully. His slender fingers had not reached the thready tip before Remo felt an increase in air pressure beside him.

He didn't duck out of the way. Eyes closed, he took his medicine, allowing the bony hand to smack him soundly in the side of the head.

Chiun's darting hand quickly retreated to his kimono folds. "That did not help," the old man announced, unsatisfied. He whirled away from his pupil, storming off down the sidewalk.

"Worked for me," Remo grumbled.

Rubbing the side of his head, he trailed the Master of Sinanju down the street.

THE MOTT STREET Community Home stood amid a cluster of seedy brownstones half a city block down from the burning headquarters of the Scubisci Family.

The name made it sound to Remo like the sort of place that had sprung up around the country starting in the sixties. Designed to keep kids out of trouble, all of those places inevitably became a focus for the kind of troubles they were supposed to distract from.

This community home was different, given the fact that its clientele was considerably older than Remo had expected.

"It's an old-folks' home," Remo said when they'd stepped through the Plexiglas front doors.

"I am in no mood for your age bashing," Chiun hissed.

As they headed down the hallway to the nurses' station, Remo shook his head.

"I just assumed from the name that it was one of those places where punks go to score drugs. The

ones with the pool table with one missing leg and
the posters encouraging the joys of prophylactic use
among the preteen set." They were at the main desk.
"This can't be right," Remo frowned. "Sweet said
a Scubisci would be here."

"And why wouldn't one be here?" Chiun said,
an undertone of intense displeasure in his squeaky
voice.

"Well, I suppose Great-uncle Phineas Scubisci
might've been mothballed here twenty years ago,"
Remo said. "But we're looking for someone a little
more current. Someone who knows who's really
pulling the purse strings on Raffair, and who maybe
knows who these guys are who keep trying to kill
me. I assumed it was old Don Pietro's grandson or
something, but this is about as far out of the loop
as you can get. Let's get out of here."

"Hold," Chiun insisted. He fixed his gaze on the
nurse behind the desk. "Does a Scubisci reside
here?"

"Room 24A," the woman nodded, pointing down
an adjacent hall.

The Master of Sinanju swirled away from the
desk.

"This is silly, Chiun," Remo said, hurrying to
keep pace with the purposeful gait of the old Asian.

"I agree. Therefore let us get it over with quickly
so that we can attend to more important matters."

The comingled smells of antiseptics and medica-
tions poured from open doorways. Remo hesitated
outside room 24A, but Chiun bullied by him.

Inside the small room were two beds. One was neatly made. The covers of the other were a crumpled mess that hung in a tangle off to one side.

An ancient woman sat in a vinyl chair near the window, an unlit cigarette dangling from between her dry lips.

She'd been plump a lifetime ago. Now the empty flesh hung off her shrunken frame like dirty sheets draped across a sagging clothesline.

Her black dress—extra large at one time—was a loose-fitting rag. The woman's ankles were too swollen for shoes. An unused black pair was tucked beneath her chair.

Rheumy eyes looked up as Remo and Chiun entered.

"You got a match?" she threatened.

Remo rolled his eyes. "Chiun, let's go," he whispered.

"Hush!" Chiun insisted. To the old woman he said, "Signora Scubisci?"

The crone pulled the cigarette from her lip. "Atsa me. You gotta match, or no?"

"Sorry, no," Remo answered.

"Eh." She shrugged, lowering the unlit cigarette. "They just take it away from me anyway."

"We beg a moment of your time," the Master of Sinanju said, bowing politely. He motioned to Remo.

"What?" Remo asked from the corner of his mouth.

"Ask her whatever foolishness it is you need to

know," Chiun prodded. "And I would appreciate it if you did not draw her a map to the Sinanju treasure house while you are doing so."

Remo felt silly. Obviously, in his last minutes of life, Sol Sweet had had the courage enough to lie. Remo was surprised. The lawyer seemed too scared to offer anything but unvarnished truth.

"Sol Sweet sent me," he began reluctantly.

A light of understanding sparked in her ancient eyes.

"Oh, the Jew," the old woman said. Without another word, she reached for the table next to her chair. It was scarred with the deep black furrows of old cigarette burns.

Resting on the table was a plain manila envelope. A gnarled hand dropped across it. She dragged it across the table, flinging it to Remo. He snatched it from the air.

There was an airmail sticker on the envelope. It was addressed to "A.S. c/o Angela Scubisci, Mott Street Community Home." Along with the zip code and street address was the legend "New York, NY. U.S.A." There was no return address.

"A.S.?" Remo asked, reading the initials.

"Anselmo." She said the name with contempt. "He issa my son. Didn't the kike tell you?"

He looked at the woman with new eyes. "He forgot to mention it," Remo said dully.

"Hah," the woman scoffed. "You know my son?"

Remo thought of the day he'd met Anselmo Scubisci. He had been on assignment, sent after the Don's younger brother, Dominic, Angela Scubisci's only other child.

"Only saw him once in passing," Remo said. A hard glint came to his deep-set eyes. "We knew your husband, though."

Both he and the Master of Sinanju had watched old Don Pietro Scubisci breathe his last.

The widow Scubisci pounded a blue-veined hand against her sagging chest. "Oh, my Pietro. Now *there* was a man who respected family. Even that idiot boy of ours, Dominic—God rest his soul—he knew where hissa loyalty should be. Not Anselmo. He don't respect hissa family."

Remo steered her away from the topic of family. "Sweet said you knew something about your son's backer."

The old woman sighed a pained, raspy exhalation. "It's in there," she said, pointing to the envelope. "All the betrayal. He no respect hissa father. All my Pietro's work, gone. That boy issa no good."

Brow furrowing, Remo tore one end off the envelope. He reached inside, pulling out a single sheet of paper. The printing was in some foreign language.

"Hey, whaddayou doing!" Angela Scubisci demanded.

He ignored her. "I can't read this," Remo said, handing the note off to Chiun.

"Atsa for Anselmo," the woman insisted angrily.

"This is the language of the Kingdom of the Two," the Master of Sinanju pronounced.

"Twenty-first-century equivalent?" Remo asked.

"Italy," Chiun replied, displeased at having to use the modern name. He frowned as he read the lines. "There is nothing of interest here. It is merely a note of thanks for some unmentioned success."

"Hmm," Remo said. "Could be from Scubisci's backer. Does it say who he is?"

"It is unsigned," Chiun replied.

"Maybe Smith can track him from this." Taking the note back, Remo stuffed it back in its envelope before shoving it in his pocket. "You know who sent this?" he asked the old woman.

Unable to move, she sat glaring at the two strangers.

"No," she snarled. "They never tell me. I only know itsa from Napoli." She tipped her head. "Whassa you name?"

Remo figured it would do no harm to answer.

"Remo," he admitted.

Her angry features softened. "Atsa good name," she said, nodding. "*Paisan.* I bet you don't turna you back on you family."

"Oh, I can tell you stories," Chiun offered coldly.

The widow Scubisci paid no attention to the old Korean.

"You work for that Jew, Sweet?" she asked Remo.

"No," Remo said. "And that anti-Semitism must make you the belle of the ball on mah-jongg night. Let's go, Chiun."

"You take that Jewboy out, didn't you?" Angela Scubisci called as they walked away.

When Remo turned back, her eyes had grown crafty.

Remo thought of how he'd left Sol Sweet, picture frame hanging around his scrawny neck.

"Actually, I sort of put him in," he admitted.

She tipped her malevolent witch's face forward.

"You goin' after Anselmo now, ain't you?" she cackled. Clapping her wasted hands, Angela Scubisci grinned, flashing black gums and a sorry trio of sharp brown teeth. "You get him for what he do to his poor father's memory," she said happily. "He think it's enough he get that kike lawyer of his to pay for me to stay here. He tella me he have me thrown out if I don' pass on his filthy, traitorous mail." Her Halloween smile broadened. "You getta him good now, Remo." She seemed delighted to say his name. "Him and those Napoli bastards."

"Napoli?" Remo asked. "Naples, right?"

Angela Scubisci spit on the shabby floor. "Don' talka to me about those *diavolo tonno*." She spit again, wiping drool from her chin with the back of one ancient hand.

"What's wrong with Naples?" Remo asked.

This time, the widow Scubisci tried to spit at him. He twisted and it slapped viciously against the ratty wallpaper.

"Chiun?" Remo asked, confused.

The old man stood near the door.

"She is Sicilian," he explained with growing impatience. "Clan warfare has divided both provinces for generations."

"And my Anselmo has got on his knees for them Napoli dogs," Angela Scubisci snarled. "Iffa my Pietro was alive, it woulda been different. The family always come first to him." She raised both hands above her head. Loose black sleeves rolled back to reveal flesh-draped biceps. "Oh, if he wassa here now, I'd make him some of the fried peppers he love so much. And after he eat, he woulda have one of his *caporegime* shoot that traitorous boy of his right inna the face."

"Must've missed a lot of Mother's Days," Remo commented aridly to Chiun.

"I am not interested," Chiun hissed. "Now come. We have dallied here long enough." In a whirl of kimono skirts, he ducked back into the hallway.

Remo looked once more at Angela Scubisci.

The old woman's withered hands were still upraised. Sitting in her chair, she was stretching toward the ceiling, muttering soft invocations.

"Oh, Pietro," she intoned, her hopeful, damp eyes turned upward, "thissa fine boy gonna pay back Anselmo for what he done to poison your memory."

She waved her prayerful arms from side to side.

At the door, Remo thought of all the schemes of old Don Pietro that CURE had been forced to thwart, of all the innocents who had fallen victim to the evil old man.

As he slipped through the door, he called back to the ancient widow of Pietro Scubisci, his tone icy cold.

"If you want to get to your husband, lady, you're reaching in the wrong direction."

**23**

"Anselmo Scubisci's not the top dog after all, Smitty," Remo announced. He was on a pay phone in the lobby of the retirement home. "Sounds like he's running things from jail for somebody else."

"Do you know who?" Smith asked.

"Nope. Mrs. Scubisci didn't know."

"*Mrs.* Scubisci?" Smith questioned.

"Or Mother Scubisci, depending on which one of her Riff Raff Sam relatives we're talking about. Weird thing, Smitty, but I was just thinking she's one of the few members of that family I've met that I haven't killed. Not that the temptation wasn't there."

"I found her to be charming," the Master of Sinanju disagreed. He was standing at Remo's elbow. He seemed to be attempting by restless expression alone to hurry the conversation along.

"I'm not surprised," Remo said to Chiun. "She's the first mom I ever met who opted for capital over corporal punishment." To Smith, he said, "The nasty old battle-ax wants us to ice her own son.

She's pissed at him for throwing in with some foreign investor for Raffair.''

Chiun shook his head testily. "Not just any foreign investor, Emperor Smith," he called. "The man he has taken up with is from Naples."

With his last word came a phlegmy sound from down the hall. A fresh wad of spit flew out the door of Angela Scubisci's room.

"I'm glad I'm not in charge of mop duty around here," Remo commented. "Anyway, Chiun's right. She wasn't upset that junior was a murderous son of a bitch, just that he'd gone into business with someone from the dreaded N-province."

"I understand why," Smith said. "It is an odd arrangement, given the fact that the Scubisci Family has its origin in Sicily."

"Sicily, Naples—I still don't know what the big deal is," Remo said.

"There is a very old rivalry between crime interests in both cities. Although it exists now throughout Italy, Sicily is the traditional home of the Mafia. The branch from which the Scubisci Family extends is quite strong there."

Remo didn't know how it came to him. But at Smith's use of the word *now,* something sparked in his brain. He felt his hand tighten on the receiver.

*"Now,"* he stressed, stunned at his own deduction.

"What is it?" Smith asked, curious.

"You said exists now," Remo said excitedly. "What about before? Like years ago?"

"I do not follow."

"Remember East Africa? The defense minister there made a deal with some kind of old Italian crime syndicate. Dinty Morra or something like that."

An instant's hesitation on the other end of the line as Smith picked up the thread. "Camorra," he announced, the shock of realization in his steady voice.

It was during CURE's last crisis. Renegade forces within the government had threatened to turn the African nation of East Africa into a haven for crime. The defense minister of that country had made a deal with an old rival of the Mafia thought to have been extinct since the early part of the twentieth century. Camorra. This underground syndicate intended to use nuclear devices to decimate the ranks of the visiting crime lords, hoping to assume dominance of the world's crime scene.

Remo and Chiun had thwarted their plans, and the secret fraternity had scuttled back into the shadows. In the intervening months, Smith had been unable to locate them, and they had made no more noises of their desire to expand beyond Italy's borders. Until now.

"Is it possible?" Smith asked. He was still amazed that something like Camorra had evaded detection for so long.

"You tell me," Remo answered. "I've got a letter here from Italy. By the sounds of it, Scubisci was getting stuff sent to his mother and his lawyer was bringing it to him."

"Bring the letter to Folcroft," Smith said crisply.

"I was gonna FedEx it," Remo said. "And anyway, Chiun says it's just some kind of congratulations thing. It might not be anything."

"I will not know that until I see it."

"C'mon, Smitty. Chiun's itching to go after the guys who torched our house. Besides, the note's in Italian. You don't know Italian."

"Actually, I do know some," Smith said. "And Master Chiun will be able to fill the gaps in my knowledge. As for the men responsible for burning your home, I have had no luck. There have been no credit-card usages by Fungillo since yesterday. Aside from a large cash withdrawal in his name from a Boston ATM a few hours after you saw him flee the scene, he has disappeared. At least electronically."

Beside Remo, the Master of Sinanju's face grew dark. "You confessed to Smith before me?" he hissed.

When Remo offered a sheepish shrug in explanation, the old man exhaled disgust. He marched away from his pupil and took up a sentry position at the main doors, glaring malevolence at Mott Street. The activity outside had grown since their arrival at the retirement complex.

"I don't know about Raffair," Remo muttered, "but my stock's dropping like a rock." He tore his eyes away from his teacher's indignant form. "Why don't you let us go after Scubisci right now?" he whispered to Smith. "For *my* sake? After all, as top dog he's ultimately to blame for what happened to our house. Maybe that'll get Chiun off my back.''

"It will not," the Master of Sinanju called. "I want he who struck the match, not he who holds the leash."

As Remo felt himself deflate, Smith chimed in.

"This time, I agree with Chiun," the CURE director said. "No one will miss a hoodlum like John Fungillo, but I would prefer not to send you into a federal penitentiary after Anselmo Scubisci."

"You've done it before," Remo said glumly. "And I still think he's the one behind these screwy attacks on me, no matter what you or his lawyer says."

"Sweet had no knowledge of the masked men?"

"No," Remo admitted. "But don't think Raffair's off the hook. It could be the guy above Scubisci who's behind it."

"Doubtful," Smith said. "If there is another figure lurking in the shadows, he would be far above the men you've met so far. I find it impossible to believe that he would be informed enough to direct these assaults against you. The first one in New York happened much too quickly."

"Maybe," Remo said grudgingly. "But we can find out for sure from Scubisci."

"No," Smith said. "When I've sent you on assignment into prisons in the past, the circumstances were different. Anselmo Scubisci alive in prison is a valuable weapon against those who might choose a life of crime. He shows that the system is working. Dead, he is not a deterrent.''

''Yeah, but he'd be out of business,'' Remo grumbled. ''Which, by the looks of it, he isn't now.''

''We will see. Please bring the letter to Folcroft at once.''

Remo was already hanging up when Smith broke the connection. He found the Master of Sinanju at the door.

''You heard,'' he sighed. ''Smitty wants us back home.'' He cringed the moment the word passed his lips.

Chiun gave him a baleful look.

''Sorry,'' Remo said, his voice small.

''Yes, you are,'' Chiun agreed icily. With one leathery hand, he slapped open the door.

Remo followed him outside, shamefaced.

This time when they hit the street, the air was filled with a pall of thin black smoke. Fire trucks and police cars were visible far down the road. The Neighborhood Improvement Association building was fully ablaze. The money Remo had thrown out into the street had slowed the arrival of emergency vehicles considerably. He felt little satisfaction in the act of vengeance as he stepped down onto the sidewalk.

His loafer soles had barely brushed the concrete when he heard the squeal of tires. He looked up in time to see an old Buick racing toward him from across the street, twin clouds of rubber-scented smoke pouring from its screeching back wheels. As the car approached, he saw the by-now familiar black ski mask behind the wheel.

"Oh, not again," Remo groused.

Gawkers watching the fire had to jump away from the speeding car's grille. The car rammed aside a parked minivan on its way toward Remo. Bouncing the curb, it plowed over a fireplug. Water gushed high into the air. When the car was nearly upon them, Remo jumped to the right while the Master of Sinanju jumped to the left in a billow of kimono skirts.

The car screamed past them and slammed smack into the broad steps of the Mott Street Community Home in an explosive burst of crumpling metal and smashing windshield.

"And I am tired of your friends, as well," Chiun snapped across the shattered hood as the engine idled to silence.

Shooting him an exasperated look, Remo leaned into the driver's-side window.

"Well it's about damn time," he announced.

Tearing off the door, he ducked inside. When he emerged a moment later, he was holding the driver by the collar of his jacket. The man's head hung limp in his ski mask, chin brushing his chest. Unlike those who had preceded him, this attacker was still breathing.

"We've got a heartbeat," Remo proclaimed.

The geysering fire hydrant had dropped the water pressure all along the line. Farther up Mott Street, the gushing fire hoses that had been dousing the raging flames at the Neighborhood Improvement Association had become pathetic spurting trickles. Eyes were already scanning the area for the reason.

"Let's get this one back to Smith," Remo said rapidly.

Carting the unconscious assailant under one arm like a trophy, he and the Master of Sinanju hurried down the street to Remo's leased car.

**24**

It was raining in Naples.

Ominous black clouds rolled in across denuded vineyards. In the distance, thunder rumbled.

Don Hector Vincenzo watched the fat rivulets of rain as they streaked down the glass of his closed patio doors.

The air had turned cold. The stone floor beneath his shoes chilled him up to his ankles.

Although he was Don of the Naples Camorra, the most powerful of all the Camorristas, he did not control the weather. In the dark center of his soul, though he would admit it to no one, he knew that there was precious little that he did control.

But that was about to change.

He eyed a single raindrop as it rolled down the length of a door pane. It seemed to take forever to reach the floor. As he watched, his mind drifted beyond the storm clouds, beyond Naples. To America.

It was all going according to plan. It would take some time—a few more years, perhaps—but in the end, he would succeed. Finally.

They had been second to the Mafia far too long.

It had not always been that way. There was a time when the Naples Camorra and the Sicilian Mafia had been equals. But that was before Mussolini.

It was not that Il Duce favored the Mafia over Camorra. Indeed, the dictator had labored to destroy both groups. But Sicily was an island, separate and safe. On the mainland of Italy, Camorra had had the misfortune of being too close.

Those had been brutal times.

Even so, the shadow organization had survived. Not as powerful as it had been, but alive. Unfortunately, Camorra could never again hope to compete with La Cosa Nostra.

While Camorra was still licking its wounds in the time immediately following World War II, the Mafia had thrived. The Americans had relied on the Mafia to help in the relief efforts. The Dons helped keep the social fabric from tearing while solidifying their own power. Weakened, Camorra could only watch it happen.

America herself had been Camorra's great mistake. The Naples syndicate had failed to expand into this virgin territory. And so, crippled by war and impoverished in peace, Camorra had struggled for decades.

No longer.

Don Vincenzo wasn't a young man. As his days on Earth dwindled, so too had his patience. Before his time ran out, he had vowed to see Camorra return to the greatness of old.

The grand scheme in East Africa had been part

of the strategy. To this day, he still didn't know why that had failed. As it was, he had been lucky to escape that backward land with his life.

But this was his second chance. At his age, perhaps his final chance. Originally, he had planned it to be his introduction to the American market. However, with the Mafia still present there, it had been an easy enough thing to turn it into a weapon of attack.

Things were not as they once had been for his enemy. The Mafia had grown big and clumsy. The dawning of the new millennium had witnessed a weakened Cosa Nostra. And in that weakness was opportunity....

Lightning crackled suddenly through the black sky, startling Don Vincenzo. When he looked out at the clouds, he saw that a fissure had appeared in the gloomy canopy. Shafts of sunlight broke through the clouds, illuminating his hillside vineyard. The fat splattering raindrops that had been striking the patio tabletops and chairs began to die.

The clouds moved once more, and the sunlight vanished. But the rain near the house continued to slow.

It would stop soon. Then the sky would clear. Perhaps the day would be warm.

Don Vincenzo pulled himself to his feet. Someone would have to be found to dry off his chair outside.

The old Don shambled off into the mansion in search of a servant and a rag.

**25**

Smith heard the soft sound of an engine running as he was reading the initial accounts of the fire at the Neighborhood Improvement Association in Manhattan. The sound came from the loading-dock area behind Folcroft.

Since it was too late for the regularly scheduled morning deliveries, Smith leaned over to the picture window. When he saw Remo and Chiun standing next to Remo's car, the CURE director's already displeased expression grew more sour.

Remo held up a finger, telling Smith to wait a minute. He shut off the engine, and he and Chiun disappeared from sight. Thirty seconds later, they were gliding into Smith's office.

"You did not tell me you burned down Scubisci's headquarters," Smith said unhappily as they closed the door.

"Tit for tat," Remo said levelly. He shook his head. "And that doesn't matter right now." He offered a thin smile. "Guess who's in the car?"

Smith frowned. He had seen no one in Remo's vehicle. "Who?" Smith asked warily. He leaned back again, craning to see the car near the loading dock.

"I don't know," Remo said. "And you can't see him 'cause he's in the trunk. But he *is* the first survivor of one of these boohawdle kamikaze attacks against me."

This finally piqued the CURE director's interest.

The three men left the office and hurried downstairs. Remo snagged an empty gurney from the hallway and rolled it with them outside.

"He's out like a light," Remo said as he popped the trunk.

Smith removed the white button that was pinned to the man's jacket. "I have still had no luck with this," he said.

Remo had pulled off the man's ski mask. His hair was light, his skin dark. Dried blood formed a crusted patch where his forehead had met the steering wheel.

When Smith reached for the man's pockets, Remo stopped him. "Don't bother," he said. "I already checked. No ID."

"Let's get him inside," Smith said, his brow furrowed.

Remo dumped the unconscious man onto the gurney and wheeled him in through the loading-dock door.

Smith left the patient in the care of a Folcroft doctor in the security wing of the sanitarium with an order to call upstairs the instant the man came to.

Ten minutes later, they were back in Smith's office.

"Now, let me see the letter," Smith said as he locked the door.

Remo started reaching for his pocket, but the Master of Sinanju interrupted. "First things first," he said, staying Remo with a bony hand to his pupil's wrist. From the folds of his kimono, he produced the yellow paper on which Sol Sweet had scribbled the names of the men who'd burned their home. "Find these three," he commanded.

Smith took the paper. The handwriting was appalling. Still, he recognized John Fungillo's name. "Presumably, these are the men who destroyed your home?" he asked, raising a thin eyebrow.

"It would be wise to first check those establishments that trade in guns and gardening supplies," Chiun suggested authoritatively. "When Romans are not shooting at one another, they are growing those suspicious pomato things that haven't the decency to be either a fruit or a vegetable."

"Yes," Smith nodded. "This should be checked first." Paper in hand, he crossed to his desk.

Remo couldn't hide his surprise.

"I know you're not doing it out of the goodness of your heart," he said as the CURE director settled into his chair. "And vengeance isn't your style, so what gives?"

"Simple," Smith said. "The men who burned your home saw the two of you on tape and were in your home. Either case makes them a security threat.''

"I should have known," Remo nodded.

"Your enemies are our enemies, O Emperor," Chiun bowed. Just in case the madman was lying to placate him, he stayed at Smith's side as the CURE director worked.

"Sweet had the only other tape of us, by the way," Remo said. "It's toast. Along with most of Little Italy if they haven't figured out how to get the water back on." He sank cross-legged to the carpet.

The CURE director had already engaged the basement mainframes in a continuous search for John Fungillo. He hoped that these two new names would help him locate the three arsonists. But after twenty futile minutes, he was forced to admit defeat.

"These men have left no electronic path to follow, either," Smith said once he was through. "Like Fungillo, they each withdrew a large amount of cash from an ATM in Boston after Remo saw them fleeing your home. Obviously, they wish to remain in hiding—at least for now." He entered some simple commands into his computer. "We will have to put them aside for now. I have instructed the mainframes to alert me the moment any of them show themselves."

The Master of Sinanju's weathered face showed his disappointment. "Very well, Emperor," he said.

Smith turned his attention to Remo. "Now, the letter, please."

Still sitting on the floor, Remo fished in his pocket

and removed the note he'd retrieved from Angela Scubisci.

"Probably just a fried-zucchini recipe," he commented, winging it to Smith. The envelope slid to a stop above Smith's keyboard.

Chiun helped the CURE director translate. When they were done minutes later, a frustrated expression had formed on Smith's gaunt face.

"There is nothing here," he complained.

"As I said," Chiun sniffed. He was still at Smith's elbow. "Unsigned platitudes from one Roman to another."

"Well, it *is* written to an Anselmo," Smith offered. "We can safely conclude that this is Anselmo Scubisci, but there is nothing specific that would point to the writer." As he stared at his monitor, the neat rows of letters reflected in the lenses of his glasses.

"This Begorra thing has been in deep cover for years," Remo said. "Makes sense they wouldn't sign a letter to the biggest crime boss in America."

"If it is in fact Camorra," Smith said. He looked once more at the envelope. "According to this, it was postmarked in Naples. Perhaps I can use the records from East Africa. If there is a crime figure from Naples wealthy enough to back Raffair, it's possible he was present for the events there three months ago. Remo, Master Chiun, I believe you've taken this as far as you can. I will complete this investigation from here."

He had no sooner said the words when the dedicated White House line rang. It was clear from the look on his face that Smith didn't want to have to take the call.

"Let it ring, Smitty," Remo suggested. "He's gone day after tomorrow anyway."

But Smith had already pulled the red phone from the drawer. With a look of thin disapproval at Remo, he answered it. "Yes, sir," he said tiredly.

"Just checking on your progress, Smith," the President of the United States said, forced affability in his voice.

"We have learned how Raffair can be a company that does not actually produce anything," the CURE director said. He quickly briefed the President on what Remo and Chiun had learned from Sol Sweet. "So it seems as if those ordinary American citizens who are the primary stockholders of Raffair have invested in a group intent on unraveling the very fabric of our own society," he concluded.

Once he was done, the President whistled softly. "Dang if he didn't know something was buggy about them right from the start," he said, impressed.

"Who?" Smith asked.

The President caught himself. "Oh, no one," he said vaguely. "Just some guy. So anyway, who's behind all this?"

"Well, as far as we can ascertain at this juncture, it is none other than Don Anselmo Scubisci."

"The Dandy Don?" the President said, a quick flicker of anger in his tone. "I thought he was strapped for cash. At least that's what he claimed when I hit him up for a campaign donation back in '96.''

"Scubisci has apparently found a backer in a foreign crime syndicate called Camorra,'' Smith explained. "It's an odd arrangement, given the fact that the Mafia and Camorra are historic enemies. I am still uncertain why a prominent Mob figure would get into bed with a sworn enemy.''

"Caligula would have married his horse had his Praetorian guard not killed him on the way to the ceremony,'' Chiun sniffed from his sentry post next to Smith. He was leaning in to listen. "Tell the bloated puppet President that the Romans are not choosy about their bed partners.''

"Neither is he,'' Remo chimed in from the floor. "I saw that pig-in-a-beret he wasn't having dictionary sex with.''

Smith gave them a withering look.

"Were those your men?'' the President asked. There was an odd strain to his hoarse voice Smith hadn't heard before.

"Yes, sir,'' the CURE director replied.

"Caligula wasn't gonna marry any horse,'' Remo muttered at Chiun.

"It is called history,'' the old Korean said.

"It's called bullshit,'' Remo disagreed.

"It is only that when not said with authority,'' the Master of Sinanju retorted. "And I am not talking to you.''

Smith slapped a firm hand over the mouthpiece. "Do you two mind?'' he whispered hotly.

"So they're both okay?" the President asked. He seemed oblivious to what they'd said.

Smith's face grew puzzled. "They are fine," he replied.

"Good, good," the President said, suddenly seeming strangely distant. "Anyway, about this Raffair thing. If Anselmo Scubisci's behind it, I think they should be closed for good. I don't want people saying organized crime rode the coattails of my economy. Could you do me a great favor, Smith, and shut down those other offices around the country like you did in Boston?"

From the floor, Remo shook his head desperately while mouthing the word "no" repeatedly. Leaning a shell-like ear toward the phone, Chiun seemed supremely disinterested in the conversation he was eavesdropping on.

Smith closed his eyes on both of them. "Very well, Mr. President," he said.

"Great," the President enthused. "Gimme a call when you're through."

There was no dial tone when the dedicated line went dead. Smith replaced the phone in his bottom drawer.

"What's he want us to do next," Remo griped, "interview strippers for the first post-White House orgy? Count me out this time, Smitty."

"It did not seem an unreasonable request," Smith said.

"It does to me," Remo retorted. "I thought we could hang around here at least until that guy downstairs comes to. And I'm a little bit anxious to pay a visit to the goon squad that torched our house.''

At this, Chiun harrumphed.

''And I've had it up to here with you, too,'' Remo snapped at him. ''It was my house just as much as it was yours. You don't own the copyright on indignation this time, Little Father. And you sure as hell didn't get the promise from some ghost of a truckload of crap getting dumped on you for the next decade, so why don't you just back off?''

The flash of injured anger in his pupil's tone caught the old man off guard. The harsh lines of Chiun's face tightened for an instant before relaxing somewhat.

''I sympathize with you for your loss,'' Smith said reasonably. ''And I'm just as interested as you in the identity of your masked assailants, but at the moment we are in a holding pattern for both. Right now, it might be best for us all if you kept busy. At least until something new comes up with either situation.''

On the floor, Remo closed his eyes, forcing calm. ''Why don't I just stick a broom up my ass so I can sweep the streets while I'm traipsing all over the country?''

''There isn't room,'' Chiun said, his eyes hooded. ''For your head would get in the way. We will go, Emperor Smith,'' he told the CURE director. ''If only to give you the solitude you need to find those Sinanju seeks.''

''Thank you, Master Chiun,'' Smith nodded. ''I

will print out a list of Raffair's national offices." He focused his attention on his computer.

"Thanks a heap, Chiun," Remo complained quietly as the old Korean swept around the big desk.

"For once the lunatic is right," the tiny Asian said, his voice pitched low enough that only Remo could hear. "Retribution will come in its time. If this distraction satisfies Smith's need to placate the departing billhilly he serves, then we will serve our emperor in this task."

Remo didn't answer. Scowling deeply, he crossed his arms.

Chiun said nothing more. As Smith worked, the aged Korean sank to the floor next to his pupil.

He offered but one more glance at Remo. When he saw that the look of brooding had not yet fled, a new expression formed on the older man's weathered face. With an air of sad understanding, Chiun focused all his attention back on his mad employer.

THE PRESIDENT SAT on the edge of the bed. At his feet was the red phone used to contact Smith. The nightstand in which the telephone was supposed to be secreted had vanished the previous day.

With a heavy sigh, he dragged himself to his feet.

The living room was empty as he trudged by. He had no idea how she'd managed that. It was as if all the furniture had been swallowed up by a black hole while he'd slept.

There were a few half-chewed photographs on the floor. On the scraps he saw his own thoughtful puffy eyes, earnest protruding chin and thoughtful bitten lip.

At least he didn't have to run from the First Menagerie anymore. The dog and the cat were in exile, locked across the street at Blair House. It was one of his last official acts as President. Probably ever. Thanks to *her,* he might never get the third term he so desperately wanted.

Past the living room, he entered the small study. The boxes containing billing records and personal files were gone, as were all the shredders. Relocated to New York.

He found a phone that his wife hadn't taken and stabbed out the number by memory.

"*¡Hola!*" said the female voice that answered.

"It's me," the President said glumly.

The woman's voice grew cold. "Oh. Ju hab news?"

Her Spanish accent was awkward. In the background, the same man's voice that the President had been hearing for more than a year continued to drone Spanish in soft, modulated tones.

"They're on their way," the President said. "I don't know which office they'll hit first, if that makes a difference to you, but they're goin' after them all."

"Eet duz not," the woman replied. "We will be ready for them. They stand in the way of my ascension to the throne and must therefore be crushed by my royal guard."

"Yeah," the President grumbled. "If that's all you need, I've got some stuff I've gotta do."

At this, the woman laughed. "For ju there is no more work. Ju are, as my people say, El Lamo Ducko."

He was pretty sure this wasn't real Spanish. He didn't have time to speak before the woman—still laughing that groin-injuring laugh of hers—slammed the phone in his ear.

He dropped his own receiver to its cradle. Since the coffee table had vanished, this phone was on the floor, too.

"New Year's resolution number one," the President muttered to himself. "I *gotta* start bein' more picky about who I sleep with."

# 26

Don Anselmo Scubisci felt the faint kiss of fear as he carefully pressed out the eleven-digit number.

He'd used the redial button the first twenty times, but the last five he had entered the number manually, each time thinking he'd misdialed the previous times.

All the lines into the Neighborhood Improvement Association were busy, including Sol Sweet's private line. Something was wrong.

Other men were waiting to use the prison phone. Not that it mattered. For the head of the Manhattan Mafia, they'd wait.

When he finished dialing the twenty-fifth time, the familiar buzzing assaulted his ears.

He slammed down the phone.

Scubisci fished out the coin from the return slot and shoved it back in the phone. He quickly stabbed out a different number. After hearing nothing but the relentless staccato buzz of a busy signal, it was jarring when the phone started ringing at the other end.

As he waited anxiously for someone to pick up, he drummed his fingers impatiently against the graffiti-covered wall. His nails were shabby. It had been some time since he'd had a decent manicure.

The phone was answered on the ninth ring. "Mott Street Community Home," a woman's nasal voice announced.

"Angela Scubisci," Anselmo barked. The frantic sharpness in his voice stung his throat, reminding him of the too-recent brush with cancer and the nodes that had been removed from his vocal cords.

There were no phones in the nursing-home rooms. Standing at the prison phone, he prayed they'd wheel his mother into the hallway fast. After fifteen minutes, the prison phone would automatically hang up.

After nearly eight agonizing minutes, the familiar angry old voice came onto the line.

"Who's this?" Angela Scubisci demanded.

Though he hadn't seen her since he'd been sent to prison nearly two years ago, he could still picture the withered old crow. Her scowling, toothless face haunted him in his dreams.

"It's Anselmo, Mama."

"You still alive?" She sounded disappointed.

"Of course I'm alive, Mama," Anselmo said. For an instant, he felt sorry for her. Such tragedy had been visited on her in recent years she had to have thought her elder son dead, as well. "I'm in jail, remember?"

"I know where you are," his mother snarled. "This notta the crazy house you lock me in."

"Then why'd you think I was dead?"

"'Cause they killa you Jew lawyer. You should see, Anselmo. Ambulance and police all over the road. I see fromma the window. It look like the day you poor sainted father pass on, God rest hissa soul."

At the mention of her dead husband, she sobbed a few obligatory times. Anselmo Scubisci hardly heard her. His mind was reeling.

"How do you know Sol's dead?" he croaked.

"They tella me."

"Maybe they were wrong. Who told you?"

"The men who killa your kike. One was a nice young man. The other I don't know. Some Chinaman or something."

Panic. Sweet had told him about the men who had visited the Boston Raffair office.

"They were there? What did you tell them?"

"Just the truth. Thatta you a no-good son. Thatta you insult the memory offa you father by lying down with them Napoli *fritto di pesce.*"

He couldn't wrap his brain around all this. Don Anselmo had to lean against the grimy prison wall for support.

"You didn't tell them *that?*" he gasped.

"About you new friends, Anselmo? Is that whatta you worried about?" She suddenly spoke in soothing, almost motherly tones.

She'd been joking. Anselmo felt a wash of relief flow over his thin frame.

The grating harpy's voice flashed angry. "Of course I tella them, you no-good Judas. I give them one of you letters from the Naples scum. They gonna come for you for whatta you done to your poor dead father's memory. They gonna come to that prison and they gonna cut that black heart outta you body. They gonna killa you, Anselmo. They gonna—"

Don Scubisci hung up the phone.

His mother's words echoed in his brain. He stood near the pay phone for a long time, his ears ringing madly.

*They gonna come for you.*

Who was going to come? Could they possibly get to him? In prison? Wasn't he safe in here, of all places?

He tried to focus his thoughts even as he attempted to dispel the image Sweet had painted of Louis DiGrotti's decapitation at the hands of the old one.

"You finished with that?" a voice rumbled.

Anselmo looked numbly to his left.

A man nearby. Large. Pointing at the phone.

"Yes. Yes, I am. Sorry."

Don Anselmo stepped woodenly aside.

No. Whoever they were, they wouldn't be able to get in here. Ogdenburg was a fortress. He'd be safe. Still, he had to make plans. Just in case.

Anselmo reached for the phone. He was startled to find someone already there. He had no idea how the huge man had gotten past him.

"What the hell do you think you're doing?" Don Anselmo snarled. "Get off that phone."

The man hesitated for a moment. He was a hulking thing with rippling muscles. He could have broken Anselmo Scubisci's neck with a snap of his huge fingers.

It seemed as if he were actually considering disobeying the Manhattan Don. But the moment quickly passed. Scowling, he replaced the phone and skulked away.

Scubisci scooped up the receiver.

Sol might be gone, but there were still people on the outside he could call. He didn't trust his mother. The old bat was crazy. He'd find out what was going on first.

Then he'd start worrying.

THE SHADES of his Maryland apartment were tightly drawn. Mark Howard sat in the corner of his living room in front of his glowing PC screen.

He'd been on-line ever since he'd called in sick that morning.

The Boston Raffair office was closed. Two bodies had been discovered there. With the counterfeiter Petito, that made a total of three in Massachusetts. The New York headquarters had burned to the ground a few hours before.

Things were happening. Thanks to him.

Mark knew he was the reason for all this. Why was still unclear, but thanks to the data he'd sent along to the White House, the blood of the dead was on his hands.

Mark's night had been a sleepless one. The

dreams of death were vivid. All the premonitions, insights and instincts of a lifetime seemed to be clicking into place.

There was a puzzle in himself. Something that he now realized he'd always known about but had pushed aside. His life was larger than he understood.

It was odd that this sense should strike him now. The mere knowledge that there was some secret force prowling across America automatically made him a security risk to that force. It was as if he were beginning to understand something important about himself at the same time that his life was at most risk.

But the picture was only half-formed. He couldn't bear the thought that he might never know who he truly was or what he was destined to become. Yet the same unseen thing that threatened him—Smith and his agents—was the thing that had brought him to this crossroads.

Fear, adrenaline, a risk to his very life. All combined were firing synapses in a brain that now seemed to have been dormant for the past twenty-nine years.

The mug that sat next to his mousepad was full. He'd poured the coffee hours ago, thinking he'd need the caffeine after so little sleep. He hadn't drunk a sip.

Mark was searching the news Web sites. Every once in a while, he'd do a keyword search for "Raffair," as well as a few other buzzwords like "crime," "bodies," "dead" and "Mafia." For some reason, early on his fingers had gone on automatic and typed the word "destroyer." Mark didn't know why, yet the feeling told him it was right. He left it in the search.

Nothing had happened since Raffair's world headquarters in New York was burned down. The past several hours had been chillingly quiet.

He ordinarily would have felt cramped or fatigued sitting so long at his computer, but for some reason he wasn't feeling any discomfort this day. It was as if he were born to sit in a chair and stare at a monitor. Even his eyes were alert. All this was good for Mark, for he dared not leave his computer for a minute.

Studying the screen, he used his mouse to highlight a news article from the online *Boston Blade*.

A blaze in Quincy had destroyed a condominium complex. Although the building had been occupied, the tenants had vanished. It was being said that the two men who lived there had to have been squatters, for there was no record of ownership. It was apparently a surprise to city officials that the place was abandoned property.

A boring little item, and Mark had no idea why it should interest him. Yet he found himself clicking and saving it to his hard drive.

As he did so, a muted electronic beep issued from his computer. His mailbox popped open.

He'd subscribed to a couple of news services earlier in the day, so he quickly clicked on the mailbox icon.

One of the services had flagged a report out of Chicago. When he read the simple lines of text, his mouth went dry.

There had been another multiple homicide at a Raffair office, this one on East Sixteenth and Clark in Chicago.

Mark read this latest report with a growing combination of dread and disbelief.

According to the Chicago police report, four men were confirmed dead. In a surrealistic twist, one of them appeared to have been fed through an office paper shredder. Police theorized that it had taken the killers hours to perform this gruesome act, and that some special massive crushing implement had to have been employed first to flatten the body. Yet there were no marks from such a tool on the floor and no evidence of the residue that the crushed body would have made.

Alone in his apartment, Mark closed his eyes.

Bodies were piling up all around the country, and they could all be traced to one source. Mark Howard.

He took a steeling breath. Opening his eyes, he attacked his keyboard. Fingers typing rapidly, he called up the list of Raffair offices and staff around the country. The same list he'd given the President.

He looked down at the first electronic page.

Boston, New York and Chicago were gone. They weren't taking them out alphabetically. Geography was dictating their path. L.A. would most likely be last. It sat alone on the West Coast. That left only a handful of others.

Mark scanned the list, much shorter now than it had been twenty-four hours ago.

New Orleans and Miami. They'd pick off the Houston office on their way west.

Howard took several minutes to commit the remaining addresses to memory. When he was through, he deleted all files concerning Raffair from his system.

Shutting down his computer, Mark stood.

No pain in his back or legs. No pain at all.

In his last days in office, the President had exposed Mark to something deeply dangerous. He could either hide and hope it all blew over or confront whatever mystery force was out there.

Fear told him to stay put, but the feeling told him to go. His subconscious had invaded his conscious mind and it was screaming one word to him, over and over and over again.

Destiny.

He'd get his plane tickets at the airport. Pulling open his top desk drawer, Mark took out something he'd bought after joining the CIA. Something he thought he'd never use.

Mark turned from the desk.

His overnight bag was in the hall closet. Gun clutched tightly in his hand, he went to collect it.

**27**

The Master of Sinanju had said next to nothing on the flight from New York to Chicago. He'd remained reticent as he and Remo dismantled Chicago's Raffair office, as well as its occupants. When they settled into their seats on the 727 out of Chicago-O'Hare, it didn't appear as if the old man had any intention of breaking his silence.

Chiun's hazel eyes were turned away from his pupil, set firmly on the plane's left wing, lest it have the audacity to drop off during takeoff with him aboard. Only once they were at a safe cruising altitude did he turn his attention inside. Still, he said not a word.

Remo wouldn't be goaded. If the old crank was giving him the silent treatment, he'd give it right back to him. No, siree, not a peep. Two could play at that game. He'd keep his mouth shut for ten damn years if he had to. He would absolutely not be the first one to snap. No way in hell—his lips were sealed, locked and the key had been tossed out the pressurized door at thirty-five thousand feet.

He folded his arms firmly across his chest and

screwed his lips shut tight. Beside him, Chiun was oblivious to his decision. The old man remained lost in private thoughts.

Remo decided it was no good giving someone the silent treatment unless they knew they were being given the silent treatment.

"I'm not talking to you, either," he announced without turning his head.

Chiun didn't reply.

There was a sudden raucous sound from the rear of the plane. Someone had smuggled on a boom box. They'd just started playing a CD with a heavy Latin beat. A group of rowdy passengers cheered the sound.

"Just so you know," Remo continued. "I don't think I deserve it from you, 'cause I'm going through exactly what you're going through, and it's not my fault about our house no matter what you think, and I really don't think it's fair that you're taking it out on me. So if you're not talking to me, *I'm* not talking to *you*. How do you like them apples?" He hugged his arms further into himself.

In the back, the revelry had become more focused. The cheering turned to singing and clapping. A conga line danced up the aisle next to Remo, led by the copilot. The man's uniform shirt was open to his navel, revealing hairy chest and belly. His head and arms swayed with the music as he danced by, a group of college-age girls attached hands to hips behind him.

"And my final word on all this before I go mute,

just so you know, is that I think it's pretty low of you," Remo said as the last of the line sashayed by. "So there. That's that. See you in the funny papers. I'll be the one without the mouth. Like that freak with the lightbulb head. Henry."

And having spoken his final, final word, he jammed his angry hands even deeper into his armpits.

For a few long seconds, the only sound aboard the plane was the blaring music and popping hiss of smuggled six-packs.

Remo was about to offer another last word when a squeaky voice chimed in beside him. He was stunned by what was said.

"I am sorry, Remo," the Master of Sinanju intoned gently.

He couldn't remember the old Korean ever uttering those words before. Remo turned to his teacher.

The old man was looking over at him, a hint of sad understanding in his eyes.

Remo's own eyes narrowed in suspicion. "If this is a trick to get me to talk, it won't work. I'm as mute as a monk."

Chiun shook his aged head. "Do not offer me such false promises," he warned. "It is unfair to taunt one of my advanced years. Besides, you were already struck dumb years ago."

There was no edge to his tone. Despite the shots, he seemed somber. And most important of all, he was talking again.

"Okay," Remo said. "So what are you sorry for?"

He still figured it was some kind of trap, but the look of sincerity never left his teacher's face.

"I am sorry for what you will have to endure," the Master of Sinanju replied simply.

Remo knew instantly what he was talking about. It made him wish Chiun was still giving him the silent treatment.

"You think this is it?" he asked quietly. "The hardship I'm gonna have to endure in the coming years?"

"I doubt my dead son made the journey from the Void merely to prophesy the burning of our home," Chiun replied. "But it begins with this. And for this and whatever is yet to come, I am sorry. You have a good heart, Remo. One undeserving of hardship. I will pray to my ancestors that it be strong enough to endure that which is to come."

Remo nodded numbly. "Thanks, Little Father," he said softly.

No other words were necessary. Chiun turned his attention back out the window. Remo stared at the back of the seat in front of him. Neither of them said another word.

When the conga line passed by this time, the co-pilot was shirtless and reeked of Budweiser. Remo tripped the stumbling man, and he collapsed under a pile of boozy sorority girls. Just because Remo's life was shit, it didn't mean someone else couldn't have a little fun.

**28**

Mark Howard had never been a field agent. Straight out of college, he had gone to the CIA as an analyst and had spent seven years toiling in the bowels of the Agency's Langley headquarters. But he had early on learned the true meaning of the term *counterintelligence.* Anything that ran counter to whatever the smart thing was—*that* was precisely what the CIA did.

It had only gotten worse when the Agency was defunded in the 1990s. Everything was falling apart, and everyone at Langley was at risk from disgruntled employees who'd been downsized out of a job. Thus Mark had bought the Heckler & Koch. He wanted to be ready if someone sold him out. Though he'd never needed the weapon, he was glad to have it now.

He didn't wear the gun on the plane. It was wrapped in its X-ray repelling holster and tucked safely away in his bag in the overhead compartment.

He was wearing a simple sweatshirt, jeans and sneakers, so no one in coach gave him a second look. A lot of people seemed to be involved in a limbo contest up near the galley. Beer cans littered the aisle.

Mark caught up on his sleep on the flight down from Washington. A flight attendant awakened him to tell him that he had to put on his seat belt for landing.

At the airport, he rented a green Ford Taurus and drove to a distant corner of the rental lot.

He shut off the car.

Mark slipped off his worn leather jacket and pulled his gun and holster from his bag. He shrugged the smooth straps onto his shoulders. The gun settled in the moon-shaped sweat stain beneath his arm as he pulled his jacket back on. At his side, the gun was a lead weight.

There was no premonitory feeling at the moment. Unless he counted the tingle of fear in his belly.

"Ready or not, here I come," Mark muttered.

Turning on the engine, he backed out of the parking lot space. As he slipped the car into Drive, he was surprised to see that his hands weren't shaking. He hoped it was a sign.

Stepping firmly on the gas, Mark Howard sped off into the warm darkness.

REMO AND CHIUN STEPPED through the terminal's automatic doors and out into the night.

Though the day had cooled somewhat at evening's fall, the mild New Orleans air was still a welcome change from the bitter cold that had greeted them in Chicago.

"I hope Smitty realizes the airfare we're racking up for this dumb-ass mission," Remo complained as they headed for the car-rental agency. "And I think half the flight crew was high. Which, the way air travel's going lately, is probably less than the FAA's one hundred percent stoned rule."

Walking beside him, the Master of Sinanju was unmoved. "Travel is a welcome distraction from waiting," he said. "You were growing too anxious."

"I'd rather wait at Folcroft than prance around America like the professional assassin's answer to Charles Kuralt, all for some President who's been giving Smitty the royal shaft these past few years."

His tone had grown angrier as he spoke. When he was through, the Master of Sinanju gave him a bland look.

"Thank you, Remo, for proving my point."

At his words, Remo felt some of the anger drain out of him. Chiun was right. He'd been storing it up ever since he'd seen Johnny Fungillo driving away from their burning house. Face growing dark, he fell silent.

A car was driving out of the lot as they headed into the small rental office.

Remo had barely pulled out his credit card when Chiun pushed his way in front of him. He addressed the smiling woman who stood behind the counter.

"We wish to retain a green conveyance," Chiun insisted.

"Oh, I'm sorry, sir," she said, "but we don't have any green units."

"I just saw one depart as we entered," the Master of Sinanju argued.

"That was our last one," she explained.

Chiun crossed his arms. "Bring it back."

"I'm sorry, we can't do that," the woman said. Her plastered smile was growing weak.

"What does it matter?" Remo exhaled.

"First your ears, then your tongue and now your eyes," Chiun said to him. "What is it like, Remo, to live in a body incapable of detecting beauty?"

"Right now, this is the body with the credit card," Remo said. He turned to the woman. "Anything's fine."

She was eyeing his lean frame with growing interest.

"Blue is nice," the woman nodded hopefully. "We have plenty of blue."

"Blue is a common gutter color favored by streetwalkers," Chiun sniffed at the woman, who was dressed entirely in blue. To Remo, he said, "Get whatever you wish. I will be outside."

"Sorry," Remo apologized once the old man had swept out the door. "He's been cranky ever since we lost our house."

The sour look that had trailed Chiun out the door faded to a lustful leer when she turned her attention back to Remo.

"Oh, that's terrible," she said with lascivious sympathy. "You can stay with me if you want. We can put your friend in a home. One with really strong locks. There's just the one bed at my place, but we'll muddle through somehow."

"Just the car will be fine," he assured her.

"Oh," she said, disappointed. "I'll slip my apartment key on the ring just in case you change your mind." She fumbled in her purse.

Remo closed his eyes, forcing patience.

He'd had this effect on women for a long time, but lately he'd been able to control his natural pheromones by consuming shark meat. But his shark tank had perished in the blaze at Castle Sinanju. Another reason to fuel his desire to see Johnny Fungillo pay. Yet here he was, wasting his time in New Orleans.

"There's electronic maps built into the dashboard of all our cars," the woman said as she handed her house keys to Remo. "I can program it to find my apartment for you." Her smile bordered on obscene.

"Program it to locate the nearest hospital," called a squeaky disembodied voice from outside. "For I am going to be ill."

FONDI "KNEECAPS" BISOL was ready to pack it in. With or without orders from New York.

The Neighborhood Improvement Association—home of the Scubisci Family since old Don Pietro had emigrated to the U.S. in the 1920s—had been torched. Burned to the ground. According to Fondi's cousin Jack, the fire department had collected Solly Sweet in an ashtray.

There were bodies in Boston. More as recently as a couple of hours ago in Chicago if the grapevine was right. Yet here Fondi Bisol sat, a sitting duck waiting to get whacked.

"You think we should start thinking about leaving?" Fondi suggested to Angelo Tanaro.

They sat in the back room of the New Orleans Raffair office. The doors were all locked.

"Solly didn't give no order," Tanaro replied. He was toying with his submachine gun.

"Solly's a french fry," Kneecaps insisted. "Sitting here's a stupid waste of time."

Tanaro clicked the clip into his SMG. "You wanna tell Don Anselmo that?"

"He probably don't even know," Fondi argued. "He's on ice in Ogdenburg."

"Pauli Pavulla says he knows," Tanaro insisted. "Says Don Anselmo's been makin' calls to him ever since they torched the Neighborhood Improvement Association."

"Pavulla's a head case," Fondi said. "He saved a bowl of cereal a month one time 'cause he said he seen the Virgin Mary in the Cheerios. What's Don Anselmo calling a guy as low and crazy as Holy Pauli Pavulla?"

"No one else to call by the sounds of it," Tanaro explained, pulling his gun apart once more. "Solly's dead, and everybody else is spread all over the country. Ain't that many trustworthy guys left back in New York. I hear Holy Pauli's the Don's ears right now."

Fondi exhaled impatience. "I hope Don Anselmo knows that psycho's probably on his knees praying to his Rice Krispies right now."

As Fondi spoke, Tommy "Guns" Rovigo entered the small back room. He wore a troubled scowl.

"We got company," he hissed.

Grunting loudly, Fondi and Tanaro climbed rapidly to their feet. Tommy Guns' face grew angry, and he placed a thick finger to his lips. The other two men fell quiet just in time to hear the sound of a dying car engine outside. It was followed by silence.

Fondi Bisol felt his flaccid stomach muscles tighten.

If what his cousin had told him was true, Jimmy Pains had been fed through a paper shredder in Chicago. And Bear DiGrotti's body had been found without a head up in Boston. Now the killers were here.

"I hope Holy Pauli said a novena to his corn flakes for us," Fondi said, trying to suppress his frightened breathing.

Guns in hand, ever alert to noises outside, the three men crept through the shadows toward the closed door.

MARK POCKETED the rental's keys. Palms sweating, he slipped a hand under his leather jacket. With a tear of Velcro, he pulled his gun from his holster.

The weapon was an alien thing, heavy and awkward in his hand. If it was supposed to give him comfort, it wasn't working.

The building was dark. Not one light on inside.

Maybe no one was there. Maybe they'd heard what happened in Boston and New York and had opted to bag out.

Another thought came to him. Maybe General Smith's agents had already been here.

Mark thought of the man in Chicago. Fed through a shredder. In spite of his too warm clothing, he shuddered.

Willing himself calm, Mark kept his arm tucked in close to his body, his gun near his hip. With cautious, silent steps, he approached the dark Raffair building.

FROM THE AIRPORT, Remo and Chiun took the interstate to Veterans Memorial Highway. The New Orleans Raffair office was west of City Park.

The Master of Sinanju was quiet again, yet this time Remo didn't press it. Between their house and Remo's future, they both had enough on their minds.

Remo hated to admit it, but losing his home wasn't so big a thing when he weighed it against the other things of value in his life. And the one thing he treasured more than all others was sitting in a simple brocade robe to his right.

"Tell you what, Little Father," Remo said abruptly. "Why don't you check the radio for a country station?" For his adopted father's sake, he forced cheer in his voice.

Chiun's reply surprised him.

"Alas, I fear that pleasure is gone forever."

The words were said with such sad importance that Remo pulled his eyes off the road. In profile, the Master of Sinanju's jaw was firmly set against all the many injustices that could be inflicted by a cruel world.

"Why?" Remo asked.

"Because I do not wish to revel in my misery," Chiun said simply. "I will always associate that sad, wonderful music with a most painful time. The wound of my loss will never heal as long as I listen to it. Therefore, I will no more."

And in his words was the pain of loss. Remo's heart went out to him.

"We're in New Orleans. How about jazz?" he suggested.

The Master of Sinanju's entire face puckered.

"Cats in a sack make more agreeable noises."

"Can't disagree there," Remo nodded. His jaw clenched.

Beside him, the Master of Sinanju appeared to be a figure of ancient tragedy. Tiny hands of skeletal flesh rested in the lap of his kimono. Hazel eyes of bitter longing focused on some unseen distant point, far beyond the road on which they traveled.

There was so little in this world that the Master of Sinanju truly liked. In one fell swoop, two of those joys had been stolen from the old Korean.

Angry now, Remo gripped the steering wheel more tightly.

Although Remo had a great desire to be the one to make the arsonists pay, he decided in that moment that the pleasure would go to his teacher. He pressed harder on the gas, hoping to hurry their trip along.

MARK TRIED the front door. Locked.

An alley ran to the right of the two-story building. He took it, slipping into shadows.

A few plastic garbage bags were thrown near a dented trash can. Dogs had torn open the bags, scattering the contents around the alley.

Mark was having a hard time catching his breath. His temples and cheeks were hot with fear.

When he reached the end of the alley, he brought the gun shoulder high. His back against the wall, he leaned around the corner, peeking in at the rear of the Raffair office.

No one around.

The old brick building sagged at the second story. Bricks from the crumbling ledge lay all around the ground.

Beneath his jacket and sweatshirt, Mark's T-shirt was soaked with perspiration. He shivered as he leaned against the wall.

Insects fluttered and swooped crazily around a suspended light that shone down on the battered rear door.

Pushing away from the wall, Mark walked toward the light. After only a few steps, he froze.

A hushed voice. Somewhere nearby.

He strained to listen. Silence.

Had he imagined it?

Mark listened a few seconds more. Nothing.

His wrist ached from clenching the gun too tightly. He loosened his grip, flexing his fingers even as he started walking stealthily once more.

Before him, the door loomed large and ominous.

REMO AND CHIUN PARKED out in front of the New Orleans Raffair office. Only a few scattered cars lined the street this late at night.

"Front or back?" Remo asked as they got out of the car.

"Rear doors are for philandering husbands and collectors of garbage," Chiun pronounced.

Twirling, he marched across the road.

"They're also for people who are sick of being shot at," Remo pointed out as he followed the old man to the front of the building.

At the door, Chiun cocked an ear. "Two," he determined.

As he made a move for the handle, Remo touched his kimono sleeve. *"Three,"* he corrected.

Chiun refocused his senses. He quickly nodded sharp agreement.

"I'll count to three," Remo said. "One—"

The old Korean sent a wood-shattering kick into the center of the door. It shrieked off its frame, screaming into the darkened interior of the New Orleans Raffair office.

"I was gonna go to three," Remo said, disappointed.

"I assumed it would take all night for you to count that high, and I am not a young man," the Master of Sinanju said.

Chiun swept inside after the door, leaving Remo alone on the sidewalk.

"Old crank," Remo muttered as the first sounds of cracking bone emanated from inside.

Face clearly annoyed, he disappeared through the open door after his teacher.

NEARLY SEVEN HUNDRED MILES away, Mark Howard reholstered his gun and wrapped both hands around the rusted doorknob at the back of the Miami Raffair building.

When he pulled, the door popped open.

He was reaching for his gun once more when he thought he saw a flash of movement from inside. He was shocked when a fat hand shot out of the darkness. The hand grabbed him by the wrist, yanking him forward. As he fell to the dirty floor, he felt a blinding pain in the back of his head. Then he felt nothing at all.

Behind him, the alley door slammed shut with the finality of a coffin lid.

**29**

Harold Smith was studying three-month-old East African flight records when his secretary buzzed him.

"Yes, Mrs. Mikulka," he said over the intercom even as he continued working.

"I'm sorry to disturb you, Dr. Smith, but Dr. Edgerton just called. That patient you were interested in is awake now. The doctor said you wanted to be told the minute he came to."

For a moment, Smith didn't know what she was even talking about. It struck him all at once.

"Please tell Dr. Edgerton to keep everyone out of that room. I will be down at once."

He had given the same order earlier in the day. Even so, as he feared, the doctor was still in the room when Smith arrived a minute later. Two Folcroft nurses were waiting dutifully in the hallway outside.

The patient was strapped to his bed. Smith had told the nursing staff that his injuries were self-inflicted and that he might do more harm to himself if restraints were not used.

The doctor stood above the man who had tried to run over Remo on Mott Street. He had removed the dressing and was examining the stitches on his patient's forehead.

"Thank you, Doctor," Smith said crisply as he entered the room. "I would like to see the patient in private now."

"Oh, Dr. Smith," the physician said, looking up. "Your patient's doing fine. As you can see, he's awake. A little groggy, but that's to be expected after a fall like this."

The man on the bed seemed disoriented. Dark eyes darted back and forth fearfully as he tried to understand where he was. He muttered a soft string of words. Smith was surprised they were not in English.

"He's been talking ever since he woke up," Dr. Edgerton said. There was a concerned look on his flabby face.

Smith's eyes darted to the middle-aged doctor. "Do you know what he's saying?" he asked, his voice perfectly level.

"Me?" the doctor said. "No. Took French, not whatever he's speaking. Oh, and some Latin, obviously," he added with a chuckle. "Dr. Smith, I don't think you have to worry about letting staff in here. I know what you said, but I doubt he's contagious. Just a bad bump on the head from that fall you said he took. That's all, as far as I can tell."

Smith didn't even hear the last of what the doctor was saying. He was just relieved that the man in bed didn't speak French. Had he, he would have just cost a Folcroft doctor his life.

"Thank you, Dr. Edgerton," Smith said authoritatively. "That will be all."

The doctor hid his agitation at the Folcroft director's tone. Draping his stethoscope around his neck, he left the room. Smith closed the door behind him and immediately dragged a chair over close to the bed.

The patient's eyes rolled in Smith's direction as the older man sat down. He continued to mumble in soft, rolling tones. Smith had to tip an ear to his mouth in order to make out what he was saying.

It was clear now what language he was speaking. Yet other than a few words here and there, it was one Smith did not understand.

"Who sent you?" Smith asked, hoping the patient understood English.

But the injured man continued to mutter in his foreign tongue. His hands clasped and unclasped weakly below his wrist straps.

Lips pursing unhappily, Smith stood. He would have to wait for Remo and Chiun to return. The Master of Sinanju would be able to translate.

He was heading for the door, ready to give the on-duty staff strict orders not to enter this room under any circumstances, when he heard a new word from behind him.

This was said louder than the rest, and was uttered with naked fear.

Hearing the word, Smith turned slowly back.

What little color he possessed drained from his gray face like sand from an hourglass.

The man was pulling at his wrist straps, still mumbling the same word over and over. Each time he said it, he seemed to grow more afraid.

Shaken, Smith quickly exited the room. He found a copy of Westchester County's *Journal News* at a nursing station beyond the locked doors of the security wing. On the front page was a story he had read that morning before coming to work. Ignoring the glances of curious staff, he returned to the empty security corridor. The man was still tugging at his wrist straps when Smith reentered the room.

"Is this what you are referring to?" he demanded. He held a front-page photograph up to the patient's nose.

When the man saw the picture, his eyes grew wide. He began spouting a stream of terrified words, none of which—beyond the one he'd noted earlier—Smith recognized. Not that it mattered. The CURE director now understood exactly what the man feared. As well as who was behind the unsuccessful attacks against Remo.

As the man cowered from the newspaper, Smith flipped it around, examining the black-and-white picture.

It was something that had been of great interest both in Westchester County and nationally for more than a year now.

The above-the-fold picture showed a house with a high fence. Superimposed over it in one corner was a large photo of a man and woman. They had been moving into the home for what seemed like forever. In just two more days, it would become official.

Smith tucked the paper sharply under his arm. As the patient continued to babble the chillingly familiar woman's name, the CURE director walked briskly from the room.

REMO HAD TO SKIP to one side to avoid slipping on the brains that were spread like a gray oatmeal paste on the floor of the New Orleans Raffair office.

The Master of Sinanju's hands were slapped firmly on either side of Tommy Rovigo's head. The pressure he'd exerted had forced the man's brain up through his balding pate like a spitwad through a straw.

With fussing fingers, he tossed the gangster away. Tommy Guns thudded to the floor, an angry red cavity where his gray matter had been.

"Call your shots, Little Father," Remo said, irritated. He danced across a cerebellum minefield, loafers searching out a clean spot.

Chiun wasn't listening. He was moving away from Remo, sweeping like a kimono-clad typhoon toward Fondi Bisol.

"Don't shred me!" Fondi shrieked in terror. He flung his gun away and threw up his hands.

As Fondi cowered in fear, Remo felt another gun zero in on his back.

"Oh, great," he groused. "A shoeful of brains,

and now we're gonna get shot at again. Told you we should've come in the back," he called after Chiun.

"If you are just going to stand there and complain, you may wait in the car," the tiny Asian retorted.

Remo opened his mouth to reply, but whatever he was going to say was lost in an explosion of gunpowder.

Twirling on one heel, he dodged the bullet that had just been fired at his back. In a heartbeat, he was face-to-face with a very startled Angelo Tanaro.

"I mean, it's not like you get treated any better when you come in the front. Am I right?" Remo demanded.

Tanaro seemed stunned that the bullet hadn't found its mark. This time, when he aimed at Remo, he held the trigger down.

Remo danced around the hail of lead. Pockmarks erupted in the wall behind him.

"See?" Remo insisted. "It ain't all champagne and peeled grapes with the front. We're always getting shot at. But does he ever listen to me? No."

Behind him, he heard Chiun's gangster scream. Before him, Tanaro was trying to track him with his gun.

He fired left; Remo moved right. He fired right; Remo twirled left. He fired right again; Remo vanished.

"Missed me," a voice said very close to Angelo Tanaro's ear.

When he turned, he found he was looking into the coldest eyes he'd ever seen.

"Say good-night, Guido," Remo said.

Pivoting on the ball of one foot, he sent a pointed toe into Angelo's throat. There was a pinch of pain at the mobster's Adam's apple. It was followed by the most horrible sucking sound Angelo had ever heard.

When Remo's foot swung away, it was trailed by Angelo Tanaro's esophagus. Ghastly and elongated, it splattered against the office wall like a slippery red snake.

The gangster fell to his knees, clutching the dime-size hole in his throat. Remo finished him off with a pulverizing heel to the forehead.

"There," Remo announced, spinning to the Master of Sinanju. "No mess to slip on. Nice and neat."

"Stop your childish prattling," Chiun insisted from across the room. He sounded distracted.

When Remo saw what his teacher was up to, he rolled his eyes. "Oh, not again," he exhaled.

There was a large paper shredder in the corner of the office. The Master of Sinanju stood beside it, a puzzled expression on his face. As he studied the device, he stroked his thread of beard thoughtfully.

Kneeling on the floor at his feet was Fondi Bisol. The gangster's hands had been crushed flat and stuffed into the paper slot.

"God, please, no," Fondi wept.

"Can we speed this up, Little Father?" Remo complained, coming up beside the old man.

"I cannot find the On switch," Chiun frowned.

"It's broke," Fondi blubbered. Tears rolled down his dark cheeks.

"You stay out of this," Remo warned. "Chiun, let's go."

A deeply displeased expression took root on the Master of Sinanju's wrinkled face. His scowling eyes darted to the four corners of the room. They lingered for a moment on the idle coffeemaker before he shook his aged head.

"Pah!" the old Korean snapped.

His hands became vengeful blurs. Daggerlike nails hummed through muscle and bone. A final scream from Fondi Bisol died to a croak in his throat.

When Chiun stepped away from the body a moment later, Fondi lay in tattered strips on the floor. His severed arms hung slack from the mouth of the paper shredder.

"And the fates conspire to rob yet another spark of pleasure from a kindly old man's life," Chiun said, glowering at the remains.

Remo nodded agreement. "Let's get going," he said. "We've still got miles to go before we sleep."

Chiun didn't argue. Leaving the bodies where they lay, the two men slipped from the office and out into the mild New Orleans night.

**30**

"When did they hit New Orleans?"

"Coupla hours ago, Don Anselmo. Took out everybody. It was a big mess, what I hear."

Anselmo Scubisci couldn't even remember who was in New Orleans. He thought maybe Tommy Guns was there.

Not that it mattered. Whoever was there was dead. Four offices had been hit so far, all around the country. There were only three left.

In more optimistic times, Don Scubisci would have considered the remaining Raffair offices to be three more chances to stop the enemies who were out to destroy him. But hope had fled when he heard what happened in Chicago.

According to his mother, the men who were doing all this were coming after him. For now, his greatest hope was that they'd continue jumping from state to state. The longer they spent going after the individual Raffair offices, the more time they gave him.

"I talked to Skins Moletti just like youse asked, Don Anselmo, sir," said the deeply reverent voice on the phone.

Holy Pauli Pavulla still sounded awed to be speaking personally to the legendary Manhattan Don.

The first phone call the day before had stunned him. Pauli had been pretty much shunned by everyone else in the Scubisci Family ever since the Miracle of the Cheerios. He thought they'd only come around once he heard back from the Vatican. But then, *whammo!* From out of the blue, a call from Don Anselmo Scubisci himself.

Such an important event was this in Pauli Pavulla's life that the letters and photographs he'd sent off to St. Peter's months ago were forgotten. After all, the Pope was all well and good, but Don Scubisci was the *capo* of them all. Pauli might be called crazy as much as he was holy, but even he knew which ring to kiss first.

"You tell Skins to get moving faster," the Don ordered. The more nervous he got, the more he rasped. "The way they're moving, there's not much time left."

"Sure thing, Don Anselmo. He says he can be ready for eleven tomorrow morning."

"*Six,*" Don Anselmo insisted.

"Uh, Skins says there's a lot to do," Holy Pauli said.

"Tell him to get it done!" Don Scubisci snapped. His angry words echoed through the dark prison. Somewhere distant, a sleepy voice yelled for quiet.

Don Scubisci huddled farther into the phone. He

had bribed a guard for these phone privileges. Of all times, he didn't want to have them revoked now.

"What did he think all that money was for?" Anselmo whispered sharply. "For *this*. Now you tell him to get it done, or I swear on my mother's eyes it'll be the last thing he doesn't do."

Holy Pauli gulped. "I'll let him know, Don Anselmo," he vowed.

"And you don't stop off at church first, Pauli," Scubisci warned. "You call Skins as soon as you hang up from me. Six o'clock sharp. I don't care how it gets done. You screw up on this, you join Skins, *capisce?*"

"Yes, sir, Don Anselmo, sir," Pauli promised. "But don't worry so much. Ain't the Gabinetto brothers down in Miami?"

Don Scubisci thought of the four hulking Gabinettos. They were throwbacks to some early stage of man. At any other time, Don Anselmo Scubisci wouldn't have questioned the outcome of a contest involving the Gabinettos. Now he only hoped they lasted long enough to buy him the time he needed.

"I'll call back in an hour," he said, his voice flat.

"Don Anselmo?" Holy Pauli asked before the Mafia leader could hang up.

"What?"

"Youse want I should say a prayer for you, Don Anselmo?" Holy Pauli offered hopefully.

Anselmo Scubisci pictured Pauli Pavulla kneeling at his kitchen table, a dozen flickering votive candles arranged around a bowl of curdled milk and Cap'n Crunch. Eyes already dead, he hung up the phone.

**31**

General Rolando Rodriguez of the Movimiento de Izquierda Revolucionaria had parked his great People's Combat Wagon in front of the darkened Raffair office. The PCW was an '88 Ford station wagon he'd borrowed from his brother-in-law, Alberto, a Puerto Rican exile living here in Miami.

His nervous sweat fogged the car's windows. He was forced to clean away the dew periodically with a grimy T-shirt he'd found on the floor in the back.

After the disaster at MIR headquarters back in San Juan earlier in the week, Rodriguez had been bumped from corporal to general. It was a battlefield promotion he was afraid he'd never live to enjoy. After his multiple failures to eliminate the man who had decimated MIR's ranks, he had but one chance left to succeed. Otherwise, *she* would have her revenge against Rodriguez himself. The general suspected he'd only lasted this long because she was distracted by other matters these past few days.

Their numbers were far fewer now. The men from the first attacks in New York and Boston were dead. The later assault near Raffair headquarters on Mott

Street had resulted in the first MIA soldier in the history of the revolutionary organization. After that soldier was gone, there weren't many left. Which was why the general himself had been forced to lead the last of his troops on this final campaign.

Rodriguez checked his watch. They should be in place by now. If the men he was after showed themselves here—and according to the information she had supplied, they would—the brave soldiers of MIR would be ready for them.

The window had fogged up again. Grabbing the torn Jennifer Lopez T-shirt, General Rodriguez wiped himself a squeaky tactical display field on the front windshield of Detroit's finest People's Combat Wagon.

"HE STILL THERE?" the gruff voice demanded.

"Yeah," said another from the shadows beside the office window. "He's wipin' off the window again."

Inside the Miami Raffair office, the three men were piled against the shadow-drenched wall.

Thanks to Holy Pauli, they'd already gotten the word out of New Orleans. With another three Scubisci soldiers dead, the Gabinetto brothers were taking no chances.

The Gabinettos were hulking brutes with broad shoulders and massive fists. Unlike their fellow *paisans,* there were no nicknames for the four sons of Francesca Gabinetto. A distinctive sobriquet for any of them would have been redundant. To say "Gabinetto" was to say it all.

Their dark, looming shapes were throwbacks to some primordial time in Earth's history. In fact, many who met them thought the Gabinettos looked as if they'd be more comfortable splashing around a Cretaceous swamp. Even their normal mode of communication, which involved a great deal of shouting and hand waving, seemed to be from another age.

This night, the shouts were silenced, the hand gestures stilled. This night, their primitive silhouettes moved with silent purpose within the confines of the warm office.

They peered out the window at the dark shape that sat behind the wheel of the battered station wagon.

"You think he's waiting for this guy?" Emilio Gabinetto whispered. As he spoke, he nodded across the room.

A body lay on the floor near the open door to the rear storage room.

Mark Howard's hands had been tied clumsily behind his back. Dried blood darkened a spot on his light brown hair. His chest moved up and down rhythmically under his blue sweatshirt. He was unconscious, but alive.

"Don't matter," replied Fabio, the oldest of the Gabinetto brothers and therefore their leader. "I figured if that was the guy what's been whackin' everybody, we'd give him to Don Scubisci for a parole present. Now there's two of 'em, it's too complicated. We'll just kill 'em both.''

"Shh!" hissed Jennio Gabinetto. He was still peering out through the miniblinds. "He's almost there."

The other two behemoths peeked outside.

A huge figure was sneaking up on the parked station wagon from behind. They watched in satisfaction as Mario, their youngest brother, crept up to the driver's door.

"We whack him, den dis guy, and maybe we can finally get outta here," Fabio grumbled. He jerked his head toward the sleeping man across the room.

Outside, their brother had reached the car door. A hand as big as a small snow shovel reached for the handle. With a wrench, he tore the door open, swinging up the gun he held in his other massive hand.

Through the picture window, the three waiting Gabinettos heard a muffled pop. Their brother was still standing at the car's open door as Fabio turned to the others.

"Okay, one of youse guys aerate him," he said, pointing to Mark Howard. "I'll get on the phone wit Holy Pauli and tell him it's done."

Fabio hadn't taken a single step toward the telephone when he heard a stunned gasp from one of his brothers. He twisted back to the window just in time to see the big shadow that had obscured the station wagon tumble over backward.

"Dey popped Mario!" Jennio Gabinetto said, shocked.

As he spoke, a figure emerged from the car. The man had pulled on a ski mask. As he stepped over the lifeless body of the youngest Gabinetto, they could see the rifle in the masked man's hands.

"Dammit!" Fabio growled. "Ma's gonna kill me."

The armed man was heading for the front of the office. Fabio was about to order his brothers to shoot through the window when he noticed another figure slip from the shadows behind the car. This one was followed by four—no, *five* more. All carried rifles braced against their chests. Each man wore a ski mask and jungle camouflage.

"I taut dese guys din't use guns," Emilio Gabinetto hissed even as he pulled his own weapon from his holster.

Fabio and Jennio already had guns in hand.

"Shut up," Fabio whispered. He was staring at the door. He'd lost sight of the lead commandos seconds before.

When the shooting began an instant later, the suddenness startled the three crouching men.

Bullets chewed the wood around the doorknob. Even as the hot lead screamed into the office, a booted foot kicked the door open. A masked commando rolled into the room, rifle up and searching for targets.

Fabio laid him out with a single shot to the forehead. The dead man was falling to his knees as the next wave of soldiers leaped through the open door.

The heavily armed men dove behind desks and chairs, all the while shooting at the Gabinettos. Returning fire, Fabio and his brothers took cover behind a row of filing cabinets.

More shooting echoed from the rear storeroom. Fabio heard the sound of another door being kicked in.

"Dere's more coming in the back!" he yelled.

As he fired at the shadowy figures, Fabio suddenly thought they might be coming to collect the guy he and his brothers had knocked out. One thing was sure; if Fabio Gabinetto was going down, he'd make this was a hollow victory.

He swung his gun toward the back of the office, ready to plant a few rounds into the unconscious man.

His eyes went wide.

The guy was gone. The open storeroom door was only a few feet from where they'd dumped him.

"Dammit!" Fabio growled. He smacked Jennio in the side of the head with his gun butt. "I told you we shoulda whacked that guy," he snarled.

As Jennio rubbed his head with his free hand, Fabio turned his attention back to their attackers. With an angry scowl, he resumed firing at the mysterious masked men.

MARK HOWARD HAD COME around more than an hour earlier. Feigning unconsciousness, he'd watched the activity in the office through slivered eyes.

There didn't appear to be any way of escape. Though his bonds were loose, he couldn't very well wriggle out of them in full view of his captors. He'd lain quietly on the floor, his body cold from his own sweat, with no hope of survival.

His shocking salvation came when the door to the office was kicked open amid a barrage of bullets.

The new arrivals quickly got into a gunfight with the men who'd grabbed him while he was skulking around the rear door of the Miami Raffair office. Mark seized his chance. Hands still tied behind his back, he had crawled desperately on toes and knees into the back room.

In seconds, Mark slithered out of his bonds and was upright, running for the rear exit. He had almost reached it when fresh gunfire erupted through it. As bullets pierced the steel door, Mark dove through an open doorway to his left. He landed roughly on the floor of a small office.

Mark was scampering to his feet just as the first gun muzzle appeared around the door frame. It moved in tentatively, like the sniffing nose of a curious animal.

He was cornered. The only door was the one he'd just come through. There were no windows. As his eyes darted around the room, Mark saw a familiar shape lying on a chair.

His heart knotted at the sight of his gun. He

pounced on the weapon, tearing at the holster's Velcro straps.

His stalker in the hallway heard the sound. The man twisted around the corner just as Mark lifted his gun. With a look a fierce triumph, Mark squeezed the trigger.

It didn't budge.

He suddenly remembered he'd left on the safety. Problem was, it was so long since he'd bought the damn thing, he didn't remember where the safety switch was.

And as he twisted and shook the weapon in helpless frustration, the masked man who had just entered the small room raised his own gun, ready to fire.

Mark's eyes grew wide. He felt his breath catch as the rifle was aimed at his chest. The world slowed to a crawl, then stopped completely. Distorted sounds came in amplified waves to his suddenly acute ears.

Shouting from out front. Fresh shock above the roar of gunfire. Nearer, the rustle of fabric as the gunman raised his elbow. Hand shifting in slow motion, finger tensing on the rifle's trigger. To the right, a deafening explosion as the wall to the small office suddenly burst in.

For Mark, the world tripped back to normal time.

In a hail of plaster dust, the upended body of Emilio Gabinetto soared through the wall. Before the gunman could fire, the flying Gabinetto had slammed into him with the force of a speeding freight train.

Scooping up the masked man bodily, Emilio continued on. The two men were crushed into a pile of indistinguishable arms and legs against the cinderblock wall of the building. With a sigh of collapsed lungs, the big bundle of knotted flesh dropped to the floor.

Mark stared at them in shock.

Through the hole in the wall, he could hear the sounds of confused shouting. Men yelled in English and Spanish.

A persistent noise like that of snapping kindling rose to his ears. Somehow, Mark instinctively knew he was listening to the sound of snapping bones.

In spite of the fear he felt, Mark peeked through the jagged opening Emilio Gabinetto had formed.

He saw a flash of something small and red flying toward a cowering Jennio Gabinetto. Before the gangster could shoot, the red dervish was upon him.

The instant the blur resolved into the shape of a tiny, kimono-clad man, Jennio became airborne. Mark's eyes hadn't yet understood what they'd just seen when the warning burst like a solar flare in his brain.

He threw himself to his belly an instant before Jennio Gabinetto soared through the hole his brother had formed.

The body pounded against the wall and bounced off, collapsing lifeless on the prone form of Mark Howard.

Mark felt the air rush out of him as the mound of dead flesh settled on his back. He struggled to pull air back in his lungs. He was trying to wiggle out from under the huge body when he heard an angry hiss of Spanish nearby.

Twisting his head, Mark saw that another commando had entered the room from the back door. Even as the firefight was dying in the front office, the man strode toward the CIA analyst.

Mark had dropped his gun in the fall. He made a frantic grab for it even as he squirmed under the body.

His fingertips had barely brushed the gun butt when the hard crush of a boot heel stomped on his wrist. He felt the sharp sting of snapping bone.

The commando swung his rifle barrel at Mark's exposed head. And in that instant before finger brushed trigger, Mark heard a shocked gasp.

"Remo, cover your eyes!" cried a squeaky voice.

From his ankle-view of the world, Mark saw a pair of plain black sandals materialize before his eyes. There was a loud crack of shattering bone, and the body of the commando collapsed in a heap inches from Mark's nose.

"What's wrong?" asked a new voice. A pair of leather loafers appeared next to the sandals. "Who's that?"

"Do not look!" implored the first. "Whatever it is, it is writhing like a Pyongyang harlot beneath that behemoth."

"Top guy's dead, Little Father."

"Worse still. Stop that this instant," the first man clapped disapprovingly. "My young son does not need to see such depravity."

"By the looks of it, this guy wasn't very well liked by anyone around here."

A pair of hands dropped beside the loafers. A face at once both cruel and curious peered at Mark Howard.

"Hiya," Remo Williams said.

Mark felt a sudden blessed lightness as the body of Jennio Gabinetto was lifted off of him.

"Okay, what's your story?" Remo asked as he tossed the three-hundred-pound corpse lightly over his shoulder. His eyes strayed to the fresh rope burns on Mark's wrists.

The CIA analyst climbed to his feet, cradling his injured arm. "CIA," he explained, panting.

"Oh," Remo nodded, the light of understanding dawning. "The Keystone Kops of the spy world. Word of advice for the future, Nick Danger? Really bad form to get smothered under a big fat guy while you're doing that dippy spy stuff you people do." And with that, he turned from Mark. "This way," he said to Chiun, pointing out into the large back room.

Chiun was standing beyond Remo. His wrinkled face offered Mark a look of disapproval. When Remo headed for the door of the small office, the Master of Sinanju spun after him, kimono hems swirling around his bony ankles.

Mark knew without a doubt that these were

Smith's men. And loud in his ears, the feeling was screaming that this was both a moment of great import and dire consequence.

By the sound of it, the two men had cleared a path to the front door. He could duck through the hole in the wall and escape into the night, without further risk to his own life. But his heightened instinct told him that there was something more to be learned here.

Scooping up his gun in his good hand, he hustled out into the big room after them.

Remo and Chiun were walking over to the far corner. The way they moved, it was as if theirs were a single mind, connected by a string of unspoken thought.

As they strode past the door leading into the front office, a huge figure suddenly lunged in at them like a wounded bison. Mark fell back into the wall, startled.

Fabio Gabinetto had been shot in one shoulder, yet he still lumbered forward. His arms were stretched out wide, ready to ensnare Remo in a crushing bear hug.

Remo didn't even seem to notice. At the moment when Fabio's arms should have encircled his chest, he simply ducked out of the way. Fabio's forward momentum couldn't be slowed. As he thundered impotently past, Remo snagged him by the scruff of the neck. His legs continued pumping as he dangled in midair from Remo's outstretched arm.

"There," Remo pronounced.

The rest rooms stood side by side in the corner of the room. Remo aimed a finger at the closed ladies' room door.

A few yards back, Mark was amazed to see that there was no sign of strain on Remo's face as he held the still cantering Fabio a foot off the floor.

"Put that down," Chiun clucked.

"Huh?" Remo asked. He looked over at Fabio as if just realizing he was there. "Oh."

Whipping the gangster around, he planted his head neck deep in the nearby wall. The body went slack, toes barely brushing the dirty floor.

Chiun was already at the restroom door. He opened it with a simple hand slap.

A man was hiding inside the small room. When he saw the two men framed in the doorway, his eyes grew wide inside his ski mask. Something flashed in his hands.

Behind Remo and Chiun, Mark Howard caught the glimpse of movement. "Gun!" he yelled in warning.

As soon as he shouted, he threw himself at the floor, aiming his own weapon between the two men. Fresh pain from his broken wrist shot up his arm.

In the instant Mark winced, Chiun's hand snapped down. The CIA agent's eyes opened just in time to see the old man's fiercely sharp fingernails sail through the commando's gun barrel. Mark watched in astonishment as a section of rifle clanked on the tile floor. It was joined by two others. Sitting on the toilet in the single-stall room, the masked man suddenly found his hands grasping air.

"Thanks for the warning," Remo said dryly to Mark. "And if you wanna make a bang noise when you point that thing at people, you might want to take the safety off."

Turning back to the commando, he pulled off the man's black mask. The terrified face of General Rolando Rodriguez cringed from his darting hands.

"Okay, I've had it up to here with you nimrods trying to kill me six ways to Sunday," Remo said with a scowl. "I want to know why you're after me and I wanna know now. Otherwise, you're going headfirst into that bowl, and I won't stop flushing until there's nothing left but a pair of really smelly Che Guevara boots."

Rodriguez wanted to lie. But he had seen the result of this man's work at MIR headquarters back in San Juan. Fresh fear of the thin young man and his terrifying Asian companion supplanted all other concerns.

"She made me come after ju," Rodriguez blurted. His soles were on the toilet seat and he hugged his knees, shrinking from Remo and Chiun. "After what ju did to MIR in Puerto Rico, ju became a threat to her ambition."

"These attacks had nothing to do with Raffair?" Remo asked, surprised he'd been wrong all along.

Rodriguez shook his head. "No," he insisted. "She just told us where ju would be. In Boston, we knew you would be coming soon, but at the places like this we were told to wait. She did not know when you would arrive, only that you would come.''

"Okay," Remo said. "Here's the twenty-thousand-dollar question—who's 'she'? The only one who knows about us is our boss, us and…" His voice trailed off. It struck him like a bolt out of the blue. "Oh," he said quietly.

He turned to the Master of Sinanju. There was a hint of a knowing look on the old man's otherwise inscrutable face.

"She's your—" Rodriguez began.

They were the only words he managed to get out before the hardened finger pierced his occipital lobe. All speech, thought and life ended at the same time for the revolutionary leader. When Remo pulled his finger free, General Rolando Rodriguez toppled sideways into the wall of the toilet stall.

Remo spun. His face was a dark thundercloud.

"Let's go," he said to the Master of Sinanju.

Behind them, Mark Howard had climbed back to his feet. He'd been listening to the commando's words with growing fascination, but when Remo and Chiun swept toward him, the CIA man backed nervously against the wall.

Chiun breezed past him without even acknowledging his existence. Remo stopped before the young man.

For a moment, Mark held his breath, unsure what his fate might be. When Remo raised a hand, he flinched.

Remo extended a cautionary finger. "Forget everything," he warned. "It beats me having to kill you."

That was it. The hand lowered and he was gone. Out into the main office. A minute later, Mark heard the sound of an engine turning over. The car faded into the night.

Only when the sound had died completely did he exhale. As he leaned against the wall, his shoulders sagged. He hugged his broken wrist as he tried to catch his breath.

He'd done it. He had faced down the fear of his own destiny and had survived.

Smith and his agents were irrelevant to his future—at least for now. Surprisingly, fate had brought him here to learn something else entirely. Something that went to the character of the man who had found him toiling in anonymity at the CIA.

MIR. The Puerto Rican separatist group. A huge controversy over a year ago. And here were the terrorists now, apparently sent after one of Smith's agents.

Mark knew the truth. And he also knew that no matter what he was asked to do by the President of the United States between now and Inauguration Day, he would not allow himself to be corrupted. Ever.

Still bracing his arm, he pushed away from the wall. His breathing was close to normal.

The authorities would be here soon. He'd better get his holster and get out before they arrived. Leaving the bodies of Fabio Gabinetto and Rolando Rodriguez, Mark C. Howard headed for the back of the tomb-silent Raffair office.

**32**

Remo called Smith from the plane.

"You were right, Smitty," he announced. "Those Puerto Rican terrorists are the ones who've been trying to kill me all along."

"I know," the CURE director replied. "The man you brought back here regained consciousness a few hours ago. I tried to call you during your flight from New Orleans to Miami, but the plane's system was down."

"The navigator probably shorted it out when he accidentally spilled his rum and Coke," Remo said dryly. "So did he tell you who's behind it?"

"Yes," Smith replied, thin distaste in his voice.

"Oh." Remo sounded disappointed. He had wanted to be the one to tell the older man. "We're giving a pass to the other Raffair offices," he said. "Chiun and I are flying back to New York. We'll hit her first and then put this whole goose chase to bed."

Smith's reply surprised him. "No," he said. "No matter what the motivation was to involve us, Raffair is still a danger. I have had no luck tracing Anselmo Scubisci's benefactor. Once you are finished here, I want you to go to the federal penitentiary in Missouri and find out from him who is behind this.''

Remo sighed. ''Okay.''

''And, Remo,'' Smith warned. ''Do not kill her.'' He wanted to make his orders clear, so he did not substitute a euphemism for the distasteful word.

''Kind of figured that,'' Remo replied. ''But I'm looking forward to this inauguration like I've never looked forward to one before, and if I miss it because of jet lag, I'm gonna insist that Chiun start listening to country music again. And since we're house guests of yours for the foreseeable future, you'll have half the staff of that nuthouse up on the roof banging down loose shingles.''

**33**

The heavy blue quilt was pulled up to her neck. Lying alone in her big comfortable bed in New York's Westchester County, she was trying desperately to banish the vexing thoughts that had plagued her this past week.

Though dawn was still a few hours away, the soft Spanish voice still droned incessantly in the background. Just as it had for the past twelve months. Even at night she'd been allowing the soft words to penetrate her brain. But though the faceless man had recited ceaselessly—day after day, week after week—she just wasn't getting it.

"*¿Esta Susana en casa? Si, esta con una amiga. Donde esta en la sala. No, en la cocina.*"

The metallic man's voice stopped short. There was a soft whir and a click, followed by silence.

From her bed, she snaked out a hand. Fumbling around the nightstand, she popped the front on the portable tape player. She pulled out the ninety-minute cassette. Printed on its side was the phrase: "Learn Spanish just like the diplomats do! It's easy, fun and *fast!*"

She flipped the tape and dropped it back in the machine. When she pressed the Play button, the man continued to recite the same dialogues she'd been listening to for months.

For some reason, the words just weren't sticking. There was no reason why she shouldn't be picking it up easier. After all, she was the most brilliant woman ever to set shoe to soil. *Time, Newsweek,* Eleanor Clift and all the major networks had told her so for the past eight years.

But in spite of her penetrating intellect, so far the only words she'd learned were *hola* and *si.* And though no one in the Movimiento de Izquierda Revolucionaria dared tell her, she still mispronounced both of those.

"Stupid language," she muttered under her sleep mask. "My first edict will be to make that filthy little island an English-only zone."

When a voice answered her from out of the night, she was stunned that it did not come from her tape player.

"Does that include the name Puerto Rico, too? 'Cause the only ones who really stand to benefit from that are the mapmakers."

When she whipped off her mask, she winced. The bedroom lights had been turned on.

Two men stood near the door. She recognized them at once. *"You,"* the First Lady of the United States screeched.

Remo's face was hard. "And everyone knows that the mapmakers are still sitting on the sacks of gold they made after Russia collapsed," he concluded.

Beside him, the Master of Sinanju offered a polite bow. "Madam," the old Asian said.

The First Lady didn't return the courtesy. In a flash, she shot up out of bed, planting her bare feet firmly on the ornate Oriental rug that had been stolen from the White House Map Room. With an ungodly howl, she ripped the nightstand tape player up and flung it at Remo's head.

He plucked it from the air, carefully pressing the Stop button before placing it to the floor.

She threw a lamp at the Master of Sinanju. The old man ducked to one side, and the lamp shattered against the wall.

Panting, she wheeled on them, all bobbing pageboy hair and flashing teeth.

"I knew it was you," the First Lady hissed. "I only met you those couple of times, but as soon as that spic Rodriguez mentioned those freaky wrists of yours, I *knew* it."

Remo looked down at his own wrists. They didn't seem so bad to him. "Yeah, well, if I had thighs like yours, lady, I wouldn't be commenting on anyone else's shortcomings," he said in an injured tone.

The First Lady didn't hear. She was drawing back her head to scream. When she opened her mouth, revealing twin rows of sharp teeth, she looked like a carefully coiffed hound getting ready to bay at the moon.

"Don't bother," Remo interrupted before she'd

even sucked in enough air to fill her lungs. "The Secret Service has gone night-night for the time being."

The shriek died in her throat.

"What are you doing here?" she snarled. "Don't tell me those MIR morons blew it in Miami."

"Your soldiers have been vanquished by Sinanju, Your Majesty," Chiun replied.

"Sinny-what?" the First Lady demanded. She didn't wait for an answer. "Do you two know what you've done? You've delayed my ascension to the Puerto Rican throne. After the revolution, those greasy little wetbacks were gonna make me their queen. Now I'm gonna have to go out and find some more wrongly incarcerated revolutionaries for that worthless husband of mine to pardon within the next twenty-four hours."

Diving across the room, she grabbed for the phone on her dresser. A strong hand was already there, holding down the receiver. She looked up into Remo's hard face.

"Couldn't you just be content being a nuisance in regular America, and spare the protectorates?" he asked.

"Let me call!" she screamed.

As Remo held the phone, the First Lady pounded her furious balled fists against his chest. As she continued to punch him, he noticed a pin lying on her dresser. It was the same one with the weird parentheses-enclosing-a-circle design that all of his attackers had worn.

"What the hell is this, anyway?" Remo asked, unfazed by her attack. He picked up the pin.

Panting, the First Lady fell back.

"It is a symbol of female gender superiority," she spit. "I was sick of you men with your phallocentric designs for everything from flagpoles to obelisks. That's a symbol of sisterhood designed by a female."

Remo looked at the button again. For the first time, he realized what it was.

"It's a woman's private parts," he said.

When he showed the button to the Master of Sinanju, the old man's eyes took on an appalled cast. Cheeks flushing, he covered his face with a billowing kimono sleeve.

"Put that smutty thing away," the old man insisted.

"It's nothing to get too worked up over," Remo said. "By the looks of it, the model was a robot."

"It's conceptual," the First Lady snarled.

"Not if it looks like that, it ain't," he said. He tossed the pin back to the dresser. "Okay, Cruella de Vil, let's get this over with."

"I will not be silenced!" she screamed, recoiling from his outstretched hand. "Everyone knew the Senate wasn't big enough to hold me! I'll be back!"

"Before then, remind me to buy stock in an earplug company," Remo said as he pinched a nerve on her shoulder.

Mouth still twisted open, the First Lady went rigid, then limp. Remo grabbed her as she fell, dumping her into a Louis Tiffany chair that had been bought for the White House by Chester Arthur.

He brought his lips close to her ear.

"You're going to forget everything you know about CURE, Harold Smith and the two men you've been trying to kill this past week," Remo said. "You're going to forget all of this stuff forever, and you won't even be remotely interested in ever remembering. Do you understand?"

Her eyes closed, the First Lady nodded. She purred contentedly. It made her sound like a cat that had just eaten a particularly succulent rat.

Remo straightened. As he turned back to the Master of Sinanju, a thought suddenly occurred to him. He leaned back over the First Lady.

"And from now on, your role model for womanhood will be June Cleaver. You will cook, clean and bake cookies with a smile on your face and a song in your heart and you won't even be remotely interested in TV cameras, public life or inciting socialist rebellions. Oh, and you'll wear a frilly white apron wherever you go. Even in the shower."

When he stood back up, Remo wore a satisfied expression.

"America owes me big time," he announced.

Leaving the soon-to-be ex-First Lady snoring complacently in her stolen chair—happy visions of vacuum cleaners and bundt cakes dancing merrily in her head—the two Masters of Sinanju slipped silently from the bedroom.

**34**

In the predawn light of a small Missouri airport, a surplus Bell AH-1 Cobra helicopter hummed to life. The drooping rotor blades grew rigid, slicing air with violent purpose. Behind it, three more helicopters growled awake.

At the same time, from hangars draped in sheets of dying gloom, a stream of black vans rumbled forth, their occupants obscured by tinted windows.

On the runways, pilots in face-obscuring camouflage paint checked instruments with swift efficiency. When all was ready, the first chopper lifted into the sickly gray sky. A single streak of orange appeared over the eastern tree line.

The second helicopter lifted off, then the third and fourth. They regrouped above the black trees. Like angry hornets leaving a nest, the fully armed helicopters swooped down across the gray tarmac, briefly joining the convoy of vans before soaring back up over the distant trees.

Windows rattled in houses a mile distant as the helicopters tore away through the chilly air.

On the ground, the vans vanished down the road, drawing the last shadows of night in their wake.

And then all was silent.

DON ANSELMO SCUBISCI WAS burning the last of his Camorra correspondence in the toilet of his solitary-confinement cell when he heard the thunder. He checked his watch—6:00 a.m.

The first lonely booms grew in frequency and intensity until the very foundation of Ogdenburg Federal Penitentiary shook. The prison Klaxons blared to life.

And as the explosions grew closer and the prison erupted in the violence of panic, Don Anselmo Scubisci sat calmly on the edge of his bed. To await salvation.

AFTER LEAVING the First Lady's bedroom, Remo and Chiun had taken a direct flight to Missouri.

Remo knew something was wrong the instant he saw the slivers of black smoke rising above the pines at highway's edge. His concern only grew worse when he saw three dozen men in orange jumpsuits running like mad through the woods.

When they broke through the trees and saw the ravaged prison wall, Remo shook his head in angry disbelief.

Ogdenburg looked like Berlin after the war. The main walls were pulverized, collapsed into piles of rubble. The ruins of a downed helicopter sat like a squashed bug on the snow before the main entrance.

Sirens blared even as more men in orange slipped through the many holes in the walls.

It looked as if rockets and truck bombs had been used to pierce the walls. One of the black vans hadn't exploded. Remo squealed to a stop beside it.

Behind the wheel was a man dressed in civilian attire. A dozen gold-and-silver crosses hung around his neck. For some reason, the General Mills logo was tattooed on the backs of his hands. He had missed reaching his target after being shot in the chest from a guard tower.

Blood gurgled from between the man's whitening lips. Holy Pauli Pavulla was breathing his last.

"What the hell is this all about?" Remo demanded, already fearing what the answer would be.

Holy Pauli gasped. "Don Scubisci..." he panted. His eyes were closed. "Had to spring Don Scubisci...."

Remo's face grew dark. "Where is he?"

At this, Holy Pauli's lips curled up. "Gone," he breathed. "Saw him get on the chopper with my own eyes. I did good by my Don." His eyes sprang open. He was staring through the cracked windshield at something far distant. "Sure, I'll step into the light," Holy Pauli gulped, his breathing becoming even more ragged. "But you silly rabbit, Trix are for...oh, wait, those ain't ears, are they?"

With a final wheeze, he slumped over the steering wheel. It honked like a desolate foghorn.

"Dammit," Remo growled. "Thanks to her, we missed out on the action. We *never* miss out on the action. I'm telling you, Little Father, those two are a curse."

Chiun was cocking an attentive ear to the cold white sky. "Emperor Smith will not be pleased that the Roman lord eluded us, but he will be even less so if he learns that we have been filmed again," he intoned somberly.

Remo listened for what the Korean had heard.

Helicopters. A lot, by the sounds of it. No doubt the press had heard about the mass escape at Ogdenburg and were racing to the scene.

"Why can't my life ever be easy?" Remo groused.

They dove into the car. Remo had to throw two convicts out onto the road before he could put it in Reverse and hightail it back down the highway.

## 35

Mark Howard had endured the pain in his broken wrist for the whole flight back to Washington. He had the bone set at Arlington Orthopedic Hospital before returning home. When he finally trudged through the door of his apartment, it was Friday afternoon.

The digital answering machine on the stand inside the door registered one phone call. He ignored the steady beep of the machine while he pulled his gun out of his bag with his good hand. He stuffed the weapon and holster far back in his desk drawer. When he finally returned to the machine twenty minutes later, he was chewing on a ham sandwich.

Mark pressed the message button, turning the volume up loud. He walked into the living room, sinking into a chair as the message played.

"Hello, Mark?" asked the familiar hoarse voice. "You there? If you're there, pick up. No? Oh. This is your President speaking. No wait, scratch that. Got in trouble identifyin' myself on tape before. Anyway, I got an important offer I'd like to make you. You probably didn't know it, but I had you

checked out these past few months. You got a real
weird personality profile there, buddy. Loyal to your
friends, dismissive of your enemies. Like they don't
rate spit. Did you know they were thinkin' of firin'
you once 'cause they thought you were hidin' something from them? But you passed all the lie detectors
for national loyalty and that secret-keeping stuff, so
they decided to keep you on.

"Anyway, I got a proposition for you that I think
we should talk about in person. I got a car that'll
come and pick you up at ten tonight. You don't have
to do anything but get in. I'll tell you what's what
when you get here. Uh, I guess that's it. You still
not there? I really hate these goddamn machines.
Okay, see you tonight."

Two seconds more of dead air and the answering
machine beeped off. With a click, it reset itself to
0 messages.

In the living room, Mark's eyes were closed. He
still held his sandwich, but he hadn't taken a bite
since the message had started playing. He suddenly
wasn't very hungry.

Mark tossed the sandwich to the coffee table. In
doing so, he bumped his cast against the arm of his
chair. He winced at the pain.

Treating his broken arm very gingerly, he pulled
himself to his feet. He needed a shower. But he'd
have to cover his cast with something first.

Mark shuffled off to the kitchen. To dump the loaf
of Wonder bread out of its long plastic bag.

**36**

The black Cobra helicopter carried Don Anselmo Scubisci across the border into Canada. A private jet bought by Sol Sweet with Raffair money was waiting for him. Before the American authorities were aware of what had even happened, Don Scubisci was far over the Atlantic. In half a day, he was on the ground in Naples.

A black limo with darkened windows was there to meet him at the airport.

The estate of Don Hector Vincenzo was a well-guarded fortress nestled safely within gently sloping hills at the fringe of Naples where the edge of the old city met the azure waters of the Tyrrhenian Sea. The limousine kicked up plumes of dust in its wake as it drove past the naked winter vineyards to the big old house.

An armed guard met Don Scubisci's car at the end of the great round drive. The Manhattan Mafia leader was led through the cool, drafty house and out onto a glass-enclosed patio that overlooked dormant vineyards.

Don Vincenzo was sitting at a white wrought-iron

table. A glass of deep red wine sat at his elbow. Beside it was a cloth bag, knotted at the neck.

"You have had a busy day, Anselmo," Don Vincenzo said. He did not look at the younger man, did not offer a seat. As the Camorra leader stared out over his fields, Scubisci stood uncomfortably before him.

No men toiled among the vines. A cold sun shone down on the hills of Naples.

"I had nowhere else to go," Don Scubisci admitted.

"So you come straight to me? Lead them to me, hmm?" He finally turned to the younger Don. His watery old eyes were flat.

Don Scubisci pressed his hands together. "Please, Don Vincenzo," he begged, his voice a painful rasp. "My own people will not accept the wisdom of my decision to join with you. They will see it as an act of betrayal. I wasn't safe in prison. Some force unknown to me has destroyed all we built together. They would have come to me eventually. This I know. I had to flee from them and from my own people."

He was practically in tears.

"Would you serve me faithfully?" Don Vincenzo asked. He tipped his head as he looked up at the sweating man.

A spark of hope. Don Anselmo nodded desperately. "This I promise, Don Hector," he pleaded. "You have my word."

"You are disloyal to your own blood, and you

expect me to believe you will remain faithful to me?'' Don Vincenzo said, with doubtful amusement.

Hope burned away. ''I—I...'' The words would not come. *"Please,"* Scubisci wept finally.

''You are Mafia. La Cosa Nostra. I am Camorra. It is my blood, my soul. We were enemies before either of us was born, Anselmo. It is the way of things.'' Don Vincenzo waved a sad apology. ''Thanks to long-ago fate, your people thrived in America. And because of that, your Mafia Families ran the world. For a time. But your power wanes. In time it will be no more.'' He smiled his row of yellow-brown teeth. ''But Camorra will thrive after you are gone.''

Don Hector Vincenzo took a thoughtful sip of his wine.

''You were weak after your imprisonment, Anselmo,'' he said, putting the glass carefully to the table. ''I saw opportunity in that weakness. Raffair was not the simple moneymaking scheme I claimed. Nor was it your stepping-stone to domination of the American market. It was designed specifically to weaken the Mafia. If Raffair was successful for a time, I reaped the benefits. If Raffair failed publicly—and such public failure always involves the authorities, Anselmo—it would be a black eye for the Mafia. Either way I win. But, I am afraid, there is no way for you to do so. I am sorry for this.''

A subtle nod. Missed by Don Scubisci. The American Mafia leader was about to plead for his life once more when it was suddenly and abruptly ended.

The bullet hit Don Anselmo Scubisci in the back of the head. His forehead yawned open, and he sprawled lifeless to the cold patio.

As bits of flesh and brain were splattering to stone, the guard who had led the Manhattan Mafia leader through Don Vincenzo's home replaced his rifle on his shoulder.

Still seated, the Camorra leader picked up the cloth bag from the table. Old fingers tugged open the string at the neck. Taking the bag by the end, he shook it a few times over the body of Don Scubisci. A fat white pigeon dropped onto the back of the dead Mafia leader.

"See that they are buried together," he instructed.

"Yes, Don Hector."

Another guard appeared. The two men dragged the body off the patio. After they were gone, another came up the side steps, pulling a garden hose behind him. He began hosing the small specks of Don Anselmo Scubisci's brains off the windowpanes.

As the man worked, Don Vincenzo took a sip of wine. Sunlight sparkled off the glass.

It was time to start thinking about tomorrow.

**37**

"There was some men come lookin' for you," Johnny Fungillo's mother told him as he stepped through the back kitchen door of her Jersey City house.

Johnny's hand froze on the doorknob. "What men?" he asked, eyes darting over his shoulder. Beyond, his mother's Mercury sat in the cold garage.

"What do I know what men?" Mrs. Fungillo asked with a frown of her great jowls. *"Men."*

She didn't turn to her son. At the stove, she continued to use a big wooden spoon to stir the caldron of tomato sauce that bubbled on the back burner.

Johnny immediately regretted coming back for some clean clothes. He left the door into the garage open. Glancing back over his shoulder, he hustled over to his mother.

"These men," he asked. "Were they young, old, what?"

"What are you doing leaving the door open?" Mrs. Fungillo asked, unmindful of the anxious look on her son's face. "It's the middle of January." She tasted a spoonful of sauce.

*"Ma!"* he snapped, grabbing her by the biceps.

She recoiled. Her son had a murderous glint in his eye.

"Whatsa matter with you, Johnny?" she asked, drawing her orange-stained spoon to her ample bosom. "You in trouble again?" She saw for the first time the big circular bruise on his forehead. "Where'd you get that?"

He shook his head angrily. "The *men*," he demanded, squeezing harder.

"They come about an hour ago," Mrs. Fungillo said, wincing. She looked down with growing concern at her son's white-knuckled hands. His fingers bit into her big arms. "One was young and the other was real old. He was some kind of Chinaman. He was real nice. You know, polite."

"God," Johnny croaked, releasing her. Stunned eyes darted from his mother's sauce-splattered glasses to the cheap linoleum floor.

Mrs. Fungillo took a step back. Regaining her courage, she raised her stirring spoon like a weapon. "You and them slobs you hang around with could learn a thing or two about being polite from them Chinese," she warned him.

Johnny didn't hear. Before she'd even finished talking, he'd regained his senses.

He flew out the kitchen door, grabbing up his mother's car keys from the hook on the wall. He dove into her car, twisting the key violently in the ignition. The garage door split into a dozen neat panels as he plowed through it. The wood was flying into snowbanks on either side of the driveway as he slid out into the road.

He hadn't gotten as far as the stop sign three houses down when he heard something that froze his heart.

"Take your first left."

The familiar voice came from the back seat. He had heard it first in East Africa three months ago. Again on the plane in Boston earlier this week.

His frightened gaze strayed to the rearview mirror.

It was him. Along with the old man from the Boston Raffair office. Dead eyes stared through to Johnny's very soul. He was naked and alone on Judgment Day.

Johnny Books grabbed for the door handle. A long-nailed hand snagged him by the scruff of the neck, pulling him back into the driver's seat.

"*Please,*" Johnny cried.

"We're beyond that," Remo said coldly. "Drive."

There was nothing else he could do. Johnny did as he was told. By the time they reached the empty parking lot behind the abandoned Newark tenement, he had told them where they could find Mikey "Skunks" Falcone and the third man who'd helped burn Castle Sinanju to the ground.

"We can cut a deal," Johnny begged as Remo dragged him out of the front seat.

"You don't have anything we want," Remo said as he hefted the thug into the air.

"Save one thing," Chiun intoned gravely.

As Johnny wept in fear, Remo flipped him upside down. He held the big man by one ankle, dangling him at arm's length above the ground.

The Master of Sinanju bent low. Johnny held his breath as the same deadly nails that had decapitated Louis DiGrotti moved toward him.

Chiun's hand slipped past Johnny's frightened, upended face. He felt a tug at his hair. Not even very hard.

Johnny strained his eyes to see what the old man was doing. All he could see was the edge of the big purple bruise on his broad forehead.

Where Fungillo's hair brushed asphalt, Chiun twirled a single lock of greasy hair between two fingers. His fingertips rolled faster and faster until they became a barely visible blur.

A tiny curl of smoke rose into the air. Johnny caught a whiff as it rose past his nose. A look of upside-down horror appeared on his reddening face.

"*No!*" Johnny "Books" Fungillo screamed, just as his greasy hair burst into flame.

Johnny continued screaming as the fire climbed up his clothes. His jacket and trousers ignited rapidly. The sickly sweet smell of barbecued flesh filled the cold air.

For a few minutes, Remo tossed Johnny from one hand to the other. Eventually, when Johnny finally stopped screaming and the flames were too much for even Remo to bear, he tossed the burning corpse into a nearby Dumpster. The trash in the metal container flamed to life.

Remo and Chiun didn't give him another look.

As the flames grew, charring to ash the body of the man who had taken their home away from the forever, they climbed into the front seat of Mrs. Fungillo's car. Leaving the fire to burn itself out, the two stone-faced men drove slowly out of the pothole-filled parking lot.

THE PRESIDENT of the United States sat in his bathrobe on the floor of the Lincoln Bedroom. Nearly everything was gone now, including the bed. The red phone was still there. He held it in his hand now as he tried to explain.

"I didn't mean for it to go bad like this, Smith," he said. "She just kind of makes things happen, you know?"

"No, I do not know, Mr. President," the disapproving voice of Harold W. Smith replied. "As for your wife's knowledge of our existence, that is as much my fault as it is your own. She inserted herself into enough crises in the past that I should have dealt with her long before this."

"Yeah," the President agreed hopefully. He bit his lip as he tried to go for the wiggle room. "It really is your fault more than it is mine."

"I did not say that, Mr. President," Smith said tartly, "and you cannot deny culpability in this matter."

The President rubbed anxiously at his face. A

smear of orange rouge stained his pale palm. "You really made her forget about you fellas?" he asked.

"Yes," Smith replied. "Not that her knowledge of us was as extensive as yours. But she knew enough to make her a security risk. Obviously."

"Yeah, that was really awful how she made me tell her where your guys would be," the President said. "But you've met her—you can understand how I didn't have a choice."

"No, sir, I do not understand," Smith said icily. "You allowed your wife to manipulate you into placing my men at risk, all for some half-baked scheme that had no hope of succeeding. You had a choice. You could have refused."

"Maybe you haven't met her after all," the President exhaled tiredly. "She's taken me down this same road a million times. From universal health care to those Puerto Rican terrorists. What she wants, she gets."

Smith would not be led down that primrose path. "Before we end this conversation—which, Mr. President, will be our last—I need to ask a few questions. First, are the MIR revolutionaries associated in any way with Raffair?"

"No," the President replied. "I asked you to check Raffair out before my wife called me about you."

"So it was you personally who supplied the whereabouts of my men to your wife, and she in turn instructed the terrorists? There were no go-betweens?"

"Yeah," the chief executive said. "Each time her boys failed, she called me again, meaner than the last time. By the end, she was threatening to stay in New York, not even come down here for the inauguration tomorrow."

"Very well, sir," Smith said. "This ends your contact with this agency. Tonight you will brief your successor about us, and later in the evening, while you sleep, my men will visit you and perform the same procedure they have already performed on your wife. You will forget forever the existence of this agency and its personnel. Goodbye, Mr. President."

"Wait, Smith," the President called. His hand tightened on the red phone.

"Yes, sir?"

Sitting on the floor in his bathrobe adorned with the presidential seal, the President shifted on his ample rump. A lost-little-boy look came to his blotchy face.

"I wasn't so bad, was I?" America's chief executive asked. "I mean, this stuff at the end wasn't too great, but I was okay otherwise, right?" All his life he had always sought approval. He listened expectantly now for an answer.

At first, Smith's voice was flat and dispassionate.

"Your actions have threatened us with exposure and put at risk the lives of my two operatives, men to whom this nation owes a debt untold for three decades of tireless, thankless service." By this point, his lemony tone was that of a disappointed New

England school marm. "Yes, Mr. President, you were bad. You were very, very bad."

And with this final admonishment over, the red phone went dead for the last time in the ear of the future ex-President.

IN HIS FOLCROFT OFFICE, Smith replaced the phone with an authoritative click. Face pinched, he slid the drawer shut.

"Guess suck-up time is over," Remo suggested.

He was sitting cross-legged on the floor, the Master of Sinanju at his side.

Smith nodded tightly. "Tomorrow at noon, we begin with a clean slate. Although we must temper that fact with the knowledge that this President will doubtless not speak kindly of us when he briefs his successor tonight."

Remo shrugged, as if it were all a matter of supreme indifference to him. "One President's pretty much the same as the next one to me," he said. "This guy was no great shakes, but I've seen the new President, so I'm not getting my hopes up. I did like that part, though, where you played us up for our thankless service. That'll come in handy at contract time, I'm sure."

From the corner of his eye, he looked over to the Master of Sinanju.

Chiun sat rigid on the worn carpet, eyes straight ahead. His teacher's silent sadness brushed Remo's heart.

"While you were tracking down the three men

who destroyed your home, I continued my search for Anselmo Scubisci," the CURE director said, changing the subject. "He took a jet from Canada to parts unknown. No flight plan was registered. I can't locate a pilot, so he cannot be traced for questioning. For all intents and purposes, Anselmo Scubisci has vanished without a trace."

"And lives to bug us some other day," Remo said bitterly. "If it wasn't for Washington's answer to Evita Peron and her San Juan ski patrol, we would have had him, Smitty."

"Yes," Smith said. "But let us view this with some optimism. Scubisci's plan was a failure. The Securities and Exchange Commission is now looking into Raffair. The stock has collapsed. Given all this, it is likely that Anselmo Scubisci's Camorra benefactor is not pleased with him. Perhaps our work has been done for us."

"I'm not too hot on leaps of faith, Smitty," Remo said. "And I remember a time when you weren't, either."

Smith leaned back in his chair, steepling his long fingers at his chin. "You will find, Remo, that the world changes as you age." His gray eyes were faraway.

The office lights were turned down low. They reflected dully on the big picture window behind Smith. For a moment, cast half in shadow and bathed in pale amber light, the figure seated behind that broad desk seemed unchanged from the first time Remo had seen him.

Smith spoke, breaking the spell. "I should inform the two of you that I have been considering suspending operations," he announced softly.

"Huh?" Remo asked. He glanced at the Master of Sinanju. This had gotten the old Korean's attention.

"The thought has been with me for some time," Smith admitted. "This posting has always been demanding, even in my younger years. And while you and Chiun have remained more than consistent in your abilities throughout our association, clearly I have not."

"You are in but the second blush of life, O Emperor," Chiun said dismissively. "Do not trouble yourself with such vexing thoughts until you have reached one hundred."

"Realistically, that is not an option," Smith said somberly. "And even if I were to stay on very much longer, I am not certain that I'm equipped to understand this new age."

"There's no new age, Smitty," Remo said. "It's always just the same crummy old one with a new coat of paint and a bigger price tag."

"I disagree, Remo. In my day, ordinary Americans would not have invested money in organized crime. A project like Raffair would never have been seriously considered by the Mafia. Such things are products of a different America. One which I am becoming less able to comprehend."

"Bulldookey," Remo offered. "Ow!" he said, feeling a sudden pinch on his thigh.

With a silencing look, Chiun withdrew his tapered nails.

"You will retire?" he asked Smith, his eyes narrowing.

Smith thought of the poison pill in his vest pocket. "In a manner of speaking," he nodded.

"Before you leave on this sunny autumn journey, Smith the Generous, Sinanju craves a boon."

"If it is within my power to give it."

"Please be kind enough to tell the new occupant of the Eagle Throne that which you just told his lard-bellied predecessor."

"I knew you were listening," Remo said. He had to slap a hand over his leg to avoid another pinch.

"The idiot is going to commit suicide," Chiun hissed in Korean. "Before he kills himself, he could at least put in a good word for us." To Smith, he said, "Your humble servants would be eternally grateful."

There was no rancor visible on Smith's tired face. As he nodded, he stood. "I will see what I can do."

"A thousand thank-yous, Emperor Smith," Chiun said, bowing his head. "Do not play us up too much, however. After all, we do not wish to appear desperate."

Smith came around his desk, his battered leather briefcase at his side.

"Where are you going, Smitty?" Remo asked, trying to dispel the mercenary air that had just descended on the dusty office. "I thought you didn't have to be back in your coffin until sunrise."

"Home," Smith replied. "And the two of you should be leaving, too. You have a plane to catch for Washington. I would appreciate it if you first disposed of the MIR agent you brought here. He is in the security wing."

"Can do," Remo nodded. He was studying the tired lines in the CURE director's face.

"When you leave, be certain to lock this room. Good night." With that, Smith left the office.

"Great," Remo muttered after he was gone. "More planes." He unscissored his legs, rising fluidly to his feet. "If there's any smuggled boom boxes on this flight, I'm tossing them through a jet engine."

Chiun rose delicately beside him. "Unless they are playing the lovely Wylander," he said.

Remo's head snapped around. "Whoa. You told me you were giving up country music."

Chiun gave him a look generally reserved for dim children and mental defectives. "Country music, yes," he said, turning on one heel. "Oxygen, no."

And as his pupil's face fell, the Master of Sinanju padded silently from the shadowy office.

**38**

As promised, the government car picked him up at precisely ten o'clock. Mark didn't even try to engage the driver in conversation for the whole ride to Washington. Lost in silent thoughts, he braced his broken arm on the armrest and stared out at the twinkling lights.

At the White House, he was ushered up to the family quarters. He was surprised to see so little furniture upstairs. A butler brought him down to the Lincoln Bedroom.

The President was waiting for him at the door. No longer capable of being surprised by anything, Mark didn't even blink when he saw the second man who was in the room.

The President-elect sat on a hard wooden chair across the room. It was an old Truman kitchen chair that had to be brought up from a musty corner of the basement. There was very little good furniture left around the mansion.

An old-fashioned phone was at the future President's feet. It was fire-engine red.

"Hello, Mark," the current chief executive said. "I'm sure you two haven't met."

He waved a questioning finger between the President-elect and Mark.

Sitting on his chair, the man who would become President the following day at noon didn't seem interested in Mark in the least. He was studying the phone at his feet, the deep lines of his forehead creased down the middle.

"We were just having a little talk before you showed up," the current President said. "It's a matter that, well, that concerns you now."

He glanced at the President-elect. The other man's face was somber. When he turned back to Mark, the chief executive took a deep breath.

"Mark, let me tell you about a little something called CURE...."

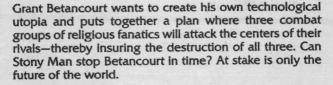

# Take
# 2 explosive books
# plus a
# mystery bonus
# FREE

# James Axler

# OUTLANDERS®

## TIGERS OF HEAVEN

In the Outlands, the struggle for control of the baronies continues. Kane, Grant and Brigid seek allies in the Western Islands empire of New Edo, where they try to enlist the aid of the Tigers of Heaven, a group of samurai warriors.

*Book #2 of the Imperator Wars saga*, a trilogy chronicling the introduction of a new child imperator—launching the baronies into war!